# WITH A BLIGHTED TOUCH

## ALSO BY J. TODD KINGREA

THE DEIPARIAN SAGA

The Witchfinder
The Crimson Fathers

# WITH A BLIGHTED TOUCH

## J. TODD KINGREA

Livonia, Michigan

## WITH A BLIGHTED TOUCH

Published by BHC Press

Library of Congress Control Number: 2023930894

ISBN Numbers:
Hardcover:  978-1-64397-361-6
Softcover:   978-1-64397-362-3
Ebook:       978-1-64397-363-0

For information, write:
BHC Press
885 Penniman #5505
Plymouth, MI 48170

Visit the publisher:
www.bhcpress.com

This book is dedicated to my friend,
Christopher Levon Kelly

an unjudgmental heart
who knows far too much
about the truths behind the story

# WITH A BLIGHTED TOUCH

# 1
## WITHIN ARM'S REACH

To twelve-year-old Christopher "Kit" McNeil, summer was the greatest time of the year. It was even better than Christmas. Sure, there was a lot of buildup to Christmas Eve and the anticipation of Christmas morning, but it was just a single day. On December 26, everything pretty much went back to normal. By New Year's the tree, brown and shedding needles, lay beside the road like an accident victim no one had bothered to help. Cardboard boxes held together with masking tape were stuffed with lights, tinsel, and ornaments, and stored away in the attic.

But summer was different. It lasted three whole months. The days stretched together, filled with bike riding, and ice cubes made from cherry Kool-Aid, and the unmistakable tang of chlorine from the town pool. Most families took vacations during that time.

Other people's families. Not Kit's. Too expensive, his father always said.

His friend Troy Wallace's family did though. Sometimes he'd bring Kit a T-shirt from St. Louis or a bottle of sand from Destin, Florida.

If summer held one drawback for Kit, it was being stuck in Black Rock without Troy. Kit had few friends, and when Troy was away on vacation, he felt lost. That week seemed to drag on forever. He slept in when he could, mowed the lawn when his father ordered him to, and rode his bicycle to no place in particular. At night Kit watched reruns on television with his mom or sat by his open window putting together plastic model kits. He drew a red star on the calendar to mark Troy's return.

Which had been four days ago.

Tonight was the first time in over three weeks that Kit had gotten to sleep over at his friend's house. Kit didn't like having Troy over to his house, because he never knew what kind of mood his father would be in. Albert Mc-Neil had made it clear he didn't care to have any more kids around.

Troy's mother had taken them to Moviehound Video & Tanning in Black Rock Plaza to pick out two movies. "Only two to make it fair," Mrs. Wallace always said. "One for Kit and one for Troy." On the way home she'd picked up a pizza for them at DiVeccio's Italian Kitchen. After the double feature of *Terror Train*—Kit's choice—and *Alligator* (which was the best Troy could find after his mother nixed *The Gates of Hell*), they had gone out to the green Coleman tent set up in the backyard. They'd walked around the neighborhood after Troy's parents went to sleep and had only just gotten back into the tent when Mrs. Wallace called to them.

"Kit? Troy? Are you boys awake?"

The boys heard the back door close and footsteps cross the yard. They pushed the flaps aside and watched her approach in her housecoat. She stopped in front of them.

"Kit, your mother is on the phone. She needs to talk to you," Mrs. Wallace said in a concerned tone.

"Huh? What for?" Kit asked.

Her mouth pinched and she motioned him out of the tent. "I-it's important."

In the kitchen, the receiver lay on the counter, the white spiral cord coiled like an albino serpent.

"Hello?" Kit said.

"Hey, it's Mom. I— Hold on."

Kit heard her talking softly to his father in the background. "Mom? What's going on?"

"Honey, I need to come and get you. We've got to go to Murfreesboro. Your uncle Arnold . . . H-he's been in an accident. We've got to go."

"Right *now*?" Kit asked. Selfishness flared in him. He didn't want to leave. As far as the boys were concerned, the night was just getting started. Kit still wanted to go bike riding around town in the early morning hours like they'd planned. He didn't want to go to Murfreesboro for something that didn't sound all that urgent to him.

"Can I just stay here with Troy?"

Kit's mother cleared her throat. "Mrs. Wallace was kind enough to offer, but no, you need to be with us. It's . . . it doesn't sound good."

"Please, Mom?" he pleaded.

"No, this is something we have to do as a family. I'll be over to get you in a few minutes. I've got a lot to do in a short amount of time, so be ready."

"But I've got my bike over here."

"You can get it when we get back."

"Lemme just ride it home. I can be there in ten minutes." He twirled the phone cord around his finger.

"I will come get you."

"I can ride home while you're doing all the other stuff you said you had to do."

There was silence on the other end of the line, followed by more muffled voices in the background. "Okay, fine. But I want you on your way as soon as you hang up. You've got ten minutes."

Kit accepted the minor victory. "Okay."

"Be careful. I love you."

"Love you too, Mom."

He handed the receiver to Mrs. Wallace. Troy followed Kit back to the tent and helped him collect his things. It was a little after one o'clock in the morning when Kit rode down the driveway and into the deserted street. The wind pushed his hair away from his forehead as he zipped down the hill out of Troy's subdivision.

*I wonder what kind of accident it was,* Kit thought.

He had always liked Uncle Arnold. Sometimes he wondered why he couldn't have been Arnold's son rather than Albert's. His uncle had always treated him with kindness and love, and he seemed to enjoy having Kit around. Kit felt guilty about his attitude on the phone. The more he thought about his uncle, the faster he pedaled.

His route took him straight through downtown Black Rock. He crept past the old brick buildings that lined the street on either side, guarded by silver parking meters. There were no cars parked along the sidewalks, and none moved on the street. The traffic lights blinked yellow.

Kit coasted to rest his legs for a moment. He looked toward the nearest building and realized someone was watching him. The person stood in the shadow of a recessed doorway that led up to a set of ramshackle apartments.

Probably one of the town winos his father was always griping about or somebody who couldn't sleep.

Kit turned to face the road again and noticed another person in front of the furniture store. And another in the doorway of the department store.

And the doorway after that.

And the one after that.

A figure lurked in every alley and entrance on both sides of the street. All had hooked noses and wide-set eyes. Everything else about them was indistinct, like a group of cookies made with the same cutter. Yet something about their features sent a chill through Kit despite the muggy night air.

He heard footsteps and looked over his shoulder. The figures were disengaging from the shadows after he rode past. They crossed the sidewalks and merged into a group that walked stiffly down the middle of the street after him.

Kit pedaled faster as the street began a gradual uphill climb. Another glance showed the group was getting larger. Breathing heavily, Kit stood and pedaled up the incline. He didn't remember this hill being so steep before. His wheels slowed; his momentum lessened. It was like riding through syrup.

His pursuers drew closer. Footsteps increased in speed and rhythm. Kit knew he shouldn't, but he looked back anyway.

The group, thirty strong by now, started to run toward him. The distance between them closed.

"Leave me alone!" Kit yelled over his shoulder.

His bicycle was barely moving forward. Sweat covered his brow as he stomped the pedals. He knew he could get off and run, but something held him to the seat. Then his momentum was gone. The bicycle wobbled.

Dozens of identical hands reached for him.

Kit yanked the handlebars sideways, and suddenly, he was moving again. He rattled down a hill into the town park. Taking his feet off the pedals so they could spin faster, he hunched over the handlebars to minimize wind resistance. Sticks snapped. His tires kicked up blades of freshly cut grass as he wove between the maple, ash, and black oak trees.

Kids often used the park as a shortcut. It didn't really save much time, but the sidewalks made for smooth riding. Kit found one, and he was glad to be off the hole-riddled ground. The air cooled his face, and a great pressure released from his chest. Chancing a peek over his shoulder, he saw his pursuers. They stood on the sidewalk at the summit of the hill. They had not entered the park.

*What the hell was that?* he wondered. *What were they doing? Why did they chase me like that?*

The moon illuminated his path across the park. He steered his bike toward the gazebo in the center and resumed pedaling.

Something surged out of the darkness at him—a vague black blur. He yelled in fright and twisted the bicycle aside. He smelled a gross yet familiar aroma, like sour milk.

The bicycle wobbled beneath him. Kit regained his balance just as the shape came toward him again from the darkness beneath a tree. Something cold touched his arm just above his shirt sleeve. No, not touched.

Clutched. Grasped.

*Rip.*

Kit and the bicycle slammed into the ground. His right side tingled, and pain flared there as if it had been set on fire. Stars twinkled at him from between the trees. Reaching across his stomach, Kit found the right side of his shirt sticky and wet. The pain spread throughout his body, radiating from his shoulder.

*Shit, I've broken my arm!* That could be the only explanation for the piercing agony that enveloped him.

He struggled to sit up.

Something crouched among the trees' shadows.

Kit squinted. The pain caused his eyes to water. He tried to separate the movement of whatever had attacked him from the inky blackness surrounding it. He saw an arm sticking out from behind a tree, but whoever it belonged to was hidden from his view.

The pain grew intolerable. He panted through gritted teeth and cradled his broken right arm, cold and sticky with blood. That must be why it hurt so bad. It was one of those breaks where the bone comes through the skin. Kit couldn't remember what it was called.

He focused harder on the tree his attacker was hiding behind. The arm was still visible, and it was holding something. Through the pain and darkness and tears, Kit tried to identify what that something was. He could make out that it was thin and slightly bent toward the shorter end. The longer section ended at a hand—

The air caught in Kit's throat. He wanted to scream but couldn't. He looked down at his quivering body. His left hand clutched the right side of his bloody shirt. Instead of an arm, there was only gleaming bone surrounded by shredded muscle and flesh.

Eyes bulging, Kit finally screamed and screamed and screamed.

Whatever was behind the tree flung Kit's own right arm at him. It spun through the air and landed at his feet. The fingers still twitched.

"AHHH, GOD!" he shrieked.

Kit bolted upright in bed. Darkness surrounded him. His heart raced. It hurt so bad that he put a hand over his chest to keep it in place. Cold sweat drenched his skin, and his breath came in great rasping gasps. The inside of his skull felt like an impacted wisdom tooth being tapped with a hammer.

With his left hand Kit fumbled for the lamp beside the bed. The light nearly blinded him. He cracked his eyelids just enough to look down at his right arm.

It lay on top of the covers, trembling as the nightmare flushed from his system. He closed his eyes and took several deep breaths. *That goddamn dream again*, he thought. Would he ever be rid of it? Kit didn't know what it meant. He *had* flipped his bike that night on his way home. But he'd never broken his arm. It wasn't ripped from his body, and nobody had chased him through the middle of town. Groaning, he fell back into pillows that stank of sweat and tried to go back to sleep. He left the light on.

# 2

## HOME AND MEMORIES OF HOME

*Wednesday, June 1, 2011*

The telephone beside his bed would not stop ringing. The shrill sound ricocheted inside Kit's skull, an angry yellow jacket trapped in a jar.

"Jesus," he growled through a mouth that tasted like fire-dried clay. His flailing hand found the plastic annoyance and shoved it off the table. "Shut th' fuggg . . . " he slurred.

The voice from the receiver sounded distant. "Kit? Kit, are you there? Come on, man. Can you hear me?"

Kit snarled at the stupid voice or thought he did anyway. It was hard to know with the yellow jacket thudding behind his eyeballs.

"Kit, it's me—Harvey. Harvey Ashton. I need to talk to you."

Kit forced himself up onto his elbow and picked the receiver up off the floor. The stagnant odor of his armpit struck him with all the subtlety of smelling salts. *Jesus, when was the last time I showered? And where the hell am I?* He looked around with bleary eyes as he raised the receiver. The stubble on his face scratched against the plastic.

"Yeah? What?" Kit demanded.

He recognized what was left of his hotel room. Three fraternities could have held their year-end parties in here at the same time, and it might have been an improvement. A mound of beer cans lay in the corner. Blankets and sheets from both beds were in jumbled heaps, half of them on the floor among pizza boxes and fast-food wrappers. Six liquor bottles were lined up

across the desk like bowling pins that had forgotten to fall. Heavy maroon
drapes kept out the light. The artwork on the walls hung at odd angles, or
maybe it was just the way he was holding his head. Sideways. Maybe the yellow jacket would fall out.

"Kit? Thank God I found you!" the tinny voice said through the plastic.

"Whaddya want, Harv?" Kit snapped. The band manager's voice cut
through the fog in Kit's brain, reminding him of why he was here.

"Look, I'm sorry. I really am. I told Kenny and Dwight this wasn't the
time. They should've waited until all the shows were over."

"Or, I don't know, maybe *not at all!* Christ, Harv, you're the manager.
They knew I had a history of episodes. It's not like I choose when it happens."

The voice on the other end sounded tense. "I know you don't, but you
had two of them last month—"

"One of those was during a rehearsal! Only the second was on stage—
and that was during a sound check, not an actual show."

"Maybe you should see a doctor?"

"I've already done that. Neurologically, there's nothing wrong."

"But twice—"

Kit sighed in frustration. "I've been to doctors ever since the damn
blackouts started and the answer is always the same. They can't find any cause
for them."

Harvey's tone was a mix of firmness and paternal care. "Are you still using?"

A pregnant pause followed.

"I'm fine," Kit said, his voice like hammered steel.

"Listen, you're a damned good guitarist. Southern by the Grace of God
was lucky to have you these past seven months, but—" A heavy sigh escaped
from the receiver. "Kit, you need help. The drugs and booze are ruining you."

"I *said* I'm fine."

"No, man, you're not. Hey, I'm your friend, and I'm telling you that you
need to get clean. You've got too much talent. I've seen too many good musicians destroyed because they thought they were fine. I don't want you to be
on that list."

Kit sniffed. His nostrils were dry as beef jerky from the coke he'd done
last night before that damned nightmare had woken him. He sat up and

swung his legs off the bed. His foot knocked over two empty tequila bottles. "Lemme ask you this, Harv. Was the note your idea?"

"Note? What note?"

"What note?" Kit repeated sarcastically. "My fucking pink slip! My dismissal!"

"I don't know anything ab—"

"They canned me by shoving a fucking go-to-hell note under the door!"

There was a slight choking sound on the other end. "Aw, shit, no . . . They didn't."

"They did."

"Kenny and Dwight didn't tell you to your face?" The manager's surprise was genuine.

Kit stood up and stretched. He nearly dropped the receiver as the cord pulled to its limit and the base rattled across the floor. He set the base back on the table whose surface was gritty with the residue of thin white lines. Several beer cans stood on the table next to the base like mourners at a graveside. Kit tried to remember what all he *had* done last night.

"No," Kit replied, "they didn't. Just slipped the note under the door. They left me here in Memphis."

"God, man, I really am sorry. They shouldn't have—"

"Tell me about it. My usual shitty luck strikes again." Kit fumbled a cigarette from the pack and lit it. He blew smoke into the uncirculated, putrid air. "So that's why you woke me up? To find out how I got kicked out?"

"Uh, no, no . . . " Harvey's tone grew somber. He hesitated. The silence grew awkward.

"What's going on, Harv?"

Harvey's long, low sigh was followed by a deep breath. "I-I've got some news. Bad news." He hesitated again.

Kit snorted. "There's no other kind with me."

"The . . . the thing is—"

"Christ, spit it out."

Another miserable sigh. "Kit, I hate to have to tell you this—and I hate to do it this way—but . . . it's your mom. She's dead. I'm so sorry, buddy."

The cigarette dangled from Kit's mouth, and the smoke stung his eyes. The yellow jacket was still there, pounding inside his head, but he tried to force his mind to work. It refused to comprehend what he'd just heard.

"Hey, you still here? Talk to me," Harvey said.

Kit gently lowered his six-foot frame back onto the bed as if worried that his 240 pounds would snap it like a twig. "M-my . . . my mom is . . . "

"Yeah, the funeral home in—where was it, Black Rock? Yeah, they've, um . . . been trying to get in touch with you for several days."

"*Several days?* W-when did she . . . When did it happen?"

"They said it was the twenty-sixth. Last Thursday. Her service was this past Sunday."

Kit was aware of the room, of sitting on the bed and holding the receiver, but suddenly it all felt alien, like reality belonged to some other time or place. The cigarette trembled in his free hand. Numbness spread from his stomach and swallowed his heart. His head swam. He didn't realize he was crying until the first tear hit the back of his hand.

"Jesus, I'm so sorry, Kit. If there's anything I can do—"

"Yeah," Kit replied in a daze. "Yeah, sure." He dropped the receiver into the cradle, ground the cigarette into the ashtray, and laid back on the bed. Memories swelled like a flooded river. He tried to pick one and focus on it, but they just kept coming. Her smile, her tenderness, her protection—how she tried to find the positives in the worst situations. She always supported him—especially when it came to his music. Because God knows his father—

Kit sat up. He wasn't numb any longer. His body was suddenly trembling with rage. "That son of a bitch!" He hurled the words at the litter-strewn room. "He didn't even have the decency to tell me."

With the fury came a fresh wave of tears. He kicked the other bed so hard the mattress flopped against the wall. Stumbling to the desk, he knocked bottles aside as he searched for one that wasn't empty. Several broke, scattering shards onto the dingy blue carpet. He found a few mouthfuls left in one bottle and swilled them down.

He let the heat of the alcohol sink into his chest, muting some of the anger. His stomach churned. *How could he not tell me? What the hell is wrong with him?*

Kit knew only too well what was wrong with Albert McNeil. At the top of the long list was the fact that Kit had always been a disappointment to his father. Nothing he had ever done was good enough. Albert had seen him as a pansy—not like the real men who worked under Albert at the factory. Kit had kept his head focused on comic books, plastic models, and his guitar, which his father had repeatedly told him would ensure his place in hell. Christ, the man had even killed Kit's puppy one day while he was at school.

Kit's gut cramped. He staggered to the bathroom. Tequila and bile raked his throat as it surged out of him. His tears mixed with the vomit in the bowl, and his body shuddered.

When his stomach was empty, Kit stood on rubbery legs, brushed his teeth, and found his suitcases. It took him thirty minutes to gather up his scattered belongings, and another ten to load the suitcases, his guitar and amp, and his tour bag into his dinged-up 2002 Honda CR-V. He pulled onto the highway, the summer sun bright even through his sunglasses. He took I-40 toward Nashville—and beyond that, Scarburn County and his home-town of Black Rock. The air conditioner blew in his face, but he was still sweating like a pig.

He drove alone but didn't lack for company. His conscience rode shot-gun like it always did. When *was* the last time he had seen his mother? He couldn't remember and hoped that was because of the drugs and not because it had been so long.

The old familiar guilt stabbed him in his heart.

It had been longer than he thought—just before this bar tour with Southern by the Grace of God. When was that—five months ago?

*Five and a half, actually.*

He reminded himself that his mother had known he'd be on the road a lot. That was the nature of the business. She had encouraged him to follow his dream. When he'd passed the audition and landed a spot in the band, she'd been ecstatic.

Still, he knew she'd been getting worse, and he'd kept right on touring. *Couldn't spare a weekend for your old mom, could you?*

Kit jabbed the buttons on the radio as a distraction. He ran through the band twice, finally settling on a country station he didn't really like.

He hated what country music had become over the past twenty years. You didn't hear Marty Robbins or Patsy Cline or Hank Williams on the radio any more. Now it was all scruffy corporate Chippendale models who sounded like pop stars in boots. This generation didn't have an Alabama or a Restless Heart.

Kit's thoughts returned to his situation. How was he going to handle things with his father? What was he going to do when he got home?

Something distasteful rose in his stomach at the word "home." He dreaded being around Albert, and he was afraid he might hit the old bastard for not telling him what had happened. But he had nowhere else to stay. After paying off his hotel bill—with a sheepish apology for the cleaning lady who'd have to venture into the disaster area—he had only seventy-one dollars in his pocket. Unless he wanted to sleep under the stars, there wasn't any other option.

Of course, Kit had no intention of staying long. He hated Black Rock and its glut of narrow-minded, redneck good old boys. There had been too many of them when he was growing up, and somehow, he didn't figure things had changed much in the past eighteen years. The plan was to say goodbye to his mother and then get back to Nashville. Maybe the reason for his dismissal from the band hadn't made the rounds. Perhaps he could snag work as a studio musician, at least until something better came along.

It was the same old pattern. Kit was always waiting for the next best thing. He looked back now and saw how he'd wasted every chance that came his way. Between the booze, the blow, and his history of lousy relationships, he really had become what Albert had always said he would be.

That thought made him depressed and sick to his stomach. He tried to think of something else. He roamed across the radio band again, but his mind kept bringing up the hurtful truth. His past *was* littered with two failed marriages, twice that many band firings, and his ongoing habit. He didn't believe he had a habit, but wasn't that what addicts always claimed?

He glanced at himself in the rearview mirror.

He looked older than his forty-two years. It wasn't just the dashes of gray in his black hair or the crow's feet around his blue eyes from squinting into too many stage lights. The lines on his face were more pronounced, those on his forehead deeper. Too much drinking had left him with chubby cheeks, not to mention the gut.

He sighed and wondered for the thousandth time how his life had become such a mess. He knew part of it was his fault. Well, more than part—maybe most of it. But Albert was responsible too. The belittling, condemnation, and beatings Albert had dished out weren't Kit's fault. He'd had no say in the matter. He was just a kid.

As the radio played something by Brooks & Dunn, Kit thought more about his childhood, and it was as if he'd opened a door in his mind. He still had a few good memories of Black Rock. Albert's oppressive, hypocritical presence hadn't been able to ruin everything. As Kit's gaze roamed the rolling hills along the interstate, the sweltering heat and music and a longing for better times caused a particular memory to crystallize.

A warm smile spread across Kit's face as he remembered summers spent with Troy. *God, I haven't thought of him in years!*

He'd met Troy Wallace in 1977 when they were in third grade. He always remembered that because he had seen Troy drawing a Death Star in his notebook, and from that moment on, they were like brothers. But it was Kit's memory of the summer of 1981 that remained the sharpest and best even though a shadow lay over it.

• • •

Seventh grade was behind them. They would be kings of the middle school in the fall, but they had three months of freedom until then. The lazy, humid days would be spent playing Dungeons & Dragons on Troy's porch, camping out in his backyard, and riding bikes. They might even go to the town pool since Stacy McCormick's sister worked there, and she filled out her swimsuit nicely.

For weeks the boys had been scheming a way to slip into the drive-in theater in August if *Heavy Metal* was going to be shown. They'd snuck glimpses of the magazine at the Hop-In convenience store, hiding it inside *Sports Illustrated* so the clerk wouldn't catch them. If the movie showed as many boobs as the magazine did, they were in for a treat.

Kit's smile slowly faded as the memory darkened. Despite all the firefly-lit nights and reruns of *The Greatest American Hero*, there remained a shadow over that summer because of the secret he and Troy still carried.

It had been early June, the first day of summer vacation. Troy had ridden his bike over and found Kit and his mom, Paula McNeil, working out back in the garden.

"Hey, Mrs. McNeil," Troy said as he rounded the corner of the house. "Hey Kit. Wanna go ride bikes?" The sun turned his thick blond hair into shimmering gold. His bowl cut had grown out, and his hair tumbled down his forehead. He was constantly raking it out of his eyes.

Kit's hair was nearly the same except that his was black, but there the similarities ended. Troy wore glasses. Kit didn't. Kit was a little taller than Troy but twice as wide. Both got their share of torment from the Dunleys. Kit was dubbed "Butter Butt," an allusion not only to his size but to the imagined homosexual relationship they accused him of sharing with Troy, whom they nicknamed "Pencil Dick."

"I can't," Kit said. "I promised Mom I'd help her in the garden."

"How long is that gonna take?"

Kit shrugged. "I don't know. Not long."

"Troy, how are your parents?" Mom asked. She brushed a strand of auburn hair from her face with the back of her floral glove.

"They're all right," Troy replied

"Well, you tell them I asked about them," she said.

Troy nodded, his hair flopping forward.

Mom stood up from her kneeling position. "Chris, you go on if you want. I can do this." She smiled.

"I still don't get why you wanna have another garden," Kit said. He looked at the small patch of neat rows that would hopefully produce potatoes, carrots, green beans, and tomatoes. "The blight got it the last two times you tried."

"Well, you know how the blight is around here. It hits someone's land one year and somebody else's the next. Maybe we'll get lucky this year. Now go on, get out of here." She waved him away with the garden trowel.

"You sure, Mom?"

"Come on, Kit. Let's go," Troy said, encouraging Kit to leave before she changed her mind.

She was hoeing the dirt and didn't look up when she said, "Where are you boys going?"

"Just riding around town. Nowhere special," Troy said. He poked Kit in the shoulder. "Hey! Wanna go to Bennett's and see if the new *Famous Monsters* has come in?"

The pharmacy on Main Street was the only place in Black Rock that carried the boys' favorite magazine. It also had the only spinner rack of comics between here and Spring City.

"Sure, but I ain't got no money," Kit said as they walked around the house.

"Kit! Be home for lunch," his mother yelled.

"Okay!"

Troy climbed on his blue Raleigh Rampar. "We'll just see if they got it. After that we can go hang out at the old school."

Kit wheeled his green Schwinn Scrambler with the banana seat out of the garage. With the sun on their faces and the wind in their hair, they pedaled into the summer that would change them forever.

• • •

In 1924 the old Black Rock school, located near the southern base of Blackpoint Mountain, had mysteriously burned down. Three stone walls were all that remained, and their eroded surfaces were decorated with graffiti. Inside the walls, rocks and logs were arranged around two fire pits. Plenty of weed-covered debris and beer cans lay scattered across the ground. Lots of teenagers came here to party.

Kit swatted at the cloud of gnats that kept pace with him and Troy. They navigated the well-worn path through weeds and underbrush until they reached the school. Troy dug into the pocket of his blue jeans and produced a crumpled pack of cigarettes. Both boys lit one. They smoked for a few minutes in the shadow of a wall.

Bees droned among the wildflowers.

"You learn any new songs?" Troy asked.

"I'm working on 'Stairway to Heaven' and some blues."

Troy jumped up. "You should learn something by Journey." He wrapped his arms around his skinny body and pretended to make out as he wailed the chorus of "Lovin', Touchin', Squeezin'." Kit pitched a rock at him and laughed.

"Seriously though"—Troy picked up his cigarette off the rock—"why the blues?"

Kit shrugged. "I dunno. Just like the sound of it, I guess. It's . . . lonesome. Makes me feel like somebody else out there knows what I'm going through."

"Your dad still being an asshole?"

"Of course. He don't know how to be anything else." Kit finished his cigarette and tossed the stub into the ash-filled ring of stone. "Shit, man, I hate this place."

"What's wrong with here?" Troy gestured at the sentinel-like walls.

"Not *here* here," Kit said. "This damn town. I can't wait to get out of Black Rock."

"Yeah, me too."

"It's like everything here is cursed, you know? Bad shit happens all the time. I don't wanna stay here and end up like my dad or like that Billings guy in town. He's what? Like forty or something?"

"Yeah, forty and wanderin' the streets, talking to himself. I wanna go live on a beach like Destin or Myrtle. That way I could watch the chicks in their bikinis all day." Troy grinned.

"Anywhere would be better than this deadass place."

Troy flicked his cigarette butt into the fire pit. "You wanna camp out in my backyard sometime this week?"

"Sure, if it's okay with my mom."

"We can ride our skateboards down the middle of the street at, like, three in the morning!"

Kit grinned. "Hey, we could go to that old graveyard by the church and tell ghost stories. Maybe pretend like zombies are coming to get us or something."

"Yeah, that's cool," Troy said. He walked around the fire pit, kicking beer cans. "I'm thirsty. It's hot out here."

"Let's ride to the Hop-In. We could pool our change and split a Coke."

Troy was about to reply but instead clamped his mouth shut. "Shh!" Troy hissed. He was looking between two of the walls at the other footpath that meandered through the weeds to the parking lot.

Voices and coarse laughter came from that direction.

Kit and Troy looked at each other in shock.

"Shit, it's the Dunleys," Troy said in a low voice. "They're headed this way."

"Let's get the hell outta here." Kit leaped to his feet.

Both boys crouched and scurried back the way they had come. They straightened up once they were in the taller bushes but kept glancing behind them. There was no sign of pursuit. Kit exhaled and wiped the sweat from his forehead. That was a close one. They stopped halfway up the hill. Only bits of the school's walls could be seen through the foliage, but the laughter and loud voices confirmed Troy had been right about the Dunleys.

Breathing heavily, Kit asked, "Which ones do you think it is?"

"How the shit should I know? There's like a hundred of them."

It was true. The Dunley family had been in Black Rock longer than anyone could remember. Nobody liked them. They were course, clannish, and dangerous, and no one seemed to know just exactly how many of them there were.

Identical twins Garrett and Johnny Dunley were two years older than Kit and Troy. They were responsible for most of the bullying that the two boys endured. The twins had a cousin, George, who was the same age. He wasn't right in the head and went to special classes.

But it was Greg and Jeff, the other set of identical twins, who terrified everyone. They were cruel and spiteful, and despite being only seventeen, both had already been in juvenile detention. Greg had pulled a knife on a teacher. Jeff had stolen a car and taken it for a joyride. The twins were following in their older brother's footsteps. At the ripe old age of twenty, Ricky Dunley was serving a five-year prison sentence for aggravated assault, rape, and burglary.

As Kit and Troy walked back to their bicycles, they heard more laughter as female voices mixed with those of the Dunleys.

• • •

Kit exited I-40 at Lebanon, just east of Nashville. He only pumped five gallons of gas because of the cost. He now had fifty-four dollars to his name.

He pulled into the parking spot farthest from the front door and rummaged through his tour bag. When he was sure no one was watching him, he slipped a plastic bag into his pocket and went inside the convenience store. Even after all these years he still thought of stores like this as Hop-Ins.

In the bathroom Kit made sure the door was locked. He opened the bag, scooped up some of the white powder on one of his keys, and snorted it. He inhaled deeply and held his nose as his eyes watered. After carefully removing any residue, he relieved himself and washed his hands. Then he was back on the interstate, heading toward his rendezvous with home.

# 3

## A BLIGHTED WELCOME

*Wednesday, June 1, 2011*

K it left the interstate and drove south along Highway 27. At Spring City, he turned west on County Road 501 and started the gentle climb to Scarburn County. It had been eighteen years since he'd last seen these domed mountains. They were brand new to him all over again, yet as familiar as a favorite pair of shoes. An occasional forestry service road or private drive disappeared into the trees as he drove through the sun-spattered woodlands.

After several miles the forest receded, and more homes began to line the road. A carved wooden sign stood among a landscaped flower bed, announcing the town ahead in bright yellow letters.

WELCOME TO BLACK ROCK, TENNESSEE

The town's name had been spray painted with a black X. Scrawled beneath it in red paint were the words:

CANCER CENTRAL

Kit slowed, not only to keep from getting pulled over by an overzealous deputy but also to give him time to look around. Things were pretty much just as he had left them.

Ahead was the car wash and Miller's Appliance Store. Just down from it stood the Black Rock Theater, Bennett's Drugstore, and the old five-and-dime building that had been empty even when he was a child. Kit stopped at the first traffic light. The courthouse stood on the opposite corner, flanked by the jail and a bank. To his right was Beckman's Diner and a church and to his left was an insurance office. The faded brick facades reminded him of age spots on an old man's head.

Time had not been kind to Black Rock. The car wash had gangly weeds sprouting from the cracked pavement. Miller's was vacant, the windows ghosted with dust. The theater marquee was busted, and the windows were painted black. A decrepit poster announced GUN SHOW INSIDE. The pharmacy, too, was long gone. Where the name had once been posted across the front was a discolored area of brick. As Kit drove on, it was more of the same—dilapidated buildings, empty storefronts, and the occasional small business desperately clinging to life. The windows of the apartments above the stores stared at him like lidless eyes.

It all weighed on his spirit like an anchor, exactly as it had when he was young. Kit and Troy had always thought that Black Rock was cursed. It had struggled to survive even in the best of times. Now a heavier, more pitiful miasma of hopelessness coated everything. Not unlike his own life.

Kit could fill up a lot of these empty window displays with the baggage of his past. You want two failed marriages? They're right here, come on in! The building that used to be the jewelry store would be perfect for showcasing the ways he had let his bandmates down over the years. He would need a couple of storefronts to hold all of his bad decisions.

The next red light caught him as well. A car pulled up on his right, paused, and turned down the road. A delivery truck waited across the intersection. Two people emerged from a lawyer's office, and someone else walked down the opposite sidewalk. Kit was glad none of them had wide-set eyes or hooked noses. They didn't look like the cookie-cutter figures from his dream, and he felt a momentary wave of relief.

He had been lucky. His was one of the rare instances when it had happened—he had managed to escape Black Rock. In the 1970s and 1980s, Black Rock had been a dead end to nowhere. Today just reinforced that. The empty buildings and all the pleasant little houses with their white fences and trellised arbors were just like him—facades covering up the real darkness within.

*How many of them are still sheltering abusers and hypocrites?*

Most kids don't know much about domestic violence unless it's happening to them. They don't know how many dark secrets people hide. But as they got older, they learned. Kit could still remember the disgust he had felt when it came out that Jim Mayview—a church deacon and Sunday school teacher—had been embezzling from the bank. Then there was the time Coach Cobb was caught taking pictures in the boys' locker room at the middle school. Sylvia Duvokavic was arrested for running a brothel out of her hotel—although to be fair, that was as much of a secret as the fact that water is wet. Kit knew that the father of at least one of his friends stopped there once or twice a month. Kit's memories contained enough salacious material for an HBO series.

*How much more was there that I never knew about?*

As he passed the park, he saw patches of blight claiming a flower bed and two trees. Something cold washed over him. Black Rock was infamous for its blight. It was a weird agricultural phenomenon that no one had been able to figure out—at least, no one had before he'd left town. He saw more blight as he drove through town.

Kit could not remember the blight ever giving him the willies when he was younger, but now something about it seemed abhorrent. *Loathsome.* He scrunched up his nose as he thought about it.

County extension agents, professors from the University of Tennessee, and scientists from the U.S. Department of Agriculture had been baffled. Patches of blight—which looked like moldy ranch salad dressing—appeared and disappeared from year to year. A garden in one yard might flourish while the one next door produced nothing. A single tree in the midst of a healthy copse would be pale and sickly, but the following year it might be lush and vibrant once more. The blight affected every type of plant in the area but had never proven harmful to animals or humans.

The only place it didn't appear was the upper reaches of Blackpoint Mountain. Kit glanced up at the granite peak, visible from everywhere in town. He couldn't remember the exact height but thought it was somewhere around 1,300 feet. It towered several hundred feet above the tallest of the surrounding hills.

Kit turned onto Tunvale Street. His street. He drove slower, but instead of looking at the houses, he kept his gaze fixed straight ahead and steeled himself. This was what he had been dreading since Harvey's call this morning.

Before he knew it, he was in front of his childhood home. He eased into the driveway behind Albert's black Chevy Silverado and sat there. The engine idled, and he took several deep breaths while his eyes roamed across the front of the house.

It was a two-story craftsman bungalow that had been constructed in 1961. A number of the gray slate tiles on the sides were chipped or missing. It needed a new roof, as did the connected garage. Despite a satellite dish on the side of the house, the broken old metal aerial still hugged the chimney like a reluctant toddler on her first day of kindergarten. The lawn needed to be mowed, and the elm by the road had the blight. The three houses to the left and one to the right looked exactly as he remembered, but now two of them sat empty with faded Realtor signs like gravestones in the overgrown yards.

Kit shut off the engine. Emotions warred within him. He hated it here so much. His mouth was dry, and his lips stuck together like a sealed envelope. He wanted to leave. Running away had always been one of the few things he was good at. The chorus of Meat Loaf's song "Bat Out of Hell" rambled through his head. His plan was indeed to be gone when morning came.

He yearned to see his mother coming out the door—except she hadn't lived here since the divorce in 1989. Even though she was originally from Scarburn County, she'd moved to Knoxville not long after. According to the funeral home receptionist, her last request had been to be buried in the place she still thought of as home.

Kit's anger swelled. A prickly rush of fear combined with an anxious pressure to avoid what was about to happen coursed through him, followed by mounting rage. He held on to the anger, nurtured it in his chest. It fed his disgust of the town and of this place in particular. No, not this *place*. His father.

Who hadn't even bothered to tell his son that his mother had died.

Swallowing the burning sensation in his throat, Kit stepped out of the vehicle. He started up the sidewalk, noticing that the porch sagged on one end. Several of the spindles were missing. It reminded him of a hillbilly smile.

A bamboo windchime hung motionless near the front door, and two rocking chairs rested on the porch.

Albert McNeil occupied one of them.

He was rocking and smoking—hopefully the oxygen tank beside him had been turned off. Kit saw his father's baggy eyes watching him as if he were a thief creeping up in the middle of the night. Beneath the nicotine-stained gray mustache, his mouth didn't move except to draw on the cigarette and exhale. The rocker slowed to a stop.

Kit climbed the three steps to the porch. Each one felt like he was walking through water. He forced himself to keep going, leaning on the fury that burned within him. The moment had arrived. He faced his father.

Albert assessed his son from head to toe. "Christopher," his father said with a hint of displeasure. "It's been a long time."

Kit clenched his fists and ground his teeth together. The longer he stared at his father's thin, gray hair and heavy jowls, the angrier he got. He finally exploded. "I can't believe you!"

His father feigned surprise.

"Don't pretend like you don't know! You didn't even have the decency to call?"

"I tried," Albert said. "You were out somewhere doing your . . . *thing.* Wasn't any way to contact you."

"Jesus, Dad! The band has a manager. And a management agency!"

"I did what I could." Albert's blue eyes turned icy, and he poked the cigarette at Kit. "Don't you come in here yelling at me, boy. I'm still your father. Exodus 20:12 says to honor thy father and—"

"I know what it says! I heard it often enough!"

"You might've heard it, but you didn't *listen.* You're still smarting off."

Kit sighed and tried to calm down. He felt himself shrink, becoming that scared little kid once more. He despised that feeling. After eighteen years, Albert still had power over him. Kit loathed that too. He cursed himself for allowing it to happen, but his inner child still cringed when he heard a certain tone of voice or caught one of Albert's looks.

*This is crazy. Look at him. He's in bad shape. He can't do anything to me, not anymore.*

Kit knew he was simply trying to rationalize his trauma. He had learned a long time ago how to handle the beatings. That just came with the territory when you lived with an abuser. Maybe Albert couldn't hit him like before, but the majority of the damage his father had inflicted wasn't physical. No, Albert's preferred weapon had been words—the kind that turned a happy, normal kid into a guilt-ridden, frightened mass of insecurity.

"Look," Kit said, trying to soften his tone, "I know you weren't expecting me. I . . . I know you don't care whether I'm here or not, and you know I don't really want to be here. I wouldn't be, if not for Mom."

"She was a good woman. Better than I deserved. *She* fought the cancer hard."

A wave of guilt slammed into Kit. He looked away, struggling to control his anger and grief. He'd not only learned how to take a beating but also how to read between the lines. One of Albert's favorite tactics was to make even the simplest statement carry a double meaning. Like a two-edged sword, Albert's simple words carried a crueler, shameful meaning. "*She* fought the cancer hard" also meant that she'd fought the cancer *alone*.

Kit looked at his father. "I-I've just come to tell her goodbye. I understand the *funeral* was really nice." He knew nothing about the funeral but could also take a swing with the double-edged sword.

His father ignored the bait and dropped the cigarette butt into a can of Ensure.

Kit looked out into the yard and took a long, slow breath, exhaling it in the same manner. His rage and incredulity lessened, a wave receding from the shore. He stuck his hands in the pockets of his jeans and leaned against the railing.

"I'd be careful if I was you." Albert gestured to the spindle-less openings along the railing. "This old thing could easily drop you out in the yard."

Kit noticed that his father's teeth resembled the railing. *God, he's even starting to look like the house.* "Listen, I was wondering—can, uh . . . can I stay tonight? I got gas on the way here, and it didn't leave me with much."

Albert snorted. "I told you that you'd never make no decent living with that guitar."

Kit bit his tongue.

"You need to get down to the plant and get a real job—something that pays good, has good benefits. You know, man's work."

"Dad, I'm in a band," Kit lied. *Or at least I was.* The last thing he wanted was for Albert to learn about what had happened in Memphis.

Albert looked at him smugly. "And don't got a pot to piss in, do you?"

"Can I stay or not?"

The elder McNeil hocked a string of phlegm over the railing and into a bush. He wiped his mouth with the heel of his hand and sighed. "Take one of the rooms upstairs. I started to use them for storage awhile back, but I don't go up there no more."

"Thanks."

"You still drinking? Doing them drugs?"

Kit summoned up his best straight face. "No, that was, uh, a long time ago."

"Good. Damn drugs are part of what's wrong with you. I won't have any of that stuff in my house. Devil's poison."

"Yeah, okay."

"And don't be playing that damn guitar all hours of the night. I ain't in the best of health anymore." Albert nodded at the oxygen tank.

*Still healthy enough for a pack and a half a day though.* "Yeah, no problem." Kit turned and started toward his vehicle.

"When you planning on getting your own place?"

Kit fumed and kept walking.

Albert coughed up another ball of phlegm and spit. "I've still got connections with the union. A call or two and I can probably get you on second shift at the plant."

As he unloaded his belongings, Kit said, "Are you charging me rent?"

"Nope. Just think it's time you quit wasting your life and take a real job. Like I did. I provided for the family. Bought this house and every car we ever owned."

"Uh, yeah, you know what? I'm not going to be staying that long."

What if his father was right? Maybe he should get a nice job, something consistent to keep the bills paid. *Man's work.*

The thought was slimy and frightening. That would make him just like his father—like most of the people in this town. He couldn't think of any hell that would be worse.

• • •

Kit carried his things up the stairs. The guest room was to his left, and the half bath was straight ahead. He turned right and opened the door to his old room. Thick, stuffy air greeted him. Inside was a bed and nightstand, a chest of drawers, the old desk he had once used as a workbench, and a pile of Albert's boxes. His old Stevie Ray Vaughan poster and a couple of *Sports Illustrated* swimsuit pages curled away from the walls. A fine layer of dust covered everything, which was not surprising since his father would never *pay* a woman to clean. In his mind that was her God-given duty.

Kit started to sweat in the confined humidity, so he crossed the room and opened the window. The air outside was no better.

Heavy. Still.

He looked at the two trees in the backyard and the chain-link fence that separated the property from the one behind. He tried to remember who had lived back there, but their names escaped him. At one point there had been half a dozen or so kids around his age on the block.

Kit dropped his things at the foot of the bed and ran his fingertips along the surface of the desk. It was marred by dozens of tiny X-Acto knife scars and pebbled with dollops of dried Testors model paint.

*Man, how many hours did I spend here, putting together all those models?*

His interest in modeling began when he'd gotten a dinosaur kit for his ninth birthday. From there he'd moved on to tractor trailers, monsters, and spaceships. The USS *Enterprise* and the X-wing fighter had been his favorites, and he'd proudly hung them from the ceiling.

Modeling was how he'd gotten his nickname. Troy had bestowed it upon him. One day Kit had been working on a model—painting, gluing, soaking the decals in water, and trying to slide them onto the plastic without tearing them or getting them stuck together. Troy had found him hunched over his desk, building and listening to the radio. Troy nicknamed him Kit then and there, and Kit accepted it cheerfully.

He had even used the nickname briefly when he worked as a disc jockey for his college radio station. "You're listening to Kit McNeil here at WMTS-FM!" That was before he'd dropped out of Middle Tennessee State University.

Another opportunity wasted.

He sat down on the edge of the bed and unpacked his clothes, tossing a couple of magazines and paperbacks near the pillows. After putting the clothes in a drawer, he turned around.

He stopped.

Another memory ignited when he saw the magazines and books against his pillow.

• • •

After he and Troy had left the old school, Kit had headed home for lunch alone. Troy had to go to Spring City with his mom and sisters.

Someone on the block had just finished mowing their lawn, and the air smelled sweet as Kit swerved into the driveway. He dropped his bike in the garage, grabbed a glass of Kool-Aid from the refrigerator, and trotted upstairs. He walked into his room and saw it.

Lying against his pillow was the issue of *Famous Monsters* he and Troy had seen in the drugstore earlier that day! The menacing Darth Vader was pointing toward a TIE fighter that was firing on an X-wing, while below Luke, Ben, and C-3PO were surrounded by stormtroopers. He hurried to pick it up, his eyes wide.

That's when he discovered the other surprise. A second magazine lay behind it—one he'd never seen before. *Guitar Player.* He stared at the cover. Country rock superstar Albert Lee stared back at him. He opened it almost reverently and read the table of contents. There was stuff about Molly Hatchet and a bunch of other people he didn't know. There were news and reports and ads for all kinds of cool gear. And sheet music! He was so engrossed that he didn't hear his mother come in.

"So what do you think?" she asked with a grin.

"Where did these come from? Are they from the library? Do I have to return them?"

"No, they're yours. I had to go to the drugstore and pick up some medicine for your father. I overheard you and Troy talking about that monster one as you were leaving this morning. The other one I just thought you might be interested in. It was the only one they had." She smiled as she watched him with her green eyes.

"Mom, this is so cool! Did you see? It's got music in it!"

She put a stack of clean clothes in the dresser. "It does? I didn't look at it very closely. I saw the title and thought of you."

"Thanks, Mom!"

She turned to leave. "Don't tell your father. You know how he is about spending money frivolously."

"What's 'frivolously' mean?"

A look of beleaguered frustration crossed her face. "It means your father is a tightwad and fun-sucker."

Kit giggled. His mother winked at him.

"You want the door open or closed?" she asked.

He kicked off his shoes and scooted into the middle of the bed. He sat cross-legged with the music magazine in his lap. "Open's good."

"It's humid up here," she said as she crossed the landing and started down the steps. "Keep your door closed when you use the air conditioner. We don't want you cooling the whole upstairs."

• • •

Now Kit stared down at the magazines he'd pitched against the pillows. He realized tears were running down his cheeks. His eyes drifted to the door, hoping to see her there once more, smiling and happy—like she was before Albert's nastier side emerged.

But there was nothing. From now on there would always be nothing. This harsh realization hit him like a baseball bat to the stomach. He collapsed onto the bed and wept.

# 4

## MARTY'S JOINT

*Thursday, June 2, 2011*

**K**it stepped into the parlor of the Dennis-Stanz Funeral Home one block south of the courthouse. Despite the bright lights and perfectly arranged furniture, the burden of death could not be hidden. The cloying aroma of floral bouquets filled the air.

The receptionist stopped typing on his keyboard and looked up. "Good afternoon. May I help you?" the young man asked with a practiced smile.

"Uh, yeah, I'm Kit—I mean, Christopher—McNeil. My mom, Paula Rhodes, was . . . "

The receptionist nodded. "I'm so sorry for your loss. Has the family made any prearrangements? If not, that's no problem. We can have someone sit down and go through everything. Are there other family members who will be joining you?"

"No, no, I mean . . . She passed away last week. The funeral was on Sunday."

"Oh, my apologies, sir. Paula Rhodes, you said?" He pecked several keys and looked at the monitor. "Yes, here we are. You're her son, Christopher?"

"Yeah. I was on the road. I'm in a band, and we were touring." He felt that he needed to justify his absence. "I just . . . found out yesterday."

"I understand. Please know that all of us here at Dennis-Stanz express our condolences for your loss."

Kit shifted his weight from one foot to the other. "Thanks. I was wondering where she's buried. I-I'd like to visit."

"Of course, sir. She's interred in Scarburn County Memorial Gardens. Are you familiar with the area?"

Kit nodded.

"Your mother's resting place is in Section 4, Row H, the seventh marker from the road. Let me write that down for you." After another expression of sympathy from the receptionist, Kit departed with the sticky note in hand.

The weather was identical to yesterday, and the early afternoon sun baked Black Rock as he drove through. The cemetery was about fifteen minutes west of town. He occupied his mind by looking for buildings and roads that he remembered from childhood.

He turned off County Road 501 onto an adjacent two-lane that snaked around the base of several hills. He passed two new apartment buildings, a convenience store, a laundromat, and a Baptist church. A metal sign directed him to turn, and the road ended at the cemetery gates. The gates stood open, and he rolled slowly through as if too much speed would disturb the dead.

He referred to the sticky note and scanned the small signs that marked sections and rows. The last time he had been here was for the graveside service of Donald Jeffs, a member of his graduating class who'd died in a freak accident at work. A forklift had tipped over and crushed him, although no one could explain how a piece of heavy machinery could just turn over on its own.

Jeffs's death hadn't been the first. By 1993, seven years after graduation, fourteen other classmates had died. Rumors of foul play were attached to a few, but nothing was ever proven. Mystery and peculiarity—like the forklift accident—surrounded half a dozen of them.

*The curse of Black Rock strikes again.*

He had often wondered if he was as cursed as the town seemed to be. Surely no one could have as much bad luck as he had experienced. It seemed that no matter what he did, eventually it all fell apart. If King Midas could touch something and make it turn to gold, Kit felt like his touch brought nothing but frustration and futility. When he had left Black Rock a month after his last visit to this cemetery, he had secretly hoped his bad luck would end when he crossed the county line.

It hadn't, of course. After a while he had resigned himself to the fact that he wasn't going to have the kind of life other people did. There wasn't going to be a nice house, a wife, some kids, or a dog. No stable income. Security. Hope. He told himself that he didn't really want those sorts of things. He was a loner. He didn't want any attachments that might make him become like his father.

But what if he *did* want something to call his own at some point down the road? What were the chances of it happening? Slim to none, he figured. So why dream about it? Why work toward it? He was snakebitten when it came to things going his way. That was why he didn't gamble. No use reaffirming what he already knew by losing hard-earned money.

Gravel crunched beneath his tires as he eased onto the lane for Row H. He stopped and got out at the seventh marker. The stone rectangle was unobtrusive, decorated with angels in the top corners. Blocks of sod had been laid over the grave and dirt still surrounded the area. Kit knelt. His fingers traced his mother's name.

Memories came unbidden. Most didn't have a lot of detail but were filled with feelings of warmth, security, and contentment—as if all the best things about her had been distilled into these sensations. Of course, there were the memories that had always stayed with him—the *Guitar Player* magazine, the Christmas he got his first amp, her face as she took pictures of him at graduation, and even the excitement in her voice when he'd told her about the audition for Southern by the Grace of God.

Remembering the magazine prompted the recollection of their library visits together.

Albert had always been a union man. He'd attended union meetings every Tuesday evening. During that time, Kit and his mother visited the library. He would pick out two or three books, and she checked them out for him.

Over the next few days Kit would devour his books. He always liked to read beside his open window when the weather permitted. Spring winds that smelled of honeysuckle and clover kept him company as he followed the exploits of The Hardy Boys. Summer thunderstorms added menace to scary stories late in the evening.

Those library trips had been something just between the two of them—something that Albert couldn't take away. He knew they went each week but didn't care. If it wasn't the newspaper or related to his job, Albert had no interest in reading it.

Kneeling in front of the headstone, Kit smiled softly at the memory of getting his very own library card. The librarian had handed him the keys to the kingdom. He could check out books on his own! The power he carried in his pocket was nearly intoxicating to an eight-year-old boy.

Those trips—and the books—had been one of the ways he learned to cope with Albert's mood swings. Reading was an escape for his mind when his body was imprisoned. He had walked the Hyborian Age with Conan and scurried through the rabbit warrens of *Watership Down* while his bruises healed. The magical world of Xanth in *A Spell for Chameleon* had mesmerized him, and he'd joined Bilbo's magnificent journey in *The Hobbit* to forget the venom of his father's biting criticisms.

His mother had always found ways to ease his suffering. She had gone behind Albert's back to bring him chocolate chip cookies and milk, comic books, and model kits. He wasn't sure if Albert had known about those things, or if his mother had endured Albert's wrath as a result. It struck him just how much of her own money she'd sacrificed back then to help offset his father's cruelties. Had she cried into her pillow sometimes the same way Kit had? How much hurt had she absorbed so it wouldn't get to him? Had she suffered in silence on his behalf? Hot tears ran down his face.

The afternoon wore on, and Kit felt no urge to leave. He walked around the cemetery a few times, visiting the markers of some of his old classmates. He also saw several patches of blight, and once again, the pale coloration and lumpy texture gave him a peculiar, disgusted feeling. He always ended up back at his mother's grave. He talked to her, apologizing for all the ways he felt he had let her down and for all the missed opportunities to spend time with her. He thanked her for everything she had done for him, for how she'd raised him.

As he purged his soul, all of his bad decisions and screwups and failures resurfaced as well. He imagined his mother listening patiently, nodding occasionally, and offering him her smile that said everything was going to be all right. He confessed everything, and she silently absolved him. His conscience didn't sting quite as much as he sat on the fresh sod and listened to the breeze in the pines. His remorse was genuine, and unburdening himself left him exhausted but freer than he had felt in ages. When gray clouds promising rain crept over the mountains, he said his final goodbye and drove away with an aching but lighter heart.

• • •

Kit had no interest in returning to the house, so he got back on County Road 501, heading west. He realized he wasn't going anywhere in particular, but when he saw the sign for Marty's Joint and an arrow pointing to an upcoming left turn, he smiled and took it.

Half a mile later the old brick building came into view. A portable yellow marquee sign with a flashing arrow read:

MARTY'S JOINT
BEER  MUSIC  POOL

FRI—SAT  6/3-6/4
THE OUTLAW POSSE BAND

WE ID.  SMOKING ALLOWED.

Kit smiled again. He'd played at Marty's Joint when he was twenty. A couple of shows had been solo, and two were as last-minute fill-ins for local bands.

His first public appearance—not including playing for his mom or Troy—had been in the high school talent show. He had performed an acoustic version of Eddie Rabbitt's "I Love a Rainy Night" and had gotten a standing ovation. A lot of people had known that he played but few had realized how good he had become. He hadn't won the talent show. That honor went to Emily Towers, who had danced a nearly flawless reproduction of the final performance in *Flashdance*, but the principal had called him back for an encore to close the show. He'd played "Pride and Joy" from Stevie Ray Vaughan's *Texas Flood* album.

Kit parked between two pickup trucks and crossed the gravel lot.

Marty's Joint had three windows and a red front door, and the place hadn't changed since the 1970s. The wood-paneled walls held the same dartboard, neon beer signs, framed photos of classic country musicians, and the

NO FIGHTING sign that had been there forever. Tables and chairs cluttered the edges of the room, leaving space near the stage for dancing. A row of booths lined the wall beyond the bar. Stained glass light fixtures dangled like gaudy earrings above four pool tables. The jukebox was dark but a radio behind the bar played Miranda Lambert's "The House That Built Me." Two men sat at a table while another man occupied a stool and talked to the bartender.

"Afternoon," the bartender said, turning from his conversation. "Getcha something?" He was covered in tattoos and hair, and his skin appeared to be made from cracked leather.

"Hey," Kit replied. "Kitchen open yet?"

The bartender glanced over his shoulder at the Coors Light clock. "About half an hour."

"Cool. Let me have a beer."

"Bottle or draft?"

"Bottle is fine." Kit searched his memory as he studied the bartender, but nothing clicked. Kit didn't remember him.

Cold bottle in hand, Kit sat down at one of the tables and watched a sports talk program on a wall-mounted television. Several men wandered in, greeting each other and throwing curious glances toward Kit's table. They were all dressed in dirty work clothes. He got another beer, and when the kitchen opened, he ordered chicken tenders and fried chips. As he ate, more men dropped in. They lined the bar like targets in a shooting gallery.

He was wiping grease from his fingers when the door opened and someone said, "I don't believe it!"

The speaker walked toward him, the grin on his face spreading by the second.

His gait seemed familiar to Kit, and he looked the newcomer up and down. The face—with a few added pounds and a beard—was definitely familiar. "Oh my God," Kit whispered as he rose to his feet.

"Kit? Is that you?" the man asked. His grin faltered briefly as the possibility of mistaken identity crossed his face.

"Oh my God!" Kit shouted. He couldn't contain his elation. "Troy! Jesus. Oh, man!"

The two old friends shook hands, pumping each other's arms. Troy slapped Kit on the shoulder.

"Holy shit! How're you doing? What're you doing here? When did you get into town?"

Kit laughed. "Whoa, slow down! One question at a time, man."

Troy pulled out a chair. "Jesus Christ, it's good to see you." He looked over his shoulder. "Reggie, two beers over here."

"You see any damned waitresses around here?" the tattooed man retorted with a smile. "Get over here and get 'em yourself, you lazy bastard."

Troy retrieved the bottles and sat down across from Kit. They grinned like schoolboys, faces flush with surprise and joy.

"When did you come back?" Troy asked after taking a drink.

Kit explained about his mother in between swigs from the bottle.

"Yeah," Troy said, "I went to the visitation. I wondered where you were."

Kit explained that as well, and a fresh wave of guilt hit him for not being there for his mom in her last days. His anger returned as he talked about what Albert had done and about the prickly homecoming he'd received from his father, but the excitement of their reunion soon overshadowed even that. They talked and laughed, catching up on the events of their lives.

"Look at you," Kit said. "When we were kids, you were so skinny you had to wear snowshoes in the shower to keep from falling down the drain!"

"Now I look like *you* did back then, Butter Butt."

"You married?"

"Yeah, on my second. You?"

"Twice divorced. Currently single."

"Kids?" Troy asked after swallowing a mouthful of beer.

"God, no! My life is enough of a mess. I can't imagine trying to be a father when I can't even get my own shit together."

"I've got two by my first wife and one with Shawna."

Kit told him about his sputtering music career and his most recent embarrassment in Memphis. Troy worked as the director of maintenance for the Spring City School District and commuted from Black Rock.

Even though they hadn't seen each other in almost two decades, Kit found it just as easy to talk to his friend now as he had growing up. The transparency felt good. After the time spent at his mother's grave and now this fortuitous reunion, Kit felt as if his soul had been washed clean. It was a welcome feeling, one he wished he could have more often.

"So much for that place on the beach you always wanted, eh?" Kit pushed his empty plate aside.

"Place on the— You gotta be kidding me! You still remember that?"

"Coming back here has jarred loose a lot of stuff."

Troy grew serious. "Speaking of that, do you remember when we used to think this place was cursed, because of all the weird deaths and stuff? Well, have I got some things to tell you."

# 5

## SOME THINGS NEVER CHANGE

*Thursday, June 2, 2011*

The door to Marty's Joint burst open, and two young men entered, talking loudly. Kit studied them as they went to the bar. Both appeared to be in their early twenties. One had a sparse mustache and goatee with long black hair that was slicked back. The other wore a ratty green fishing cap. He had a hawk nose and wide-set eyes—the unmistakable features of a Dunley and like the people who chased him in his dream.

Kit looked at Troy. "Which one is that?"

Troy needed no clarification. "That's Scotty."

Kit pursed his lips and shook his head.

Troy lowered his voice. "You remember Garrett, right? That's one of his boys."

"They just keep reproducing, don't they? What about the other one?"

"Gabe Beecher. Another local good old boy."

Kit was more than familiar with the type. He and Troy had grown up among them. Guys like that had bullied them for not playing football or not following NASCAR. They had terrorized Kit and Troy for liking Dungeons & Dragons and for simply being smaller, easier targets. Kit and Troy hadn't dipped Skoal or gone hunting. They hadn't driven pickups with lift kits and rebel flag stickers on the rear windows.

Scotty and Gabe took their beers to the far side of the room and sat at a table, still laughing and talking louder than was necessary. Kit couldn't help watching them. He remembered his first run-in with the Dunley family when he was eight years old. It had scared the hell out of him.

• • •

Kit was walking home from elementary school with a folder of papers tucked under his arm and his Marvel Super Heroes lunch box thumping against his leg. He was lost in thought when he rounded a corner and saw Garrett and Johnny, the twins, loitering farther down the sidewalk. Panic surged through his chest, and he froze. Kit prayed they hadn't seen him. He was just about to creep back around the corner when one of them spotted him.

"Hey! Hey, you! Come here!" The command was cold and dripped with menace.

Kit searched the street in front of him for an adult but saw no one. His gaze landed on Bennett's Drugstore. Without thinking, he ran as fast as he could.

"Get back here, you little turd!" one of them yelled.

Their pounding feet and cruel laughter made him run faster. His lunch box cracked against his knee, and he clutched the folder to his chest to keep from dropping it. As he dashed across the street, he saw Garrett and Johnny closing in fast. They leered at him in eager anticipation.

"Yer dead!"

"Stop runnin', you little puke!"

Kit threw open Bennett's glass door. The bell jangled like a dinner chime on a ranch. He scuttled down the greeting card aisle and cut back through the cold and flu section. The air he sucked in smelled of medicine and perfume. Hands on his knees, he peered around the magazine shelf and tried to breathe as softly as possible.

Garrett and Johnny bounded in. They split up and started down the aisles.

Heart hammering, Kit edged around the shelf. He surveyed the area between him and the door. He imagined getting halfway to safety before the Dunleys leaped on him.

From the back of the store, a man's voice called, "Hey, what're you kids doing over there?"

"Nothin'," one of the twins replied. Kit realized this was his chance. It was now or never. He dashed outside, the bell betraying his departure. He ran as fast as his legs could carry him. As he rounded the corner at the end of the block, he heard the bell chime once more followed by coarse laughter.

"We'll get you next time!" one of the twins shouted.

"Gonna beat you to a pulp!" yelled the other twin.

Kit ran the rest of the way home surprised that he hadn't wet himself.

• • •

As the memory receded, Kit realized his heart was beating faster. He drained his bottle and looked at Troy. "You said you had something to tell me?"

Troy nodded. He started to speak just as the door opened. A diesel truck roared into the parking lot, a jackhammer on wheels blaring country music. Troy waited until the door closed again.

"Do you remember Tyler Daniels from our graduating class?" Troy asked, adjusting his silver-rimmed glasses. His voice had turned serious again.

Kit eyed the nicotine-stained ceiling as he searched his memory. "Maybe, vaguely."

"He was the kid in our class who studied overseas our junior year. Went to England or Scotland, somewhere like that."

Kit recalled a face, faint as gossamer in a mist. "Yeah, I think I do now."

"He died a few days ago—May 22. Car went off the road. He was wearing a seat belt and still got thrown thirty feet into a tree. The *only* tree within *seventy* yards."

"Damn," Kit replied in a low voice. Now he remembered Tyler Daniels. Before they'd gone to high school, Kit and Tyler had often thumb wrestled in their middle school homeroom. "How did it happen?"

"Not sure. The police think he swerved to avoid something in the road. Probably a deer."

Kit shook his head. "Damn. How many people from our class are dead now—eight or ten?"

Troy's eyes widened. He shook his head slowly. "You've been gone a long time, pal. I've been keeping track. Gruesome hobby, huh? Since we graduated, a total of—"

A bottle shattered.

Turning toward the sound, Kit and Troy saw a man at Scotty and Gabe's table. Beer bubbled on the floor amid shards of brown glass.

"Hey, sorry, Gabe. I didn't mean to do that. I was just goin' to take a leak an' my arm—"

Kit watched Gabe shoot out of the booth like he'd been catapulted.

"Well, you might not've meant to do it, but you *did*, peckerwood! You owe me a fuckin' beer, Lew!" Gabe pushed the man in the chest.

"Ease up, it was just an accident," Lew replied, his voice hard.

"You callin' me a liar?"

"You're the one who left the bottle too close to the goddamn edge of the table, Gabe!"

Kit saw movement, but it was so sudden and swift that it took him a second to catch up with it. A loud pop followed. Lew's head snapped back. He staggered as blood ran down into his mustache.

"Scotty! Gabe!" the bartender bellowed. "Don't you fuckin' start! I told you last time I wasn't puttin' up with no more of your bullshit!"

Two men jumped up from the bar and hurried toward the ruckus. They stepped beside Lew, who snarled and wiped blood from his face with his sleeve.

Scotty rose from his chair, his beady eyes locked on the newcomers. He turned his hat around backward. "Back off. You don't want no part of this."

The bartender was on the phone.

Lew grabbed Gabe and slammed him against the wall, but Gabe just laughed. He pounded Lew in the side, his fists driving like pistons. Lew doubled over, coughing up blood. A knee to the face and Lew was on the floor. He tried to protect his ribs, so Gabe switched and kicked him in the head.

Scotty shot forward and knocked one of the two guys, who had come over from the bar, backward over a table. He pivoted and started punching the other man. Scotty fought like a man possessed.

Barstools clattered to the floor as more men headed for the brawl. Tables were pushed aside. Chairs fell. Curses and heavy breathing filled the air.

"Some things never change," Kit said, shaking his head. He was surprised to see Scotty holding his own against five stockier men. They landed punches, but Scotty didn't seem to register the pain. He kept grinning like a lunatic and returning blows. Kit thought there was something feral about his expression.

Amid the scuffling and grunting and swearing, Kit watched several men try to separate the combatants. More fists flew. Bodies collided, slammed into tables, and bounced off walls.

In the end it took eight men to restrain Scotty and Gabe. A couple other guys helped Lew to his feet. He grimaced in pain as he clutched his rib cage, and blood covered his face. Scotty and Gabe seethed with rage. More curses and promises of retaliation flew back and forth.

"Put it away, Reggie," someone said as the door opened.

Kit turned and saw the bartender with a shotgun. Two police officers entered.

"We've got this," one of the officers said. He was a Hispanic man in his midtwenties.

An older woman followed him. She was taller than her fellow officer, thin, not unattractive, and about Kit's age. Her brown hair was cut short, and her hard eyes did not miss a thing. "Good thing we were in the neighborhood," she deadpanned to Reggie.

Kit watched her as she walked across the room. There was authority and power in her stride, determination in the steely set of her face. He guessed this wasn't the first time she had been called on to deal with a Dunley.

"That's Laura Richie," Troy said. "The other officer is Marquez Cambeiro."

Deputy Richie put a hand on Kit's shoulder as she navigated her way through the crowd of gawkers to confront Scotty and Gabe.

"I might've known," she said in disgust. "Hands behind your backs."

"Hey, we didn't do nothin'," Gabe complained. He licked at the blood trickling from his lip. "We was just havin' a beer when that sonuvabitch"—he pointed at Lew—"came over here an—"

"Shut up, Gabe," Deputy Cambeiro ordered. He had his nightstick out. "We know what happened."

"Fuck you!" Gabe yelled.

"I said hands behind your backs," Deputy Richie repeated. Her mouth was a grim line etched into her iron face. "I won't tell you again. Next time I'll put your ass on the floor."

Gabe spat bloody saliva at her feet. "Ain't you got nothing better to do?" His voice dripped with disdain. Then his expression changed as quickly as a television channel. He put his hands up in surrender. "We were just having some fun, Lady Cop."

Scotty acted as if he wanted to step forward.

"Give me an excuse, Scotty," Deputy Cambeiro warned. He raised the nightstick.

Scotty shook his head in disbelief. He turned slowly, putting his hands behind his back. "This ain't over," he promised.

"Yeah, yeah." Deputy Cambeiro took out his cuffs.

Gabe's eyes were wild. He glared at Deputy Richie and bobbed up and down like a boxer ready for the bell. His sneer exposed yellow teeth. He clenched and unclenched his fists.

He reminded Kit of someone on angel dust.

"Gabe," Scotty said in a low, even voice. "Let it go."

Gabe's face scrunched in confusion as he stared at his buddy. His voice dripped with disappointment. "You serious, man?"

Scotty nodded with an arrogant grin. He winked at Gabe as the deputy turned him toward the door. "Another time, another place. Don't forget, you and I got all the time in the world."

Cursing, Gabe thrust his hands behind his back. Deputy Richie cuffed him and marched him across the floor. Deputy Cambeiro and Scotty followed.

With the excitement over, tables and chairs were reunited. Barstools were righted so the men could reclaim their territory and discuss the fight. Reggie put his shotgun back under the bar.

As soon as the door clicked shut, Kit looked at Troy. "Imagine that," Kit said sarcastically, "a Dunley getting in trouble with the cops. That Gabe looks like a nutjob too."

"He is. White trash troublemaker," Troy replied. "They're like animals. Most people around here think they did it."

"Did what?"

"I guess you do need some catching up. Two people from the area have disappeared in the last year. Tyson Collinsworth, from Spring City, went missing about a year ago, and Meredith Walston from Black Rock vanished early last month."

"Yeah, it wouldn't be much of a stretch to imagine them being responsible for something like that," Kit said.

"The problem is that no bodies have been found. There's no evidence linking those two fuckups to the disappearances. Sheriff Owens and the TBI have hauled them in several times over the past few months. I guess they're trying to rattle their cages to see if they turn on each other or let something slip."

Kit raised his eyebrows. "The Tennessee Bureau of Investigation?"

"Sure. County officials asked for their help. Word is the FBI is in the loop too."

Kit shivered despite the dense, smoky air and lowered his voice. "Do, uh . . . do you remember the summer of '81?"

"Yeah, I do."

"And what we saw out there in the woods?"

Troy nodded and picked at the label on his beer bottle.

"Was she . . . was Melody Sellers ever found?" Kit's chest tightened. He really wanted an affirmative answer.

"Nobody has heard from her since then. Far as I know, we were the last people to see her with the Dunleys that summer."

# 6

## MELODY SELLERS IS MISSING

*Thursday, June 2, 2011*

**W**ith Scotty and Gabe gone, the bar returned to normal. Kit went to the restroom, stepping cautiously around the blood and the broken beer bottle on the floor that had launched the donnybrook. When he returned, Troy was leaving a tip on the table.

"You leaving?" Kit asked, unable to hide the disappointment in his voice.

"Yeah, just got a call from the wife. She needs a few things from the store. How long you gonna be around?"

Kit shrugged. "Not long. I visited Mom today. Guess there's not much else to keep me here."

"Why don't you stick around for the weekend? I'm busy all day tomorrow, but what if we went out to eat on Sunday? I'd invite you over to the house and grill some steaks, but our kitchen is all to hell right now. We're redoing the cabinets," Troy said as they stepped outside.

The humidity had lessened, but after the air-conditioned confines of Marty's Joint, it still smacked them in the face like a wet sponge. The clouds Kit had seen from the cemetery must've dumped a quick shower somewhere nearby.

Kit thought for a moment. He didn't relish the idea of being around Albert any longer than was necessary, but who knew when he might see Troy again? Kit smiled. "Yeah, okay, I'd like that."

"How about Mexican?"

They settled on Sunday at Tres Sombreros. After shaking hands and saying their goodbyes, Troy drove off in his green Ford F-150.

Dusk threatened from the east, chasing the sun over the mountains. Kit felt better than he had in a long time. Running into his old friend had been a balm for his withered soul. The circumstance that had brought him back to Black Rock was horrible. He knew he would never be the same again, but the time with Troy had grounded him. It was a reminder that even the darkest times could be endured with the support of a good friend.

He drove toward town, the muggy air fresh and clean as it rushed past his open windows. It carried the unmistakable cool, earthy scent of distant rain. He didn't want to go back to Albert's. Kit had gone out of his way to keep his distance. If they weren't together, they couldn't fight. No need to hear in person what his mind replayed for him nearly every day.

Kit felt so good at the moment that he didn't want to spoil it. Albert was probably sitting in his recliner, watching some hunting or fishing program. Kit had never understood the desire to watch someone else catch fish.

On a whim, he decided to drive up to The Sweet Spot. Everyone called it that since couples often went there to be alone. It also happened to have one of the most scenic views in all of Scarburn County. As he reached the outskirts of town, he stopped at a convenience store and bought a six-pack before driving up Campbell Mountain.

The road was an asphalt serpent around the contours of the mountain. The air smelled of evergreen and wet clay. Shadows gathered quickly between the hills as the sky faded to dusty purple. Kit turned onto the nameless, two-mile gravel road that climbed to The Sweet Spot.

The flat area was a little smaller than a football field on the southern face of the mountain. At nearly eight hundred feet above sea level, it was still dominated by Blackpoint's summit nearby. The domed hills of east Tennessee were a lumpy verdant blanket spreading away from the mountain. A few low, pensive clouds smeared the charcoal sky.

Kit was surprised to find The Sweet Spot empty tonight. There should've been a few cars up here, their occupants less concerned with the view than with each other. Of course, with all the electronic distractions available, he wondered if anybody still came up here for good old-fashioned making out.

He got out and felt the caress of the soft breeze and couldn't help but take a deep breath. He climbed onto the hood of the CR-V. Leaning against the windshield, Kit opened a beer and watched the stars come out.

His thoughts drifted back to the incident in the bar. A Dunley and some redneck getting hauled away by the cops wasn't anything new or even particularly interesting, but now that he had time to play it back, something about it made him uneasy. He thought about Gabe's face, twisted with fury over something as innocuous as a spilled beer. Then there was the nonplussed arrogance of Scotty, whose attitude suggested that everyone was beneath him.

*How were they able to hold their own against a group of nearly a dozen men?*

The Dunleys had always been rough and mean, but that display reminded Kit of someone on bath salts or bad Ecstasy. Both had seemed almost impervious to pain, and the vicious joy on their faces still disturbed him.

While his old fears of the Dunleys had resurfaced when Scotty walked in, something else gnawed at Kit. It was what Troy had said. Had they *really* been the last people to see Melody Sellers with the Dunleys that summer?

• • •

It had been a rainy morning in late June 1981. Kit and Troy had gotten together after lunch. With the afternoon sun on their shoulders, they rode through puddles, trying to spray each other with water. After a while they ended up at their hideout in the woods. It was a mass of bushes they'd cut back in places, giving them an igloo-like shelter.

After discovering it back in 1979, they had worked for four days to get it ready. Kit had smuggled Albert's handsaw and hedge clippers out of the garage since the hideout was closer to his house. When they finished, their secluded place became a playground, confessional, dream incubator, and home away from home. Beneath the thick bowers they had tried their first cigarettes. They kept a metal box hidden beneath a pile of stones that contained the three *Playboy* magazines they'd found behind a dumpster. Once, Troy had successfully smuggled a bottle of whiskey out of his grandfather's house. After downing a quarter of it, they'd puked themselves silly.

In that secret place they'd talked about movies and comic books. They made grand proclamations about the future, envisioning their lives as adults. They laughed and farted. They discussed who they would rather repopulate the earth with if there were a nuclear war—Erin Gray from *Buck Rogers in the 25th Century* or Maren Jensen from *Battlestar Galactica*. They agreed that Cheryl Ladd was a lame replacement for Farrah Fawcett on *Charlie's Angels*, but their loyalties were divided over Bo Derek and Brooke Shields. Troy had the hots for Bo, Kit for Brooke.

That sweltering afternoon they relaxed in their hideout, sharing the last cigarette in the pack.

"I need to take a dump," Troy said. He stood and brushed off his jean shorts.

"You're supposed to leave one, not take one," Kit replied with a smirk.

Troy held out his skinny arm. "Just give me the damn TP."

That was a necessity since there wasn't a bathroom nearby. They had almost learned that the hard way, so they kept a roll in a plastic bag inside the metal box for emergencies. "You gotta think," Troy had said after the near miss, "even the Hall of Justice has to have bathrooms. Superman and Batman have to take dumps." This had led to a protracted discussion of Superman's alien origins, and whether or not he actually needed to relieve himself like humans did.

As Troy walked away with the plastic bag, Kit dug out a *Playboy*. It was the August '79 issue, his favorite. The scrumptious babe Candy Loving graced the cover in a silver bunny jacket and scarlet hot pants, looking coyly over her shoulder. He was searching for his favorite page when Troy reappeared.

"Somebody's coming!" Troy said.

"Huh?"

"I heard voices!"

Kit put the magazine down. "Who is it?"

"I don't know. I didn't wait around to see."

"They coming this way?"

Troy looked over his shoulder. "I don't think so."

"So no big deal."

"I've got an idea," Troy said with a grin. "Let's pretend to be the Hardy Boys."

"Ugh, seriously, man? We haven't done that in years."

"Come on, it'll be fun. We can follow whoever is out there and make up a story like we used to."

When they were nine or ten years old, they'd liked to pretend they were Parker Stevenson and Shaun Cassidy from *The Hardy Boys* television series. They'd find someone nearby—a woman carrying groceries, the janitor cleaning the school, two men unloading a truck—and dream up a crime they were committing. Then it was up to the amateur sleuths to figure out what was happening and how to stop it.

"Okay, fine," Kit said after thinking it over, "but I get to be Shaun Cassidy."

They hid their box and crept out from beneath the overhanging foliage. Troy led the way while Kit followed with less enthusiasm.

"Where we going?" Kit asked.

"Shh!" Troy hissed. "It was right around here that I heard the voices, Joe."

Kit played along, getting into character as well. "How many voices, Frank?"

"Two, maybe three." They continued through the trees, fleshing out the details of the mystery they were going to solve.

The ground was still damp from the morning rain. Both boys slipped and stumbled several times. Suddenly, Troy halted, and Kit nearly bowled him over.

"Hey," Kit said, "how 'bout a little warning next time!"

"Shut up!" Troy said in a low, firm voice. *"Hide!"*

They slipped behind two wide tree trunks and waited.

After a moment, Troy sucked in a deep breath of air. "Oh shit."

"What is it, Frank?" Kit asked, still playing his role.

Troy cut him off with a wave of his hand. "Stop, stop. I'm not playing now. And keep your voice down!" He peeked around the tree. "Take a look."

Kit heard the voices now. He looked around the tree. "Oh fuck—"

"Don't make a sound," Troy instructed, as if Kit were planning to scream or set off fireworks.

No more than fifty yards away, Greg and Jeff Dunley, the seventeen-year-old twins, walked through the woods. Greg wore a black AC/DC T-shirt and jeans, and Jeff had on a plain white T-shirt and a pair of camouflage pants. A dark-haired girl, who looked about their age, walked between them, dressed in shorts and a blue halter top. They were talking, but

Kit couldn't hear the conversation. Greg occasionally laughed, while the girl snickered a lot and clung to Jeff's arm. She appeared to have trouble walking. The trio slipped out of sight among the trees.

When Kit was sure they were out of earshot, he let his breath go in a *whoosh*. "Let's get the hell out of here."

"No, wait!" Troy exclaimed. "Let's go see what they're up to!"

"Are you nuts? You know what would happen if they caught us."

Troy gestured at the trees. "We'll be hidden. They won't even know we're around."

"That girl looked like she was drunk." Kit stared at the place where the trio had disappeared.

"Or high. Come on, let's go see."

"No, man. I think that's our cue to skiddoo."

"Don't be a pussy, dude."

Kit shook his head. "Not a good idea . . . "

"Fine, I'll go by myself." With that, Troy crept forward in pursuit.

Kit didn't want to do this. It was stupid and dangerous. Even if they did see something, what did it matter? It wasn't as if they could tell anybody. They'd be dead meat if the Dunleys found out.

He watched Troy moving from tree to tree.

Kit couldn't just abandon his friend. What if something happened to Troy? What if Greg or Jeff found him? A chill ran through Kit. Everyone knew the Dunleys were mean, but just how far would they go?

*Well, Ricky is already serving time in the pen.*

That clinched it. "Hey, wait up," Kit said.

They followed the trio for ten minutes, using the trees and undergrowth as cover. Greg and Jeff moved easily through the forest, guiding the girl by the hand. They conversed and laughed as if they were on a picnic.

When Greg stopped, Kit and Troy slipped into hiding spots. Kit climbed a few steps up the hill and hunkered behind a rock. Troy stepped down and clung to a wide tree trunk. They watched Jeff pull a piece of cloth from his back pocket. Greg said something to the girl, and she giggled nervously. Jeff put the cloth over her eyes and tied it behind her head.

Troy shifted to get a better view. The muddy ground slipped out from under him, and stones tumbled down the slope.

Greg and Jeff spun around.

Kit's heart thudded in his chest. He watched Troy hug the tree trunk like a drowning man clings to a life preserver. His friend's face was a blanched mask of terror. Kit motioned for Troy to stay down.

Greg walked toward Kit's and Troy's hiding places.

If he caught them spying—

Adrenaline surged through Kit's body, but he forced himself to stay still. If he made a break for it, Greg would be on him in a minute.

Troy's panicked eyes pleaded for help.

A switchblade appeared in Greg's hand. He was less than fifty yards away. Through the foliage, Kit watched him survey the area. Greg's face was as hard as the mountain they stood upon.

"Whoever's out there, you better show yourself *now*!" Greg's bellow rang out like a gunshot in the quiet woods. Kit flinched.

"I know you're out there, motherfucker!" Greg shouted.

Kit willed himself to be smaller as panic spread through him like a virus.

"C'mon, let's go, Greg!" Jeff yelled. "It's just an animal."

Kit watched Greg. He shifted his weight from side to side, his blade poised in front of him, and scanned the landscape a final time. "I swear to God if there's *anyone* out there, I'll find out who you are and gut you like a fucking fish!" Greg spat and walked back to the others.

Kit's chest hurt from holding his breath. His pulse roared in his ears like a jet engine. He continued to watch Greg, Jeff, and the girl. She seemed hesitant now. Skittish. Unsure. When she started to take the blindfold off, Jeff stopped her. The Dunleys said something, and Greg took her by the arm.

"Psst!" It was Troy.

Tearing his gaze away from the trio, Kit glanced at Troy, who was pointing behind them. Kit nodded but signaled for him to wait. He looked back at the trio.

The girl tried to pull away from Greg. He yanked her close, threw his arm around her waist, and started walking. When she reached for the blindfold again, Jeff smacked her hand away.

Kit waited until they were out of sight. Then he waited another minute just to be sure before motioning to Troy. They fled down the slope, casting frightened glances over their shoulders. They didn't stop until they reached their bikes at the edge of the woods. Kit bent over, hands on his knees, gulping air. Troy leaned against a tree. Both boys were soaked with sweat.

"What was that?" Troy asked between breaths.

Kit shook his head and shrugged.

"What were they doing with that girl?"

Kit shook his head again.

"Do you know who she was?"

"No, man. Pretty sure she's in high school though." Kit looked back into the shadowy woodlands as he picked his bike up off the ground. "All I know is we almost got killed. When you slipped—"

"Don't remind me. I nearly shit myself. You think Greg saw us?" Troy swiped damp hair away from his eyes.

"Nah."

"What makes you so sure? He could have."

"Stop spazzing. If he saw us, we wouldn't be here right now."

Troy nodded. "Should we . . . I mean, do you think we ought to tell somebody what we saw?"

"Like who?" Kit threw his leg over his bicycle.

"I don't know. The police? Our parents, maybe?"

"You know how much trouble we'd get into?" Kit's father would make his life hell if he knew about the hideout. "And what if the Dunleys found out we snitched?"

They pedaled down the road.

"What do you think they were doing with her?" Troy asked, his tone curious and frightened.

"I don't know. Maybe they were just going somewhere to get stoned."

"But why blindfold her?"

"Maybe it was a surprise. Hell, I don't know, Troy."

"I think, maybe, we oughta tell somebody."

But the moment Troy said it, Kit knew they were both too scared to do it. If they told someone, word would eventually get back to the Dunleys, and one way or another, they'd figure out who'd ratted on them.

Kit veered onto the sidewalk as Troy pedaled behind. They rode through the Mountain Heights neighborhood toward town. Kit rolled to a stop beside the subdivision's entrance sign.

"Look, I've been thinking," he told Troy. "We didn't actually see Greg or Jeff do anything, right? I mean, blindfolding somebody ain't against the law."

"But what if they—"

"Hey, we don't know what they were doing. We didn't *see* anything bad. It'd be different if we saw them kill her or something."

Troy pondered this for a moment. "Yeah, but it sure looked to me like she didn't want to go with them all of a sudden."

Kit shrugged. "Maybe she was just pretending—you know, like we do as the Hardy Boys. Maybe it was some sort of sex game."

"Yeah, maybe . . . "

"I'm not going to risk pissing off the Dunleys just because we saw some girl being blindfolded and led through the woods. Nothing happened." Kit stared hard at Troy. "We gotta be together on this. You good with not saying anything?"

Conflict raged across Troy's face, but in the end, he pushed the hair out of his eyes and nodded. "Okay, yeah. You're right. We didn't really *see* anything." But uncertainty lingered in his voice.

"Just a couple of assholes taking some girl for a hike."

Troy nodded again.

"Then we're good. Just forget it."

And they did. The episode slipped from their minds as other experiences pushed their way in. Everything returned to normal.

Until a few days later.

They were riding through town when Troy skidded to a halt. Kit circled back to join him.

Troy didn't say anything. He stared at a photocopy tacked to a telephone pole. The picture in the center was large and grainy but recognizable.

Kit's mouth went dry.

Heavy, black letters screamed:

MISSING PERSON
HAVE YOU SEEN MELODY SELLERS?

SEVENTEEN YEARS OLD. BLACK HAIR. GREEN EYES.
LAST SEEN ON JUNE 29 WEARING A BLUE HALTER TOP,

SHORTS, AND TENNIS SHOES.

PLEASE HELP US FIND OUR DAUGHTER.

CONTACT THE BLACK ROCK SHERIFF'S DEPARTMENT
IF YOU HAVE ANY INFORMATION ON
MELODY'S WHEREABOUTS.

• • •

Leaning against the hood of his vehicle, Kit watched a shooting star. He finished his fourth beer, crushed the can, and pitched it to the ground.

Back in school Melody Sellers had a loose reputation and had been known to run with the wrong crowd. A lot of guys back then claimed to have had sex with her. When she didn't turn up, most people figured she had run away, although her parents had denied that. Some thought she had gone to Nashville or Atlanta and became a prostitute. That wouldn't have been surprising, given what people said about her.

Kit remembered what he had told Troy the day they saw the flyer. "Being missing doesn't mean she's dead." Despite more flyers, newspaper stories, and increased law enforcement, no trace of Melody Sellers was ever found.

Kit and Troy had considered dozens of conversations about how they could share their secret and still remain anonymous, but they'd come up with nothing. They were kids. Adults didn't listen to kids. Besides, there was nothing to link that afternoon on the mountain to Melody's disappearance.

But what if Troy was right? What if they *were* the last people to see Melody alive? Kit assumed she was dead after all this time. If she had run off or started turning tricks, somebody would have heard about it. Someone would know if she was alive. But if she was dead . . . if the Dunleys had done something to her that day—

A heaviness settled in Kit's stomach. Troy had mentioned two more missing people and the possibility of Dunley involvement. All of Kit's old doubts resurfaced again—all the things he and Troy hadn't done or should have done differently.

*Maybe we could go back to where we saw her. Maybe we could find a clue or something.*

The idea was ludicrous. What could he expect to find after all these years? A big sign pointing to her corpse? He couldn't hope to find something the police hadn't after all this time. Nothing would be left after thirty years.

Shaking his head, Kit slid off the hood and started picking up his empty cans. Nocturnal insects chirped among the weeds. Stars glistened overhead.

He grabbed a can but immediately dropped it. "Damn," he said with a snarl and held up his hand. A split metal edge had sliced his finger. The cut wasn't deep, but it bled enough to drip on the ground. There was his wonderful luck yet again. Cursing, Kit tossed the plastic bag of empties onto the passenger seat and drove away.

● ● ●

Hidden among the thick foliage, he stood close to the edge of the parking area. Lidless, milky eyes watched the man put things in a bag. This one would be good. He could smell the hot, salty blood through the man's skin.

*She* needed the blood to break the seal.

His two sisters joined him as the man got into his metal box.

To say they were siblings was only partially correct. They had been family once. Long ago. Now they were merely extensions of *her*. All three of them were her, and she was all three of them. She had assumed these smaller forms because they were the only part of her that could cross the seal, like fingertips poking through a hole in a wall. She had tried to use the adult bodies but had been unsuccessful. So the little ones were her eyes and ears and hands until she could be free once more.

She had thought the one who came to her—the bearer of the blood— would release her. He had shown fealty and promised to worship her, but he had been inconsistent with the offerings. She needed more blood and could not wait for him to bring it. She would get it herself. With the children.

The three waited until the red lights on the metal box disappeared before stepping into the parking area. Their pale, bare feet barely made a sound on the gravel.

They crept to the spot where the man had been. Crouching, they sniffed the air. The boy's spidery finger touched the gravel and brought the dark spot up to his nose. He sniffed again.

This blood was known to *her*! She remembered their meeting. After all these years, he was home again! A low growl of pleasure seeped from the boy's throat. A tongue resembling a white slug tasted the blood. He grinned at his younger sisters, his teeth like gray needles in the dark.

# 7,
## THE CURSE OF BLACK ROCK

*Sunday, June 5, 2011*

"Tell me more about these disappearances," Kit said to Troy as they waited for their dinner. They sat near the front window of Tres Sombreros and had the restaurant almost to themselves. There were only four other patrons. Hispanic music played over the PA system while the two friends munched chips and salsa.

"I think they're part of the curse," Troy replied.

"Do you really think this town is cursed? I mean, that's what we used to pretend as kids."

"I believe there's more to it than just make-believe." Troy lowered his head as if ducking to avoid an imaginary line of fire. "I'm not 100 percent sure it was just our imagination. You remember how we used to talk about the strange things that happened—all the extremely aggressive diseases people got and that time all the cows out at the old Lyle place just up and died? The blight?"

Kit nodded and sipped his Corona.

"I don't think all that was just random bits of bad luck," Troy said.

"What about all the bad luck I've had? Maybe I'm cursed too," Kit said with a chuckle.

Troy reached into the silver gym bag he'd brought and pulled out a three-ring binder. "Take a look at this." He pushed the salsa aside as he laid the binder on the table.

"What've you got there?"

"These are the notes I've been keeping on Black Rock."

"Notes?" Kit asked as he took a chip. "As I recall, you hated taking notes back in school."

"Well, it's mostly newspaper stories, online research, reports, rumors—that sort of thing. Since we always wondered about this place, a number of years ago I started collecting information related to the town. This is what I've got so far."

He flipped several pages in the binder. Each had clippings, an occasional photocopy of a person or place, and notes in Troy's scrawly print. Kit guessed there were thirty or forty pages.

"Tyson Collinsworth disappeared from Spring City last year," Troy said. "He was twenty-two years old and last seen leaving the job site he was working at with the electrician's union. Last month it was Meredith Walston, a junior at the University of Tennessee in Knoxville. She'd come home for the weekend—a short break before finals started. She headed back to school on Sunday, May 8. Police found her car abandoned just before you cross the county line, but no sign of her. The police and the Tennessee Bureau of Investigation have nothing. No bodies have turned up, and there have been no ransom demands. Zilch."

*Just like Melody Sellers,* Kit thought. Except these weren't the type of people who were likely to just up and skip town. Collinsworth had a decent job, and Meredith was in school.

"And those two? They're just the tip of the iceberg." Troy paused to take a drink of beer. "Do you remember how many people were in our graduating class?"

Kit shook his head. "Um, no, not really. Maybe a hundred or so?"

Troy turned another page. "The class of 1986 had 129 graduates. You said the other day you thought we'd lost maybe eight or ten?" He paused. "Try fifty-four."

Kit's eyes widened. "*Fifty-four?* But that's—"

"Impossible? No, but damned close to it." Troy scooped salsa onto a chip. "That works out to 42 percent of our graduating class. You remember that we lost two in '86 before the year was over." He ran his finger along a column of names and dates. "De'Andre Phillips was the first on July 28, 1986. A little over a month after graduation."

"I remember that. He was a good basketball player. Gave me a ride home one time."

"Then we lost Mikayla Davidson in November, and we lost two more classmates every year until 1991, when we lost four. By the time our ten-year reunion rolled around, *twenty-two* of our classmates were dead."

"Damn!"

"That's not all." Troy adjusted his glasses and flipped to a new page. "There were six kids who lived on your block when we were growing up. You're the only one still alive."

Kit lowered the beer bottle and swallowed slowly, his eyes still wide.

The waitress appeared with their meals. She set the chicken con queso down in front of Troy; the #14 Special went to Kit.

"Can I get you anything else?" she asked, her braces flashing.

"No, we're good. Thanks," Troy told her.

Kit waited until she was gone. His gaze pinned Troy to his chair. "Are you sure? About all of this?" Kit gestured to the binder.

Troy filled a tortilla and took a bite. "Yep."

"Man, that's just . . . That's messed up."

"What're the odds that there would be so many deaths from one graduating class in such a small community?"

Kit glanced up while cutting his enchilada. "Did they all die here in Black Rock?"

"No, but the *way* some of them died is another thing."

"You mean like Donald Jeffs?"

Troy pointed his fork across the table. "Exactly! How the hell does a forklift just turn over and crush someone when there's nobody else around? You remember Dustin McGovern? He drowned back in '05."

"That's not so unusual. Lots of people drown."

"True. But McGovern drowned *in his bed*."

Kit gave a half grin. "Now you're just shitting me."

Troy solemnly shook his head. He ruffled through a few pages and tapped his finger on a newspaper obituary. Around a bite of tortilla, Troy said, "Wife found him dead in their bed. Autopsy showed enough water in his lungs to fill a five-gallon aquarium."

"No fucking way. You're just making that up."

Troy continued as if Kit hadn't said anything. "It's not in the obituary, obviously, but I heard that McGovern was dry as a bone when they found him. Yet his lungs were filled with water."

He turned the page. "Carmelo Vargas died while on maneuvers with the army in '02, and before you tell me that a lot of people die in the military, you should know Vargas died of hypothermia. In Iraq."

"*What?*"

Troy chewed, took a drink. "I've got all of them in here. Allie Davenport, 2000, car crash. Marvin Moses, '99, electrocution. Phillip Trainor in '98, hit by a train. You remember Layne Preston, the girl who won the county beauty contest? Died in '96 from *old age*."

Kit nearly spit out his beer. "Old age? Oh, come on, man! How is that possible?"

"It's something called 'progeria.' It's a disorder that causes premature aging. Normally, it shows up in childhood. Affected kids show signs of accelerated aging—baldness, hunched posture, brittle bones. Layne was twenty-eight years old. She had a heart attack because she had the heart of an eighty-year-old."

Kit stopped eating. "But she didn't have . . . She didn't show any symptoms while we were in school."

"No. In fact, she didn't have a single symptom until she was twenty-five! It's like she aged half a century in less than three years." He shook his head. "Then there's Tyler Daniels, the most recent victim of the curse on May 22."

Kit frowned. May 22. Why did that seem familiar?

"What's wrong?"

He shrugged. "Not sure. Something about that date sticks in my mind, but I can't place why. So our class has lost fifty-four people in the span of twenty-five years?"

"Yep."

"Has this curse affected any other classes?"

Troy loaded another tortilla. "Not quite as dramatically, but from what I've pieced together, yeah. Of course, there's a perfectly normal number of natural deaths that have no bizarre element whatsoever, but for a town this size, people frequently die in damned strange ways. Not only that—did you know that Scarburn County is the worst in all of Tennessee?"

"Worst what, county?"

"Yep."

Kit laughed. "No surprise there."

"No, seriously. I did some digging online. Tennessee has got ninety-six counties. Scarburn ranks dead last in every good category—things like graduation rates, test scores, stuff like that—but it's first in every bad category. We have the highest numbers for divorce rates, fatal automobile accidents, teen pregnancies, drug use—"

"No way," Kit replied as he swallowed his food. "Not possible. Not compared to Nashville or Memphis."

"It's true. I got all the data from the state website."

"Man, you need a hobby or something." Kit didn't intend to sound dismissive, but it was all a bit hard to accept. Black Rock *was* a strange place with a lot of unusual things associated with it, but Troy's facts and figures seemed surreal. Yet they also made a quirky kind of sense. They answered a lot of questions, like sand that fills up the space between rocks.

Kit tried to smile but faltered. "We used to run around pretending to solve all the crimes in Black Rock."

Troy scratched his beard. "Even back then we knew something was off."

"Didn't we pretend that all the weird stuff and deaths and nutty rumors were because of aliens?"

"Uh-huh."

Kit looked out the window. The streetlights had come on as dusk gave way to night. A few cars drove by. In the alley on the other side of the street, blackness loomed like the onset of depression. He thought of his dream, the almost mannequin-like figures with wide-set eyes and hooked noses that chased him. He had to suppress a shudder.

*Blackness . . . black . . . May 22.* It came to him.

"May 22," Kit said. "I had a blackout that day."

Troy raised his eyebrows. "Wow, you still have those?"

Kit nodded. "Once or twice a year. Although a couple of years ago, I had nine in less than twenty-four months."

"What's your doctor say?"

"Same thing I've heard from doctors all my life. Neurologically, there's nothing wrong. I've never hit my head hard enough to cause any trauma."

"Those started when you were twelve, right?"

"Yeah, right after I wrecked my bike in the park on the way home from your house." The cold, dark memory stabbed Kit's mind like a splinter under a fingernail. He stared past Troy but didn't see the restaurant at all.

"Hey, you all right?" Troy asked. "You just went white as a sheet."

Kit didn't want the memory. It wiggled beneath the fingernail of his mind, working its way loose. The figures in his dream hadn't followed him into the park. They had just watched. For some reason he imagined that they had been smiling.

The urge to flee welled up inside him. He needed to get out of town fast, get as far away as possible.

*Coming back here was a mistake.*

He'd first felt this desperate desire to flee as an adolescent. It had caused him to bolt from town when he was twenty-four. The urge to get in his vehicle right now and drive was nearly overwhelming. It didn't matter where he went. He just needed to go. Everything Troy had told him only reinforced what he had known all along—this place was screwed and always had been.

*But why?*

"You sure you're okay, buddy?" Troy stared at him with concern.

"Yeah . . . I'm okay. I'm good."

Troy was skeptical. "You don't look okay. For a minute there you went pale and looked like you were going to jump up and fly out of here."

The waitress returned—a convenient distraction—and collected their plates. Troy asked for the check.

Kit remained silent and took slow breaths to calm himself while Troy consulted his binder.

After a moment, Troy lowered his voice. "Let me ask you something. You said you'd had nine blackouts in a two-year span. When was that?"

"2007 and 2008. Why?"

"How many blackouts each year?"

Kit scanned the restaurant as if the answer would appear on one of the television screens broadcasting soccer games. "Let's see, in 2007 I had five and four in '08."

Troy returned to the page of their deceased classmates. His eyes darted back and forth. He didn't look up when the server dropped off the check. "You're not going to believe this."

"What?"

"In 2007, five of our classmates died."

Kit stared at Troy as if his friend had suddenly turned to glass. "Yeah, so?"

Troy consulted the binder again. "In 2008, we lost four."

"So . . . what're you saying exactly?"

"I don't know, it's just . . . Those are two really bizarre coincidences."

"Are you suggesting that I really *am* cursed?" Kit glanced out the window. Across the street, in the shadows—

"Let's take this one step at a time," Troy said. "May 22 was your last blackout. Did you have any more last month?"

Kit looked away from the window and nodded. "Had one May 3."

The color drained from Troy's face. He glanced up, looking spooked. "Rico. Rico Genz died that day."

Kit didn't remember Genz.

"Any blackouts in 2010?"

Kit didn't want to remember. He didn't like where this was going. His reply was terse. "One. I don't remember the day though. Early spring, I think."

"Could it have been March 29?"

"Yeah, maybe. Why? Who the hell died that day?" Kit grew testier. He kept glancing out the window. Across the street, the buildings seemed to hunch forward, as if they were advancing toward him. *Just like the people in my dream.*

"Juliette Kaseko."

Kit whipped his head around. "Juliette? She was my lab partner in Biology I." He paused. "Why're you telling me this? I haven't seen any of those people"—he jabbed a finger at the binder—"since I left this place."

"There's a pattern here, Kit."

"There's no pattern, man! Just your overactive imagination," Kit snapped.

Troy stared at him.

"*What?* Oh, so you really think that every time I have a blackout someone *dies*? Shit, Troy. Thanks for finding a way to heap *more* guilt onto my shoulders. I was beginning to run out." Sarcasm dripped from his words.

Something moved outside the window, drawing Kit's attention. The legs of an icy centipede skittered up his spine.

A figure was watching him from across the street.

"Y-you see that?" Kit asked, his voice cracking. The figure continued to watch him—arms at its side, head slightly tilted. Whoever it was must've been wearing a lot of white. Kit began to tremble.

In some antediluvian part of his brain a wave of overpowering, unutterable terror poured through his system. It was the dread humanity has sought to escape with illumination and activity and noise that forever lurks just beyond the edge of the light. It was the primal horror of man huddled in a cave during the first eclipse. It was a creak in a dark house, the chill in a graveyard, the petrifying awareness of being followed but seeing no one.

"See what?" Troy followed his friend's gaze.

A minivan passed by. Vacant windows stared back. Heavy shadows bled across the street.

"O-over there, between the buildings—"

Troy peered through the glass and shook his head. "Nope, nothing."

Kit risked a glance. A streetlight flickered on, and florescent silver light puddled on the sidewalk in front of the buildings. The shadows wavered, drawing back as the light nudged them.

There was nothing else. Kit lifted his beer bottle with a quivering hand and sucked it dry.

"What happened?" Troy asked. He looked back and forth between Kit and the street.

The beer helped calm Kit. He took a deep breath. "N-nothing. I just thought I saw someone over there staring at us."

"Probably just the waitress's reflection in the window. You seem pretty jumpy. You sure you're okay?"

"No, I don't guess I am," Kit said, grumbling. "I mean, you've all but said I'm responsible for our classmates' deaths."

Troy raised his hands. "Whoa, hold on, I didn't say that. I just think it's a weird coincidence."

Kit glanced out the window again, dreading the centipede's touch. It didn't come, and he breathed a silent sigh of relief.

Troy went to pay the check as Kit stared across the street. He sifted through his memories. The town park came back to him.

It had been a Friday night. He'd been playing Atari with Troy, planning to sleep over, but something had happened—he couldn't remember what. Some sort of family emergency. They had to leave immediately for Murfreesboro. Kit's mom had planned to pick him up, but he'd told her he had his bike. He could be home in no time.

"I'll leave the porch light on for you," Mom had said. "Be careful."

It was past one in the morning when Kit pedaled through downtown. The traffic lights flashed, shooting jaundiced caution beams through the darkness. The warm air tousled his hair. He approached the park and cut straight across like he always did. Sticks snapped under his tires.

The gazebo in the center of the park appeared out of the darkness. He was going around it when something small emerged from the shadows. It reached for him. Kit screamed and jerked the handlebars to the side. A tree branch touched his arm.

The bike wobbled beneath him, then pitched sideways. He flew off the bike, and his head thumped against the ground. For a moment, everything became a shifting gray fog. He imagined someone bending over him, but that was impossible. It was late after all. He was the only person in the park. The cool grass against his cheek and the soft, metallic *tick, tick, tick* of his bike tire as it slowed down dispelled the fog.

"Oh, man." Kit groaned. He sat up and looked around. He was alone.

He rubbed his upper arm, just beneath the sleeve of his T-shirt. Something *had* touched him there. He looked around, trying to find the branch that had brushed against him, but none were close enough. Besides, whatever had touched him had felt cold and wrinkled and spongy. He studied his arm in the pale light but saw no sign of injury. He searched the patches of shadow and light that stretched across the park, wondering if someone had pulled a prank on him. Maybe they pushed a stick through the spokes of his tire, causing him to wreck? But if that was it, why was nobody laughing?

Because he was alone.

And suddenly, without knowing why, a rush of fear forced Kit to his feet. He *wasn't* alone. There was something out there, watching him, and it had *touched* his arm.

Fighting back tears, he vaulted onto his bike and rode as fast as he could out of the park. It felt like he was being followed, but he refused to look back. That's how people in movies died. He pedaled furiously, not stopping until he saw his mother waiting for him in the welcoming comfort of the front porch light.

• • •

Kit turned away from the gloomy buildings outside the restaurant, his heart slowing as the memory passed. He rubbed the spot on his right arm that had been touched so long ago.

Probably just the waitress's reflection in the window, Troy had said.

Kit wished to God that was the case, but what he had seen was too small to be the waitress. It wasn't any bigger than a child—a toddler to be precise. Then his memory filled in a gap he hadn't known was missing.

In the split second before the bike had dumped him, he'd heard a child-like giggle from the shadows.

# 8

## COUNTY ROAD 501

*Monday, June 6, 2011*

Deputy Laura Richie gunned the cruiser along County Road 501. She had just finished her last call of the day. Deke Mitchell was beating his wife again, and like all the previous times, Pamela refused to press charges. Laura sighed. Nobody deserved that. To top it off, half the town knew the son of a bitch was cheating on his wife as well. Laura would have loved to have five good minutes in a room alone with the scumbag.

She rubbed one eye and then the other. She had pulled a double shift today, mainly because Sheriff Owens had his back against the wall with the Meredith Walston case. Laura didn't mind except that it meant less time with her husband and young son. Owens was an easy man to work for—more than that, he was a *good* man to work for. He treated his deputies as equals, not as gophers or raw cadets. He had always been flexible with her schedule when her son was sick, so volunteering for an extra shift came easy. But the day was quickly catching up with her, and she wanted to have her paperwork finished by midnight so she could get home.

She pressed the accelerator coming out of a curve. Trees and fence posts zipped past, blurry specters in the headlights. She slowed for the next curve, accelerated again, and slammed on the brakes. She whipped the steering wheel to the left. Tires squealed. The cruiser shot across the westbound lane and onto the gravel shoulder, kicking up dust. She spun the wheel and managed to keep the car from flipping. It stopped diagonally across the eastbound lane. Dust plumed red in the taillights.

Catching her breath, she flipped on the blue lights and looked in the rearview mirror. She had just barely managed to keep from running over the body. Picking up the mic, she said, "Dispatch, this is unit two-seven. Repeat, this is unit two-seven."

The radio squawked back. "We read you, two-seven. What's going on, Laura?"

"I'm eastbound on County Road 501, about two miles past the old gas station. Got a body lying in the road."

"Copy that."

"Send a backup unit if one is available and an ambulance too."

"Roger, will do. Be careful, Laura."

"Copy that. Thanks, Blake."

Climbing out of the car, Laura unsnapped her holster and turned on a flashlight. The taillights turned the asphalt into a grungy red carpet.

The body was about ten yards behind the car. Even from this distance, she could tell it was a child.

Two forces jolted through her at the same time. The first was familiar. Her maternal instinct always appeared when kids were involved. This was someone's baby. Somewhere, a mother was beside herself with terror and anguish. Laura couldn't imagine how she would feel if it were her son lying there.

The second feeling was a rush of possibility. Could this be the missing Walston girl?

As she moved closer, assessing the scene as she went, she realized the body was too small. Meredith Walston was twenty-one. This pale form was definitely female, but Laura estimated the child to be around ten or twelve.

The stringent flashlight beam painted the girl's flesh pallid. Her hair was patchy and brittle as if she had been undergoing extensive cancer treatments. She lay face down on the road and was dressed in filthy, tattered rags that looked like they belonged to a different era.

Laura knelt. "Can you hear me? I'm a police officer. My name is Deputy Richie. Can you tell me your name?"

No response.

She balked when she touched the girl's shoulder. It felt like flesh that had been underwater for months—cold and soft. No, soft wasn't right. *Spongy.* When Laura was a little girl, her brothers had taken her to a haunted house. One of the rooms had openings in the wall where you could stick your hands into bowls of mashed-up Jell-O (brains), spaghetti (intestines), and peeled grapes (eyeballs). Laura recoiled like she had just handled the Jell-O again. She gasped. Her fingers had left faint indentions in the jellied flesh.

*What the hell happened to this girl?* She'd never seen skin like this, not even on drowning victims.

Steeling herself, she held the tofu-like wrist and searched for a pulse.

Nothing.

She pushed the button on her body mic. "Dispatch, come in. Blake, this is Richie, over."

"Go ahead, Laura. You okay? You sound spooked."

"The body in the road? It's a child. It's not, repeat *not*, Meredith Walston. But I'll be damned if I know just what it is."

"Say again?"

"Where's that ambulance? I can't find a pulse."

"On its way. Backup too. Sit tight."

"Copy that."

If she wanted to find a heartbeat, she was going to have to touch the body again. She breathed through her mouth to keep from gagging. The girl stunk like . . . There was something familiar about the odor. Ripe. Like rotten cottage cheese. Where had she smelled it before?

Setting her jaw, she put her hands on the chilled, mushy flesh and rolled the body over.

"Oh, *Jesus*," she whispered.

The little girl had no eyelids. Her eyeballs rested in their sockets like cue balls, pupils black as obsidian.

"What happen—"

Squelching like diarrhea, the eyeballs rolled to fix on her. The child's mouth fell open in what might have been a grin. Thin, pointed teeth protruded from gums with the consistency of clam's flesh.

Laura screamed.

The child bolted upright and sank her teeth deep into Laura's neck.

The deputy tried to scream again but couldn't. Her shredded throat produced only a gurgling whimper. She fell back, hot blood pouring through her fingers and down the front of her uniform.

The child stood up, lapping the blood from around her mouth.

Laura tried to push herself away as the emaciated albino advanced on her. She fumbled her gun from the holster—

Gelatinous, icy hands grabbed her from behind. Gasping and blubbering, Laura looked around. A male child, as cadaverous and repellent as the girl, was dragging her off the road.

She tried to fire her weapon but realized she had dropped it. Her twitching fingers reached in its direction, but it got farther and farther away.

The stench was overpowering as the boy pulled her down the embankment and across a ditch. As her vision grayed, she saw the little girl following. Grinning.

In the overgrown field, Deputy Laura Richie saw one final thing before she died. Dressed in the same style rags as the girl, with the same grayish-white complexion and grotesque eyes, a toddler waited. She managed a final, gurgling moan before the three of them ripped her flesh apart with teeth and nails.

• • •

Kit cursed for the third time since leaving the town of Melvine on Highway 127. He had hoped to score some coke, but the contact he had been put in touch with was dry or so he claimed. Even telling the guy that he was a Black Rock native—something that had made Kit's stomach sour to admit— had made no difference. Fuming, he turned onto County Road 501 toward Black Rock.

This was the last straw. He was leaving tomorrow. No more delays. He was through with the close-minded, small-town thinking, coupled with the ever-present "good old boy" attitude. Even his reunion with Troy was not enough to offset all the deception and hypocrisy that thrived here.

His money was almost gone though. He had twenty-six dollars left. He could stay here and mooch off Albert for a little longer, but that wasn't much of an option. No, he needed to get back to Nashville and catch up on the bills.

Maybe Troy could float him a few bucks?

*Sure, sponge off your friend, why don't you?* Kit was disgusted with himself.

If Malcolm Willis still owned the furniture store, maybe he would let Kit do a little work in the warehouse like he did in high school. Just a couple of days—enough to tide him over until he could find something back in Nashville.

Kit was getting tired of just scraping by day after day. He had to get his life in order.

He rounded a curve and slowed when he saw the flashing blue lights. A police car sat halfway across his lane. He eased closer and saw the driver's door was open, but he didn't see an officer. A dark puddle on the road caught his attention. Something lay near it. He was about to keep going but stopped in the cruiser's headlights.

*Was that a handgun lying near that puddle?*

He got out and walked behind the patrol car. Sure enough, a Smith & Wesson M&P 9mm lay beside . . . Was that a pool of blood?

Careful not to touch anything, Kit knelt. Using the meager light from the taillights, he couldn't be sure, but it looked like blood. A trail of it ran across the shoulder of the road and down the embankment.

A siren sounded and grew in volume. Two sirens.

Kit stood up. Another police car and an ambulance raced toward him. Good. At least someone was here to see to this. He turned and started back toward his vehicle.

The cruiser skidded to a stop, and two officers leaped out and drew their guns.

"Stop right there!" one of the officers shouted. "Keep your hands where I can see them!"

Befuddled, Kit did as instructed.

The ambulance halted behind the police car and two paramedics climbed out.

"All right, nice and slow," the other officer said. He looked older than the officer who had shouted. "Get on your knees and put your hands behind your head."

"Officer, I—"

"Down! On your knees!" the younger officer bellowed.

Slowly, so as not to aggravate the situation, Kit knelt and laced his fingers behind his head.

"Are you armed?" the older cop asked as he stepped closer. "Do you have any weapons we need to know about?"

"No," Kit said. His heart beat faster. He saw that the older officer was a sheriff, and his name tag said OWENS.

The younger officer, who Kit assumed was a deputy, searched the vacant cruiser with his flashlight, turned to the sheriff, and shook his head.

The paramedics looked around, seeming perplexed.

The deputy moved around the car, using his flashlight to illuminate the blood and the gun. "Sheriff," the deputy said in an angry, cold voice, "I've got Laura's weapon back here."

The sheriff's face tightened.

The deputy followed the trail to the shoulder. "There are drag marks down the embankment. Looks like she was taken over into that field. Laura!" He kept yelling her name.

"Where's the body?" one of the paramedics asked the sheriff.

"I'll bet *he* knows," the sheriff said, his jaw clenched.

The paramedic looked around. "No, I mean the child's body. We were told to prep for a kid."

The sheriff glared at Kit. "Where's the kid?"

"Man, I don't know anything about a kid or any of this," Kit said. "I just rounded the corner and saw the car sitting here."

"Looks like you got pulled over," the sheriff growled. "What did she get you for? DUI?"

"No, no! I haven't been drinking. I didn't do anything except stop to see—"

Sheriff Owens eyed him with suspicion. "Why *did* you stop, Mr.—"

"McNeil. Kit McNeil. I mean, Christopher McNeil." White light like an exploding star blinded him.

Sheriff Owens kept the beam in his face. "You want to pick one, Mr. McNeil?"

"My name is Christopher. Kit is just a nickname."

"You still go by a nickname? I'll ask again. Why did you stop?"

Hands sweating behind his head, Kit nodded in the direction of the gun and blood. "I was driving by. I thought I saw something in the road. The gun. I thought somebody might be in trouble."

"You were coming to the rescue, is that it? Where's Deputy Richie?" the sheriff asked, his voice harder and less courteous.

"I don't know who that is. There was no one here when I stopped."

"Ben," a paramedic said to the sheriff, "there's no kid here."

The deputy returned. He looked like he was in his late thirties, and he had an angular face. His name tag read ELLIS. Kit figured that Sheriff Owens had to be at least sixty, given his gray hair, lined face, and belly.

Deputy Ellis narrowed his eyes and gestured toward the field. "I'm going down there. She may still be alive but unable to respond." He looked at Kit with barely controlled fury on his face. "You better pray to God that she is."

"What did you do with the child's body, Mr. McNeil?" Owens demanded.

"What kid? I told you I don't know anything about a kid or your deputy. Swear to God." Kit's nerves tingled. He was glad his hands were still behind his head. Otherwise, they'd be trembling like a diabetic with low blood sugar. "There was no one around when I got here."

Sheriff Owens chewed the inside of his lip as he studied Kit. "Did Deputy Richie bust you on a DUI? You mouth off and get into it with her? Did you shoot her with her own gun?"

"Wh-what? No, no! I haven't killed anybody! And I haven't been drinking!"

"So you say. Don't move." Sheriff Owens walked behind him.

After a moment, Kit heard a gun chamber being checked and magazine ejected.

Sheriff Owens returned wearing blue nitrile gloves. "Mr. McNeil, I want you to stand up. *Slowly.* Keep your hands in view."

Kit did so, shaking. He made sure to keep his hands away from his body.

"Tell me again what happened," the sheriff said.

Kit took a deep breath. "I was driving along. I came around"—he pointed behind him—"that curve. I saw the car sitting here just like this. Door was open, lights were on. As I slowed down to pass, I saw what I thought was a gun on the road. I pulled off the road over there"—he gestured to his CR-V—"and went to check. I saw the gun and the . . . I didn't touch anything."

"Forensics will tell us that."

"Then you guys pulled up. That's it, I swear to God."

Sheriff Owens nodded toward the rear of the police car. "That weapon has a full clip. My deputy never chambered a round or fired a shot. Mr. McNeil, when you came out of the curve and approached the vehicle, did you see anything in the road?"

"No, nothing except what I just told you."

"Mr. McNeil, my deputy and I are responding to a call for backup from this location. Dispatch was told there was a child lying in the road."

"I swear I didn't see any kids."

"There are tire marks veering onto the shoulder. My missing deputy tried to avoid *something* in the road. It looks more than suspicious that just as we arrive, you're here, bent down over her gun and a pool of blood."

"I know how it looks, but I just saw it. I didn't touch anything. I didn't see a body—not a kid, not a deputy, nothing."

"Where are you from, Mr. McNeil?"

"Nashville. Originally from Black Rock though. I grew up here."

Sheriff Owens raised his eyebrows. "Oh? And where are you staying?"

"I'm at my dad's house. Albert McNeil. I came to town to . . . pay my respects to my mother."

The sheriff nodded. "That's why the name sounds so familiar. Your father is Albert McNeil?"

"Yes, sir."

The radio on Sheriff Owens's shoulder crackled. "Ben, the drag marks do go into the field. I'm following them."

"Damn it." Owens groaned under his breath. "Okay, stay alert, David." He looked at Kit. "Where were you coming from?"

The mic crackled again.

"Ben! Ben, I've— Oh my God!" The deputy's voice sounded shrill through the radio.

"David, what's going on? Talk to me!" Sheriff Owens said. "Mr. McNeil, you come with me. Don't try anything."

They moved to the shoulder. Owens was careful to keep them away from the drag marks.

Across the ditch a flashlight beam bobbed in the overgrown field.

"She's here, Ben!" the deputy said through the radio. "It's Laura! Oh, Jesus . . . oh shit—" The sound of retching came through the radio before it went silent.

The paramedics slid down the embankment, flashlights on and first aid kits rattling against their legs. Deputy Ellis emerged from the field and staggered past them. He climbed back to the road. Burrs were stuck to the legs of his pants, and tears filled his eyes.

Kit saw the deputy's ashen face and shivered. The pallid complexion reminded him of something—

"David, are you okay?" Owens asked. Kit saw the concern on the sheriff's face.

"Yeah, s-sorry, Ben. It's just . . . damn, I didn't expect to find her like *that*."

"Like what?"

Deputy Ellis looked down into the field where the paramedics' flashlights glimmered like will-o'-the-wisps. "She's . . . she's been shredded, Ben. It looks like someone took a fucking razor to her—hundreds of times."

One of the paramedics rejoined them. He shook his head. "I'm sorry, Ben. She's . . . "

Sheriff Owens hung his head and rubbed the back of his neck. Tears formed at the edges of his eyes.

"Well, I know it's not *him*," Deputy Ellis said, nodding at Kit. "There's not a drop of blood on him. Whoever did that to Laura would've been . . . covered in it."

"I'm not so sure about that," the second paramedic said as he crested the shoulder of the road.

Owens looked up. "What the hell do you mean, Andy?"

"Okay, keep in mind we just did a cursory examination. We'll know more when we can—"

"Andy," Sheriff Owens said, waving a hand at the paramedic. "I've got a missing coed, a missing kid's body, and now a dead officer. Get to the point."

"Sure, sorry, Ben. Anyway, the damage indicates a massive amount of blood loss. That's likely the cause of death, but"—he looked at his shoes before turning apologetic eyes toward the officers—"there's no blood down there. Anywhere."

"What're you talking about?" Deputy Ellis said. "You saw her body!"

"We did," said the other paramedic, whose name tag read TOM. He was the taller of the two paramedics. "But Andy is right. For that kind of deep tissue damage, there's not enough blood."

"That's crazy," Sheriff Owens said, shaking his head.

Andy pointed to Deputy Ellis. "David, you were just down there. Look at your shoes. Shouldn't they have blood on them? Look at ours."

Deputy Ellis's black shoes had dirt on them but no blood. He held up one leg and studied the sole. "Th-that's not possible. There should be blood— lots of it."

"Exactly," Andy said. "And that's not all."

Everyone stared at him.

"Her injuries are consistent with cuts made by a razor, but the entry points are round. Pointed. Like an ice pick, but much smaller. More like large needles."

"Are you saying somebody stuck needles in her and *then* cut her with a razor?" Sheriff Owens asked, an edge of incredulity hardening in his tone.

Andy scuffed his shoe against the asphalt. "Well, this is where it gets really weird. The bruising of the skin, the shape of the wounds, the piercing . . . Ben, I'd bet my retirement that they're bite marks."

"Bite marks?" the sheriff and deputy exclaimed.

"There are noticeable impressions, avulsion—"

"You mean skin was *removed*?" Owens asked.

"Chunks of it. We, uh, found a few near the body," Tom said, his tone dropping with each word.

"You're kidding, right?" There was a desperate quality in the sheriff's voice, begging for this to be some sort of sick joke or just a shoddy assessment carried out by flashlight. He removed his glasses and pinched the bridge of his nose.

"Teeth marks," the sheriff muttered under his breath. "Jesus . . . "

He put his glasses back on and scowled at the paramedics. "So what kind of animal do you think we're talking about? Rabid dog? Mountain lion? Bear?"

The paramedics looked reluctant.

"Uh, no. It . . . They aren't *animal* bites, Sheriff," Andy said.

"The impressions are identical to those of children," Tom said, "and there are at least three distinct sets."

• • •

Kit pulled into the driveway and shut off the engine. He sat for a moment, staring at Albert's house without really seeing it.

*Of all the unlucky—*

He pounded his fist against the steering wheel. "Damn it!"

Thanks to being in the wrong place at the wrong time, he would not be going to Nashville—or anywhere else for that matter—anytime soon. He should have just ignored the damn police car and kept going.

Sheriff Owens had called in two more deputies to cordon off the crime scene. He ordered double the usual number of photographs and requested a forensic odontologist from Nashville as soon as possible. They'd swabbed for DNA on the bite marks. Things had been moving so rapidly that it seemed like Sheriff Owens almost forgot that Kit was still there. He hadn't, and released Kit to go home with the one caveat that crushed Kit's spirit. "Stay in town. We'll need to talk to you again."

Kit didn't think that the sheriff actually believed he was guilty, but with the pressure his department was under and losing a deputy like he had, Kit could understand why the sheriff needed him to stick around. But it didn't make Kit like it any better.

Why had he experienced that momentary chill when Deputy Ellis returned from the field, his face wan as a 25-watt light bulb? What was so special about that moment and the color that he—

*The color! That pasty, doughy complexion was like . . .*

Like what had been watching him outside the restaurant! It hadn't been wearing white clothes. That had been its skin!

Dread crawled up the back of Kit's neck. Fear sent his heart racing. Spurred by his mounting sense of terror, he felt there was something in the seat behind him. He looked in the rearview mirror.

Nothing.

He turned and looked in the back seat. Nothing. Yet the terror still gripped him.

He looked outside at the shadowed yard. Nothing.

Panicked, he jumped out and hurried up the sidewalk. The porch railing leered at him with its spindle-less grin. He fumbled the key into the lock.

*What if it was just waiting for me to turn my back? What if it's coming up behind me right—*

Kit threw the door open and all but fell inside. A bass drum pounded in his chest as he shut and relocked the door. Sweat stood out on his brow. He leaned against the door and tried to get his breathing under control.

The house was dark. He turned and peered through the window in the door, expecting to see the pale thing on the porch.

But there was nothing.

# 9

## ENEMY AND ALLY

*Tuesday, June 7, 2011*

The day burned as hot as an acetylene torch. Kit drove his father's Chevy Silverado with the air conditioner on high. Albert was not feeling well and needed a prescription picked up.

"Go get it for me," Albert had said in his usual brusque manner.

"I'm low on gas," Kit had replied. He felt like a teenager again begging for gas money.

"Take the truck. It's got plenty."

He had spent the morning at the police station, giving his formal statement to Deputy Paul Mitchell, an African American in his early thirties. Despite a history of barroom donnybrooks in his younger days, Kit had no misdemeanors on his record. He breathed a silent prayer that there weren't any felonies for drug possession either. Before Kit had left, Deputy Mitchell had reiterated the sheriff's instruction to remain in town.

The diesel engine rumbled as he waited at the stoplight. He felt self-conscious driving the damned thing, as if by doing so he had capitulated, and the rednecks had won. He passed the empty shell that had once been Bennett's Drugstore.

It had closed in the mid-1990s, something that Albert never failed to lament. Kit had endured a five-minute diatribe on the front porch as he'd tried to leave. The disappearance of small-town America. According to his father, it was because of all the illegal immigrants and the liberal Democrats who wanted to take America apart piece by piece. Kit couldn't even get away from the vitriol of partisan politics in the cab of the pickup. Albert's radio was tuned to an ultraconservative talk station that warned true patriots to stand firm in the fight against tyranny. Kit had turned it off and listened to the air-conditioning instead. Better cool air than hot air.

Black Rock had two pharmacies now. One was inside a chain grocery store; the other was family owned. Kit had no doubt which one Albert supported. He passed the grocery store and pulled into the parking lot of a small building with a forest-green awning. As he got out, his gaze drifted up the road, and he saw it.

The only strip mall the town had ever had.

Memories shook loose. Black Rock Plaza had once boasted an auto parts store, thrift shop, shoe store, and appliance store. But for a kid growing up in the '80s, what made it *the* place to hang out was the arcade, the burger joint, and—best of all—Moviehound Video & Tanning. It had been the only place where you could rent a VCR and three movies for the weekend for $14.99. How many hours had he spent browsing the VHS boxes lined up on wooden shelves that smelled of furniture polish? As an added bonus there was a better-than-average chance of spotting some of the hottest high school girls at any given time since it had a tanning salon in the back.

Kit smiled at the old plaza as he remembered the time in 1983 when he and Troy had been trying to decide between *The Evil Dead* (again!) and the newly released *Creepshow*. Jennifer McCormick, Christa Gardner, and Nancy Martin had sashayed in for their tanning appointments. The boys had tried to sneak into the tanning area, but because it was near the family section, their efforts were stymied by a mother and her two children browsing the shelves.

Now, like so much of the town, the shops stood forlorn and unwanted like fat kids waiting to be picked for teams in gym class. Weeds sprouted from the buckling pavement. Kit stared at the far end where the door that had once led to the arcade stood. Many a quarter had been sacrificed on the altar of Asteroids in the quest for the holy grail—the high score with his initials at the top.

Kit collected Albert's prescription and was on his way back to the truck when he heard the commotion. Two rows over, a woman was attempting to get past two young men. No matter which way she moved, they blocked her path. Kit was too far away to hear anything specific, but he knew the sounds of harassment.

He had never considered himself heroic. He used to cross the road to avoid having to walk past any of the Dunleys. He had taken the longer route between classes—even though it almost always made him late—in order to stay clear of the older students' lockers. He had done his best to be invisible because getting involved always put you on someone's shit list. He had been on the receiving end of enough harassment to last a lifetime, which is why his next action stunned him.

He turned and walked toward the woman.

He could see she was frustrated to the point of tears. She clutched her purse and tried to knock away the groping hands.

The boys hooted and made lewd comments. One wore his hair cropped close to the skull. He must have been blond because in the sunlight he looked almost bald. The other's hair was darker, spikey—

Kit almost laughed out loud. *You've gotta be kidding me! Billy Ray Cyrus called from 1992. He wants his mullet back!*

The woman was about Kit's age with professionally styled medium-length auburn hair. She wore light-green capris and a matching top. Her antagonists wore dirty jeans, T-shirts, and boots. Both had hawk noses and wide-set eyes.

*Damn it!*

They were Dunleys. That was all Kit needed. He wanted to turn around and go back to the truck, but his legs refused to go any direction but forward.

One of the Dunleys managed to snatch the purse away from the woman. They played keep-away with it but stopped and looked up as Kit approached. The woman's face, a mix of impotent fury and helplessness, beseeched him for aid.

"What's going on here?" Kit asked with more authority and audacity than he felt.

"The fuck is it to you?" Buzz Cut demanded. He held the purse by its strap.

"Mind your own business," Mullet added.

"Come on, leave the lady alone," Kit said with a calm, even tone. "She's just trying to go to the store." The rational part of his brain—the part that had encouraged him to spend his childhood and adolescence trying to hide from the Dunleys—screamed at him to leave.

Mullet turned from the woman and faced Kit. "You deaf as well as fat, old man? Walk the fuck away. *Now.*"

"You got any idea who we are?" Buzz Cut asked, his eyes narrowed. The prospect of enlightening a newcomer to the Dunley legacy gleamed on his face. He dropped the purse.

Kit raised his hands in surrender. "Yeah, I know who you are, and I don't want any trouble. Just leave the lady alone, okay?"

"Fuck you, fat ass!" Mullet snapped. "We do what we damn well please!"

Kit glanced behind the Dunleys, praying for someone else to come along. This would be the perfect time for Sheriff Owens to show up. Kit saw the woman retrieve her purse while the Dunleys were still focused on him. She rummaged through it behind their backs and pulled something out.

Kit saw what she had and couldn't help but smile.

"You think this is funny, bitch?" Buzz Cut demanded, squaring his shoulders.

At that moment something unlocked inside Kit, and a cocktail of excitement, adrenaline, and nerves flooded his system. It warmed him like hot chocolate on a wintry day. He ignored the part of his brain that was trying to get him to flee. All he felt now was the pressure of a once-in-a-lifetime opportunity.

He released the pressure with a blast of bawdy laughter.

The Dunleys stared at him.

Kit pretended to wipe away a tear. He fixed a steely gaze on the Dunleys as heat burned in his stomach, in his heart, and behind his eyes.

"Actually, yeah," Kit replied. "It's hysterical."

Kit's laughter died. His smile faded. His tone became a crowbar breaking a lock.

"I grew up here. Even back then you lot were the biggest troublemaking sons of bitches in the county. Everybody hated your family. Probably still do. If Black Rock is the butthole of nowhere, then you're just the fucking dingleberries hanging off it," Kit said.

Kit waited until their Neanderthal-sized brains caught up. As they did, the Dunleys' expressions darkened. Mullet's lips peeled back, and Buzz Cut worked his jaw from side to side.

*Wow, that felt good! But now what do I do?*

"Hey!" the woman called.

Mullet whirled around.

Arm outstretched, she pressed the plunger with her thumb. Pepper spray spewed into Mullet's face. He shrieked, staggered back into a car, and collapsed in the parking lot.

Buzz Cut looked at the woman and was about to hit her when Kit moved, putting every bit of his size behind the punch. His fist slammed into Buzz Cut's throat. The force lifted Buzz Cut off the ground. He landed on his back and wrapped his hands around his throat as he gasped for breath. He coughed and gagged as every attempt to breathe was emphasized by wet, whistling sounds.

The woman returned the pepper spray to her purse. "Nice right hook."

"Thanks," Kit said, shaking his hand. He had forgotten how much punching someone hurt.

In his late twenties Kit had gone through a period—he referred to it as his *Road House* phase after the Patrick Swayze movie—where he didn't shy away from a fight. It was as if all his pent-up anxiety and low self-esteem had exploded in a series of bar fights. It also could have been because he'd had a big mouth, a chip on his shoulder, and an even bigger load of childhood baggage that always popped open at the wrong time. Getting into a scrum gave him an outlet for his anger.

It wasn't until Kit fractured his wrist in 1999, just before he turned thirty, that he realized he was on the verge of losing the one thing he loved most and did well—playing guitar. So fighting was out, and drinking became his new outlet. He could sure use one now.

"Are you okay?" the woman asked.

"Yeah, I'm fine."

"Thank you so much! Nobody around here will do anything about those damned Dunleys."

The Dunleys still moaned and coughed as they writhed on the ground. She studied him. "Did you really grow up in Black Rock?"

Kit nodded.

"You look familiar. Did you graduate from here?" Her brown eyes kept analyzing his face for some point of connection.

"Yeah, good old Black Rock High, class of '86."

"Hmm, 1986 . . . You're . . . Chris McNeil, aren't you?"

Kit smiled and nodded. As he examined her features, recognition clicked into place. "You're Courtney, right? Courtney Shefford?"

She grinned.

"Oh, wow. It's been a long time," Kit said and immediately regretted it. *Of course, it's been a long time, you idiot. Still as smooth as a chain saw blade with the ladies.*

"Yes, it has."

He hadn't completely forgotten her. Courtney Shefford had been part of a clique in high school that came across as little angels in public, but rumor had it that behind closed doors, they turned into devils. Of course, Kit had never had any firsthand knowledge of that. He had never had the confidence to ask any of them out. Courtney and her friends had always been out of his league. His heart beat quicker as he looked into her eyes.

*It's just the adrenaline being flushed from my body,* he thought, trying to convince himself.

She was several inches shorter than him and thin. She definitely worked out. She had been in the class of '87, so that would make her forty-one now. She had great eyes that balanced a small nose, and he liked the slight bit of middle-aged weight she carried in her cheeks. He didn't see a wedding band.

"You got out of here, didn't you?" Courtney asked. "Where'd you go?"

"Uh, Nashville, mostly. Other places too." He didn't volunteer any names.

"It was your music, wasn't it? Even before we graduated, I just knew you would make it big. I remember your performance in the talent show that one year. Wow, I'll bet you know a lot of stars!"

The attention and interest flattered him. Had she been watching him all through high school? Had she felt this way back then? Why hadn't she ever said anything?

He heard scuffing on the pavement and ugly, raspy breathing. Kit turned.

"You're dead, motherfucker!" Mullet shouted. One eye was swollen shut, and his face was as red as a baboon's ass. Spittle flecked his lips. He helped Buzz Cut—whose complexion was grayish blue and whose breath still gurgled in his throat—to their black Dodge Ram pickup. It was splattered with mud, had an empty gun rack in the window, and bumper stickers that proclaimed "One Big Ass Mistake America" and "Dale Earnhardt #3 Never Forget." As they rolled out of the parking lot, Mullet flipped the bird at Kit and shouted, "This ain't over! You're so fucking dead!"

Courtney shook her head as she watched them drive away. "Can you believe that family is still breeding? Anyway, what about your music career? How's it going?"

Kit felt awkward, as if he had brought home a bad report card. What was he going to tell her? She seemed to have the idea that he had been touring the world with Garth Brooks or some other superstar. Did he dare tell her the truth—that instead of stardom he was a messed-up guitar player who didn't have two nickels to rub together and couldn't keep a spot in a band? That he had spent more on booze and blow than he had ever made? That the most exotic place he had ever played was the Cagun Cooter strip club outside Opelousas, Louisiana?

*Yeah, better leave that one out altogether.*

She was still waiting for an answer.

Kit rubbed the back of his head. He looked down at her shoes. "It's been . . . okay. Not great, really, but at least I get to do what I love." He had to get the focus off himself, change the subject. He looked up. "So what've you been up to all these years?"

"Oh, you know, the usual. Living and working."

"Where do you work?"

"I'm a paralegal at a law firm over in Spring City."

"Hey, that's great! Married?"

She smiled half-heartedly. "I was. Do you remember Doug Best?"

The name barely registered. Kit thought he had been one of the jocks back in school but wasn't sure.

"We got married in '94, but after a while . . . well, things just weren't working out. We divorced in 2003."

Kit nodded. "I'm sorry about that. I've had two divorces of my own."

"Do you have any kids?"

"Nope. You?"

"Two daughters. Jillian is fifteen and Whitney is twelve." She raised her eyebrows as if to say, "Help! I'm surrounded by overdramatic, hormonal teenage girls!"

Kit gave a mischievous but lighthearted smile. "Is it true what they say about daughters being twice as bad as their mothers?"

"Oh God, I hope not!" She laughed. "No, they're really good girls. They take after their father more, I think, than they do me."

"I was just kidding. I'm sure they got your best qualities."

"That's sweet of you to say. Did you know they never found Melody Sellers?"

The abruptness of the question caught Kit off guard. He stiffened at the mention of Melody's name and hoped Courtney didn't notice. "Uh, yeah. Troy was telling me that the other day."

"Troy Wallace? That's right. You two used to be inseparable. I see him around town from time to time." Her voice lowered and she stared at the surrounding mountains. "It's been thirty years since Melody disappeared. I have dreams about her sometimes. She hung out with us a lot."

Growing more uncomfortable by the moment, Kit avoided her gaze and stared at a plastic bag lying in the parking lot. "Yeah, everyone was really freaked out that summer."

"Our parents were afraid to let us out of the house. Everyone just knew there was some sex maniac on the loose." Courtney paused. "Do you remember the last place Melody was seen?"

Kit's throat constricted to the size of a BB, and his heart skipped a beat. His tongue felt thick in his mouth. Of course, he remembered. He and Troy were the last ones to see her—with Greg and Jeff Dunley—that summer. How could he forget? They hadn't told anyone that they'd seen her. Maybe if they had, Melody might still be alive. But they had been too scared of what the Dunleys would do.

*What do you think they're going to do to you after today's little incident?*

Kit lied, "Uh, no, I don't remember. Like you said, it's been a long time."

"It was right over there"—Courtney pointed behind him—"at the arcade. We were all hanging out, and when she left, everyone assumed she had gone home. It wasn't until later that we found out she never made it home."

*I know where she went.*

"I think about her every time I go in here." Courtney looked at the pharmacy as if it had just dropped out of the sky. Then her mood lightened as she moved on from the memory. She fluttered her hands as if waving away smoke. "Listen to me, running on like this. I am so sorry! I came here to pick up a few things, and here I am wasting your time and babbling on about stuff that happened thirty years ago."

"No, hey, it's all right. No problem. It's really great to see you again. Sorry it had to be because of those two douchebags."

She laid a hand on his forearm. "Oh, it was so good to see you too! Maybe we can catch up some more another time. Thanks again for your help!"

"Yeah, see you."

He watched her walk toward the pharmacy. The sun on her hair. The swing of her hips. Those moments in high school when he had thought about asking her out but didn't dare. Dan Fogelberg's song "Same Old Lang Syne," about two people awkwardly trying to reconnect, popped in his head. He didn't want to be like Dan in that song. He didn't want another missed opportunity to feel guilty about. As he had done earlier, he acted on impulse. His heart thundered like the bass line of Van Halen's "Hot for Teacher."

"Courtney!"

She turned and shielded her eyes from the sun.

"You, uh, wanna get some coffee? Maybe have dinner sometime?" The words poured out of him just as they would have back in high school—rushed, awkward, hopeful. He felt like every person in the world was watching him in that moment. The words hung in the humid air, vulnerable as bone china.

"Sure, that would be great! What's your cell number? I'll text you, and that way you'll have mine."

Just like that Kit imagined that his luck had started to change.

# 10

## SUSPICIOUS MINDS

*Wednesday, June 8, 2011*

"**C**hris, get the door!" Albert barked above the din of the war movie on television.

As Kit walked down the hall into the living room, he saw two people through the window in the door.

*Please don't let it be Mormons or Jehovah's Witnesses.*

It wasn't. It was worse. Kit's spirit sank.

"Morning, Mr. McNeil," Sheriff Owens said pleasantly enough, although there was a hint of hostility just beneath the surface. "This is Agent Donovan Mack of the Tennessee Bureau of Investigation. May we come in? We'd like to ask you some more questions."

Agent Mack flipped his credentials open and held them in front of Kit. He was a six-foot, two-inch African American dressed in crisp black pants, a jacket, and a tie. He looked to be in his late forties or early fifties. His hair showed faint traces of gray.

"Uh, yeah, sure," Kit said, taken aback. He moved aside to let them enter. A quick glance showed his father scowling at him from his recliner.

Sheriff Owens and Agent Mack stepped into the living room and surveyed the space.

Kit gestured toward the cracked faux-leather couch. "Please, have a seat. This is my father, Albert McNeil."

Albert muted the television and tugged the oxygen line from his nose. "What's this all about, Ben?" he demanded. He looked from the two men to Kit.

"Sorry for the intrusion, Albert," Sheriff Owens said as he removed his hat. "Hopefully, this won't take long. We just have a couple of questions for Chris."

"Hopefully? Why?" he asked in a querulous voice. He looked at Kit. "What have you done, boy?"

"Chris, Agent Mack has been working with us on the Meredith Walston case. When I informed him about the incident out on County Road 501, he wanted to talk to you."

"Sure, okay," Kit said sitting down in a club chair. "I already told you guys everything that happened though. I gave my statement yesterday."

"I've read it, Mr. McNeil," Agent Mack said formally. His voice rumbled like a boxcar in a tunnel. "I'm sure you did tell the department everything." His simmering brown eyes roamed over Kit's face as if it were a counterfeit bill. He wore his hair with a short fade and had a perfectly trimmed mustache and goatee. "But it's been a couple of days since the incident, and sometimes things come back to people over time."

"What happened on 501?" Albert demanded.

Sheriff Owens gave him a brief, generic account.

"Why ain't I seen this in the paper or on the news?" asked Albert.

The sheriff's shoulders fell as he spoke. "We're keeping the details out of the media right now out of respect for Laura's family. A statement will be re-leased soon."

Albert glared at Kit but said nothing. The oxygen line swayed under his jaw like a chin strap.

"Mr. McNeil, tell me what happened the night you found the police car," Agent Mack said. While phrased politely enough, it wasn't hard to miss the command in Mack's tone.

Kit retold the story step-by-step.

"Before Sheriff Owens arrived, did you see or hear anything out of the ordinary?" Agent Mack asked. "Did any vehicles go by? Did you hear any machinery or see any lights?"

Kit shook his head. "It was quiet."

"I want you to think hard," Mack said. He leaned forward and placed his elbows on his knees. "Put yourself back there on the road. It's night. You've just stopped. You're getting out of your car—"

"Yeah, I thought I saw a gun in the road. I didn't know if someone might be in trouble. I pulled over and walked to the back of the patrol car—" Kit paused.

"What is it? What do you remember?" Sheriff Owens asked.

"There was a smell," Kit said. "I'd forgotten about that."

"What kind of smell?" asked Owens.

"Nasty. Spoiled. Like yogurt or milk that's gone bad. Funny thing is, it's kind of a familiar smell."

"Can you explain that?" Agent Mack said.

"It was like something I've smelled before but not in a long time. Something from—" Kit halted again, eyes darting across the carpet as if searching for something. "From my childhood."

"Go on," Sheriff Owens told him.

"The blight," Kit said. "That's it! It smelled like the blight. I can remember running through patches of it in the woods when I was a kid. If you disturbed it, the blight gave off this awful smell like something rotten."

The sheriff agreed. "It's got a pretty distinctive odor."

"You smelled that when you got out of your car?" Agent Mack asked.

Kit shook his head. "No, it was behind the patrol car. Just for a minute. Then it was gone."

The sheriff and agent exchanged a look.

"Does that mean something?" Albert asked, chiming in.

The TBI agent ignored the question and pinned Kit to the chair with his gaze. "Mr. McNeil, where were you on Monday, June 6, between the hours of 1:00 a.m. and 3:00 a.m.?"

"Huh, what? Where was I—"

Agent Mack repeated the question.

"That was the night of the . . . Look, I told you. I came across the police car on my way—"

"I said between the hours of 1:00 a.m. and 3:00 a.m., Mr. McNeil. Sheriff Owens released you from the scene on County Road 501 at"—he checked his notebook—"12:49 a.m. Technically, it was Tuesday, June 7 by then. Can you account for your whereabouts during that period? What did you do after you left the scene?"

Kit felt his heart speed up. Prickly heat began to dance along his arms and chest. "I-I came straight home. My father hasn't been feeling good. I was up with him a lot that night."

"Don't you go draggin' me into your screwups, boy!" Albert said.

"Albert," Sheriff Owens said, "can you confirm the whereabouts of your son that night?"

Albert's scowl hardened. He nodded reluctantly. "Like he said, he was right here. He had to help me use the—" He pursed his lips and looked away for a second. "Anyway, he helped me that night. It was around two thirty in the morning. I remember that."

"You say you came straight back here?" Agent Mack asked. "It's a twenty-six-minute drive from the location of the incident on 501 to this house. Did you stop anywhere on the way? A convenience store or a friend's house maybe?"

"N-no, I didn't stop. I came straight back here," Kit said.

"What time did you get in?" Owens asked. His eyebrows were level across his forehead.

"It was about 1:15 a.m."

"You're sure?" Agent Mack's tone was ice-cold.

Albert shifted in the recliner. "What's all this about, Ben? Does he need a lawyer or something?"

Agent Mack replied before Owens could answer. "Only if he's got something to hide." He never took his eyes off Kit.

The prickly heat had surged up his face and past his ears. Kit felt like he was sitting in a bathtub full of needles. "I'm not hiding anything!"

*Nothing except Melody Sellers. And what's left of that cocaine upstairs. Wouldn't that look good if they found it?*

"Something bothering you, Mr. McNeil?" Mack asked.

Kit shook his head. "No, it's just I-I don't know what this is all about."

Mack sat back and casually put his arm across the back of the couch. The upholstery squeaked like rubber. "What's your connection to Meredith Walston?"

"I don't have any connection to her," Kit said. "I've never met her."

"You've never hooked up for anything—sex, drugs?" Agent Mack asked.

"No!" Kit told the TBI agent.

"What about Tyson Collinsworth? How do you know him?" Mack continued.

Kit sat forward, clasping his hands to keep them from shaking. "I don't! I'd never heard of him until I got back here."

"Look, I'll ask this just one more time, or you can both get out. I'm a law-abiding American, and I know what rights I got," Albert snapped. "What the hell is going on here, Ben?"

Agent Mack watched Kit like an eagle seeking prey while Albert and the sheriff talked.

"You know about the disappearances of the Collinsworth boy and Meredith Walston," Sheriff Owens said to Albert.

"Sure. Heard you had Scotty Dunley and Gabe Beecher in custody for those," Albert replied.

"No," Owens said. He smoothed his hair into place. "They were brought in for starting a brawl out at Marty's Joint. Unfortunately, when all the parties were interviewed, seems that no one wanted to press any charges—not even Reggie, the owner. Of course, while we had them, we tried to shake them up to see if we could get them to give us something on the disappearances. We got nothing. And with no one pressing charges, we had no choice but to cut them loose."

"My money would be on those two," Albert said. "You better keep an eye on them."

"Oh, we are," Agent Mack replied.

Albert said, "Then why're you here badgerin' me and the boy with all this?"

For a moment, Sheriff Owens and Agent Mack said nothing. On the television, the Allies were breaking through the German lines in a silent, monochrome confrontation.

"Truth is, Albert, Chris—" The sheriff hesitated. When he spoke again, his throat worked up and down as if he were swallowing broken glass. "There's been another murder. Eleanor Davenport's body was discovered last night by her neighbor. She hadn't been seen since Monday afternoon."

"And you think *I* did it?" Kit blurted out, shock and horror in his voice. *There's the old McNeil luck again. Just when I thought things were starting to look up.*

Agent Mack wasn't moved. "We're considering *every* possibility."

Kit threw himself back in the chair, disgusted. "I don't believe this."

"Eleanor Davenport?" Albert asked in surprise. He dropped his head. "That's not right . . . "

Kit was astonished to see genuine sorrow on his father's face. The woman's name wiggled through his mind. He thought it sounded familiar—the way the name of an old pet hamster or goldfish did—like something once known but now barely remembered.

The TBI agent addressed Albert. "Mr. McNeil, your son had time to stop by the Davenport home on Monday night. It's on the way."

Albert shook his head repeatedly. "Nope, nope, no way. That boy of mine—he ain't no killer. For God's sake, Ben." His expression pleaded with and shamed the sheriff at the same time.

Sheriff Owens nodded as he removed his glasses and pinched the bridge of his nose with two fingers. "I know, Albert. I'm just doing my job."

"Eleanor Davenport was a fine woman. Her husband was a member of the union. He died three years ago." Albert paused, eyes flitting back and forth between the two lawmen. He sighed and put the oxygen line back in his nose. "How'd she die, Ben?"

Sheriff Owens looked at Kit. "Well, I'm not at liberty to say. It's an open investigation. Although there were some—similarities—to what happened out on 501."

Kit tensed. He hadn't seen the deputy's body, and from the descriptions he had overheard from Deputy Ellis and the paramedics, he was glad of that. The words painted gory images in his mind.

Sheriff Owens stood up, rolling his hatband between his fingers. "Chris, I want you to stay in town like I said before. It looks a might odd that just after you return to town, we've got a dead officer and senior citizen, both murdered in the same way. If I find out you've been lying to me or trying to play me, I'll have you locked in the darkest hole I can find. Are we clear?"

Kit nodded. "I-I told you . . . I swear, I don't know anything about any of this."

Agent Mack stood up but kept his eyes on Kit.

"Something fishy is going on around here," Owens said on his way to the door.

"Hey, it's Black Rock," Kit replied, trying to lighten the mood. "This is fishy central."

Agent Mack stopped. "What makes you say that, Mr. McNeil?" His eyebrows lowered, sharpening the creases in the center of his forehead.

*Damn it, keep your mouth shut!*

"Nothing, really. It's just something my friend and I used to talk about when we were kids. We used to think Black Rock was cursed because of all the weird stuff that happened over the years."

"Such as?" Mack asked.

The sheriff answered before Kit could explain. "It's nothing important, Don. He's just talking about stuff like the chemical spill back in '77, the old school that burned down in the '20s, and the blight. Kids in small towns like to believe theirs is somehow haunted or cursed. It gives an air of mystery and danger to living there, and feeds overactive imaginations. Black Rock is no different."

"Aren't you a little old to be looking for aliens in cornfields?" Agent Mack asked Kit.

"Oh, hey, no . . . I wasn't—"

Mack smiled for the first time since arriving. "It's okay, Mr. McNeil. Just a joke."

Kit saw them off the porch and went back inside.

Albert stood up and leaned on his oxygen tank. "What the hell are you up to?"

"What are you talking about?"

"Boy, you know damned well what I'm talking about! How dare you bring the police *and* the TBI into my house! Do you know what this'll look like at my next union meeting? You got any idea what the board of deacons at the church will say when they find out?"

Kit's mouth fell open.

"How'd you get mixed up in them disappearances? And what about these murders? A deputy? Eleanor Davenport, for God's sake—"

Kit threw his hands in the air. "I don't believe this! I didn't have anything to do with any of that!"

"Damned government seems to think you do! Or do you suppose the TBI sends agents to escort every small-town sheriff around? Good God, boy, do you know what people are going to say?"

The old familiar burn started in Kit's chest. Anger and the desire to flee. He struggled to keep them in check. He needed to figure out how to use them instead of letting them control him, but his anger tumbled out anyway. "Do you even give a shit that two people have been murdered this week?" Kit shouted. "Or are you just worried that your precious little image will be tarnished?"

Albert's face reddened. He pointed an arthritic finger at Kit. "You watch your mouth in this house, or I'll knock it into the goddamn yard! I've had just about all I'm gonna take of your lip. Honor thy father, boy."

Kit spun around and stomped into the kitchen. After a moment he heard the television blare again. He leaned against the sink, and his body trembled.

*God, I've got to get out of here!*

• • •

Outside in the driveway, Sheriff Owens and Agent Mack sat in the patrol car.

"Well?" the sheriff asked.

Agent Mack stared out the windshield at the bedraggled house. "I think he's telling the truth. His reaction to possibly being linked to the disappearances or the murders was too visceral to be faked in my opinion. He could be a damn good liar, but I didn't get that impression. I don't think he's got anything to do with these cases except for the bad luck of coming upon the scene of your deputy's murder. We've run him through ViCAP without a hit. State records have him with a couple of bar fights when he was younger, but no charges were ever filed on any of them. His recent financial activity shows him on the road with his band. Tour information from the booking agency puts him around Paducah, Kentucky when Meredith Walston went missing, and the band manager corroborated that."

The radio squawked. "Sheriff, this is Givens. Do you copy? Over."

Owens picked up the mic. "Go ahead, Regina."

"Just thought you'd wanna know. The autopsy on Laura just came back. The ME also sent over a prelim on Eleanor Davenport."

"That was quick. All right, we're heading that way. Anything I should know about?" Sheriff Owens backed into the street.

"Yeah, but I don't know if you're gonna believe it or not."

Agent Mack looked at him with a frown.

"Come on, Regina. I'm not in the mood," the sheriff said.

"Sure, sorry. Laura's cause of death was exsanguination, just like we suspected, but there was less than five ounces of blood left at the scene. Now here's where it gets even freakier. There are three different sets of child-sized bite marks all over the body. Although how or why kids could do that much damage—"

"Anything else?"

"Yeah, there were traces of blight in the wounds."

Sheriff Owens shot a sideways look at Agent Mack. "What? There were a few small patches of it on the far side of that field, but none anywhere around the crime scene."

"We found those kids' footprints leading back and forth across the field," Regina continued after a burst of static. "Maybe they walked through those patches on the way to the road?"

Owens sighed. "Yeah, maybe . . . Okay, I'll look at it when I get there."

"One more thing," she said. "The prelim on Eleanor Davenport? Exsanguination and a few ounces of blood at the scene. And the doc says there's traces of blight in her wounds too."

"Okay, thanks." Sheriff Owens replaced the mic and shook his head. "This is getting stranger by the day."

"Fishy central," Agent Mack said as he watched houses and trees go by through the window.

# 11

## COME OUT AND PLAY

*Thursday, June 9, 2011*

**K** it set his guitar aside. He had been playing for an hour. Blues mostly. He needed something to take his mind off the argument with Albert earlier in the evening. As usual, it had revolved around his life choices.

"Boy, you've got to land somewhere. You can't keep running the roads, hoping to make a living with that guitar. You need to get a real job. Look at you. In your forties now and nothing to show for it. People your age should have good jobs, a house, money in the bank. You need to make something of yourself."

Kit was well acquainted with the deficiencies of his lifestyle when compared to his peers, but he had never cared what other people thought. He had never been one for chasing dollars and climbing ladders. He enjoyed seeing new places and meeting new people, and there was nothing in the world that could compare to standing on stage, the music flowing out of him, knowing that the audience was cheering and clapping and dancing because of something he was creating.

He would take that over a regular job any time. The nine-to-five routine just wasn't for him. George Thorogood had it right—find a band and some good songs and party every night. Of course, the all-night partying had vanished once Kit had hit his thirties, and his bad habits had kept him from ever being able to take the next step musically. If he didn't get his life straightened out, he was looking at more of the same. Near misses and squandered opportunities. And he certainly wasn't getting any younger.

It sickened him to know that in a roundabout way, Albert was right at least partially. Kit had no place to settle down. He had no prospects for improving his future. He was still living hand to mouth and making no progress. Kit was just existing—no plan and no clue how to get one.

"Not everyone is cut from the same cloth," he had told his father. "Everybody follows a different path."

Albert, his breath like an ashtray, had brushed Kit off. "That's an excuse, boy, for not manning up and taking responsibility."

"No, it isn't! Just because you spent your life working at the factory and being part of the union doesn't mean that everyone has to do that."

"You trying to imply that factory work is *beneath* you?"

"I didn't say that. Don't put words in my mouth."

"But that's what you meant, ain't it?"

Kit sighed. "No, that's not what I meant! I'm not denigrating what you did for a living or anyone else for that matter. I'm just saying there are all kinds of vocations. You did your job at the factory. Great! Other people work as nurses or salesmen or teachers. Those jobs are important. Necessary. Being a teacher isn't a lesser kind of work just because it's not in a factory."

Albert wagged his finger. "But you're not a teacher, are you, boy? Or a salesman or a nurse. No, you traipse through life under the delusion that you can just play music and people will support you."

"That's not true. You know—"

"What I know is that you ain't amounted to nothing in forty-two years because you won't get your head out of the damned clouds."

It had gone on like that for another fifteen minutes before Kit had stormed upstairs, just like when he was a kid. At least now Albert couldn't charge up the steps and knock him around.

After putting his guitar in its case, Kit unrolled the plastic bag and upended it. A pitiful flurry of white powder slipped out. This was it, his last snort. Maybe this was a good time to quit. He wasn't addicted, not in the sense that he *had* to have it all the time. He felt he could quit whenever he wanted.

This was his first since the drive up here. That had been . . . eight days ago? Over a week. He hadn't had any withdrawal symptoms, so he knew he wasn't hooked. If he really wanted to turn his life around, this was a great way to start. He could certainly use the money he would save. As he inhaled what little remained, he made the decision that this would indeed be his last.

With the window open and crickets serenading him, he drifted off to sleep, feeling good about his decision.

• • •

Kit bolted upright in bed. Had he heard something, or had he been dreaming?

He strained his ears. The nocturnal insects were quiet. That was odd. He glanced at the alarm clock. The green numerals read 3:32 a.m. He was about to lie back down when he heard it.

*Tap, tap, tap.*

It was faint. No wonder he had mistaken it for a dream. *Or is it the coke?* He tilted his head, trying to identify the sound.

*Tap, tap, tap.*

It was coming from downstairs. Was his father up? Did he need something? Albert did well most of the time considering he had COPD, high blood pressure, and heart failure. He was good about taking his meds, although he still smoked too much. Could he have fallen? Was he trying to get Kit's attention?

Throwing the sheet back, Kit padded across the carpet. He had left his door open since it helped pull air in through the window. He paused on the landing and listened. The house was quiet.

He crept downstairs and walked to his father's room. Cracking the door, he peeked in. Albert snored gently. Maybe it was a water pipe? Could the refrigerator be getting ready to go out? Kit had no idea how old it was.

*Tap, tap, tap.*

Kit almost came out of his skin. Heart racing, he closed Albert's door and looked down the hallway. The sound came from the living room.

*What's in there that could be causing it?*

He stepped into the living room. The streetlight at the end of the driveway cast a silvery aura through the drawn curtains, emphasizing the shadows that lurked throughout the room. He looked for anything that might be the source of the noise.

*Tap, tap, tap.*

Once again, he jumped. It was coming from the front door. Someone was knocking.

*Who the hell?*

He pressed his face to the wood and peered through the window.

The porch was empty, but there was a peculiar odor. Sour. Rancid. Adrenaline picked up speed in his system. It was what he had smelled out on County Road 501—the stink of the blight.

*Tap, tap, tap.*

Kit leaped back from the door as if he had been electrocuted. He clamped his hand over his mouth.

The sound came from the lower half of the door, and he thought he heard a soft voice.

*What did it say? Something about . . . coming out?*

The doorknob rattled.

A shadow moved on the wall opposite the front windows.

Kit watched, petrified.

Silhouetted by the streetlight, a small figure moved in front of the windows, the shadow mimicking its movement on the wall. The figure stopped. The head came close to the glass. Two hands cupped the sides of the face. The intruder was blocking out the light to get a better look inside.

A chill scurried down Kit's spine. He watched the small form against the window. It was searching for something. For *someone.*

His heart galloped like a racehorse. Why was he imagining that the person was searching for him? That made no sense. Who would come looking for him at this hour? And why was he still smelling blight?

*Tap, tap, tap.*

The knob twisted from side to side.

Then he heard the voice again. High, singsong but garbled, as if the speaker had a mouthful of ice cubes.

"Come out and play."

Kit's blood froze.

The figure in the window hadn't moved. Kit knew somehow that it was imperative he was not seen. He flattened himself against the wall to the right of the front window behind the door. The smell was getting stronger. Kit could almost taste its foulness coating his throat. He peeked out the window in the door again. The primal part of his brain bellowed for him to flee, but he looked down instead.

A little girl stood in front of the door.

*Tap, tap, tap.*

The soft rapping sounded like hammer blows since he was so close to the door. Sweat broke out on his back and neck.

The little girl raised her head slowly and looked straight at him. "Come out and play."

Glistening round eyeballs stared up at Kit from lidless sockets. In the ethereal illumination from the streetlight, he could see that her hair was long but patchy. Wispy. Her flesh had an albino aspect and was mottled with gray blemishes. Her skin reminded him of white sponge cake or moldy ranch dressing.

*BANG, BANG, BANG!*

"Come out and play!"

He managed to hold back a scream as he tore his eyes away from the *thing* on the doorstep. Leaning against the wall, Kit held both hands over his mouth as if his breath might try to escape. Feet padded across the porch to the front window.

A second shadow moved across the living room wall. The little girl tried to peer through the window as the other figure was still doing.

Kit slid down the wall behind the club chair. It was easy to do since his legs had turned to cooked spaghetti. He needed to make himself as small as possible.

The hazy gray forms crept to the end of the porch and returned. The doorknob moved back and forth once more. Then nothing.

Silence thundered in his ears. The smell dissipated. Kit waited, the sweat drying on his skin. His heart felt like it would burst. He looked around the shadow-filled living room, down the hall—

*The back door! Jesus, is it unlocked?*

Scrambling to his feet, he ran to the kitchen. He threw his weight against the door. He breathed a sigh of relief. The dead bolt was already in place. Kit risked looking through the window. He saw a small shape—smaller than the girl—standing in the backyard.

Two child-sized figures appeared from either side of the house. The little girl and a boy. Both appeared to be dressed in tattered rags.

*Have they been in an accident? Maybe they need help.* That would explain the ghastly visage he had seen moments before.

The third figure, a toddler, joined the boy and girl. They stood side by side. Almost as one, they turned their heads, looked up at the back of the house, and walked forward.

*What are they looking at?* Something about the toddler reminded him of the figure he'd seen in the alley across from the Mexican restaurant and he shivered.

All three children moved out of Kit's line of sight. The smell reappeared. He heard a faint scrabbling against the slate tiles, as if someone were rubbing up against the house. *What're they doing? Why're they looking—*

Kit's stomach dropped. The hair on his arms stood up. His heart shuddered like a prisoner testing a cell door.

*My window!* his brain roared. *It's open!*

He fled down the hallway and bounded up the stairs to his room.

Something moved outside the window.

He scrambled across the room, grabbed the window casing, slammed it down, and threw the latch to lock it.

The waxen, deformed head of a toddler appeared over the sill like an unholy sunrise.

Kit staggered back against his bed.

The toddler looked through the glass. Bulbous eyes found Kit cowering on the floor. He saw a tiny hand reach up and try to open the window. When it didn't move, the toddler scowled in a way that made the eyeballs seem to pop out of their sockets, then it disappeared from sight.

Kit couldn't stop shaking. He refused to take his eyes off the window, although he didn't know if he could handle seeing that cruel, pallid face again. When nothing happened after several minutes, he scooted backward across the carpet and out the door. On the landing, he hauled himself to his feet and nearly fell down the stairs in his haste. He ran to the kitchen and took a knife from the block on the counter. Only then did he check every window downstairs. He didn't see any children.

*Jesus Christ, could they come down the chimney?* They were certainly small enough.

*Or up through the basement? What the hell are they?* He moaned in terror.

*Get a grip, get a grip!* No, the chimney was blocked off and had been for years, and he had locked the basement door.

Summoning his courage, Kit double-checked the front door. He peeked out through the door's window at the tranquil night. He smelled nothing. The crickets had recommenced their night songs.

Kit collapsed in the club chair, trembling, with the knife clutched to his chest. He watched the living room window until exhaustion overtook him, and he slept.

• • •

"Get up!"

The voice stabbed through Kit's sleepy brain like an ice pick to the eye. He blinked. Sunlight streamed into the living room, and Albert stood over him.

"I want you out of here."

"Huh? What—" Kit mumbled, trying to get his bearings.

*What am I doing in the living room? Why am I holding a knife?*

The events of the early morning rushed back to him. His eyes widened as he looked from the door to the front window.

"Did you hear me? I said I want you out of this house." Albert scowled down at him. With the oxygen line running from his nose back behind his ears, Albert looked like his head had been bisected.

"Wh-what? Why?" Kit managed to ask as he sat up. His neck and shoulders ached from sleeping in the uncomfortable chair.

Albert pointed his finger in Kit's face. "I told you when you showed up that I wasn't putting up with none of your bullshit! I told you no playing that damn guitar at night. Now I find you down here like this. You lied, boy. You're still on them drugs."

"No, I'm not. I-I can explain this," Kit said as he held out the knife.

Albert sneered. "Oh, this oughta be rich. What were you going to do? Slit my throat while I slept?"

"Of course not! There was . . . Last night, I heard . . . " His voice trailed off.

What exactly had he heard? Now, as dust motes drifted in the sunbeams and birds chirped outside, he wasn't sure. Had he been dreaming? Had that last little bit of coke left him with a parting gift of paranoia? God, he needed a nose full right now.

Albert folded his arms. "Heard what, boy?"

Kit looked at the front door. He remembered standing there. He had heard . . . somebody knocking. That was it! And when he'd looked through the window to see who it was—

*Come out and play.*

Sweat broke across Kit's forehead. His body shook as he relived the terror of those dead eyes looking into his, of the doughy skin and the stench. The toddler at his window. He shivered.

Albert thrust his chin forward. "That's what I thought. You're strung out on something. Get the hell out of my house!"

"No!" Kit shouted, louder and harsher than he had intended. He didn't want to go outside, no matter how cheerful the birds sounded. "No, I'm not on anything!"

"Bullshit! What's that white junk under your nose? It ain't powdered sugar. Look at you. You're going through withdrawal." Albert sounded almost pleased.

"It wouldn't be withdrawal if I just took something—which I *didn't*! I-I heard someone knocking last night. I came down to check. I got the knife just in case."

"You didn't hear nothing 'cept them drugs in your head!"

Kit stared at the door. "There was someone there."

"Who? The cops again? The TBI? Maybe it was Mrs. Ortega from across the street bringing me one of her casseroles."

"It was kids," Kit said in a low, haunted voice.

"Kids? Okay, sure. It might've been some kids playing a prank. What were you going to do? Stab them?"

"They . . . weren't ordinary kids," Kit said under his breath.

Albert leaned closer. The smell of cigarette smoke drifted off his clothes. "What did you say?"

Kit shook his head. "Nothing. It doesn't matter."

"That's the first damn thing you've said that makes sense." Albert walked to the front door, unlocked it, and yanked it open.

Kit tensed and gripped the knife tighter.

Morning light flooded in. Albert stared outside for a moment, then turned.

"You're done here," Albert said. "I want you out of here by lunchtime today. I've had all I'm going to take of your drugs and lies. You understand me, boy?"

Kit didn't reply.

"I asked you a question, boy."

"Yeah . . . okay," Kit mumbled. A numbing awareness descended on him.

*Where am I going to go? I can't leave town.* He didn't have enough money for a hotel, but he had to find somewhere safe before nightfall, before the darkness came back.

Before *they* came back.

# 12

## A BURDEN FINALLY LIFTED

*Friday, June 10, 2011*

Kit punched in Troy's phone number and waited. He leaned back in the ancient desk chair, its slick red upholstery patched by duct tape. It squeaked like a nest of terrified mice. Around him in the Family Discount Furniture office were two desks, three filing cabinets, a small television tuned to a DIY show, several boxes, piles of folders and invoices, and four chairs. It smelled of old paper and varnish.

Troy answered.

"Hey, it's Kit. Got a minute?"

"If you make it quick."

"Absolutely. I was wondering if I could talk to you today after you get off work."

"Anything wrong?"

Images of gruesome albino children and wavering silhouettes flashed through Kit's mind. *Come out and play.* "Nah," he lied, "nothing that can't wait until later."

"Okay, where do you want to meet? Marty's Joint?"

Kit pushed a paper clip around on the desk. "No. Can you come by Family Discount Furniture? I'm doing a few odd jobs for them."

"I can be there around five," Troy replied. "Will that work?"

"Absolutely. Thanks, man. I appreciate it."

Kit put the receiver back in the cradle of the old touch-tone phone. Given the age and condition of the store, he wouldn't have been surprised to find a rotary one hanging on the wall, its cord knotted like mating snakes. The furniture store was something of a monument in Black Rock, having been passed down through the Ellistan family for generations. The current owner, Vince, had been a classmate of Kit's. He had put in a good word for Kit with his dad which had landed Kit a part-time job in high school. Vince had always been impressed by Kit's musical ability. He had even tried taking lessons from Kit once but didn't have the aptitude to get beyond the basic chords.

Kit had come into the store right after it opened this morning. After he and Vince had exchanged stories and memories, Kit had asked if there was anything he could do to make a little money, and he needed a place to stay for a few days. Did Vince know anywhere he might be able to crash?

Luck was with Kit for a change. Vince needed someone to load and unload the trucks, make deliveries, and keep the place clean. Then Vince surprised him again. Kit could stay in an unused, upstairs office if he didn't mind moving a bunch of stuff that was stored there. It had one window that looked down into the back parking lot and plenty of dust, but at least it was right beside a bathroom.

"I've always wanted an on-site security guard," Vince had teased.

Kit was overjoyed to find something so quickly. Vince told Kit that he could rummage around in storage for any old pieces of furniture he wanted to manhandle into the small space to make it more comfortable.

Kit had just started to organize the receiving area when Vince called him to the front of the store.

As soon as he walked onto the showroom floor, he recognized Deputy David Ellis from the incident on County Road 501. He was talking with Vince. Kit's heart dropped.

"Mr. McNeil," the deputy said. "Sheriff Owens would like a word with you over at the station."

"Uh, okay. What time?"

Ellis hooked his thumbs in his belt. "The sooner the better."

Vince smiled but Kit didn't feel any warmth from it. In fact, Vince looked like he was having second thoughts about his hospitality.

Kit returned the smile with his best "I'm sorry" expression and said, "I'll tell you all about it when I get back."

Family Discount Furniture stood two blocks from the police station. Kit walked the short distance alone. Deputy Ellis had gotten in his car and gone the other way. Plump, motionless clouds stuck to the sky like gel decals on a window. The intolerable humidity made him start sweating—a reminder that in addition to giving up drugs, he really needed to start exercising.

Ten minutes later Kit found himself sitting across from Sheriff Owens. Between them, a jumble of paperwork littered the desk. Agent Donovan Mack, dressed exactly the same as before, walked in with a Styrofoam cup in hand. He greeted Kit and leaned against a filing cabinet, casual yet poised for action.

Sheriff Owens asked Kit to run through the events from Monday night one more time. He obliged. He had seen enough cop shows to know that Owens was looking for discrepancies in his story. Agent Mack interrupted several times to ask questions or seek clarification. The agent was cordial, but his face remained stern.

As Kit responded to their questions, one thought pervaded his mind: *Should I tell them about last night?*

Sheriff Owens, Kit had discovered, had come to Black Rock from Atlanta, so he might be more open to something out of the ordinary. Kit knew the man was no fool. No doubt he had seen plenty of horrific things during his time down there.

*But children with no eyelids climbing the side of a house? Come on, get real. He'll think I've lost my mind.*

Maybe it was like Albert had said—just bored kids playing a joke. Of course, there was no way Kit would ever be able convince *himself* of that. Kids don't climb up the sides of houses, and they don't have bulging eyes and doughy flesh. He tensed to keep from shivering as the scene in the living room replayed in his mind.

"Ahem, is everything okay, Mr. McNeil?"

Agent Mack's deep voice shattered Kit's thoughts like a rock through plate glass. He realized both men were studying him with the kind of look cops get when they have a whiff of something suspicious. Kit gave a forced chuckle, but it sounded unconvincing even to him.

"Yeah, uh, I didn't get much sleep last night. Just tired is all." He put on his best smile, hoping they'd go back to the event on 501. At least with that he had nothing to hide.

Sheriff Owens said, "Mr. McNeil—"

"Call me Kit. Or Chris. 'Mr. McNeil' sounds like my father."

Owens sat back in his chair. "Very well, Kit. I'll be straight with you. I don't think you had anything to do with Deputy Richie's death. I believe you came upon the scene like you said."

Kit smiled and felt some of the tension release from his body. "Thank you. I—"

Agent Mack raised a hand that looked as big as a catcher's mitt. "But there's *something* you're not telling us. Your left leg hasn't been still since you sat down."

*Shit! Calm down.* Kit stopped bouncing his leg and offered an apologetic smile.

"Was there something else that happened on 501 that you're not telling us?" The sheriff's eyebrows lowered as if his forehead could no longer support them.

Kit glanced out the window. The trees and manicured lawn of the courthouse luxuriated in the midday sun. He thought he saw a small patch of blight near the sidewalk. When he looked back, both men still waited for his reply.

"No," Kit said in a small voice. "It's . . . it's something that happened a long time ago."

Sheriff Owens leaned forward. "Tell me."

*You better not do this!*

Kit ran his tongue along his upper teeth as he formulated his thoughts. "How long have you been in Black Rock?" Kit asked the sheriff.

Owens sized up the question before responding. "Fourteen years. I moved here in '97 when I took this job. Why?"

"So you've been around long enough to know that Black Rock . . . has something of an unusual reputation," Kit replied.

"Such as?" Sheriff Owens said.

*Don't do it! You're getting in over your head!*

"You probably know about the weird things that have been said about the town. It's haunted. Cursed. That more people die in Black Rock than anywhere else in Tennessee. That there's always been a 'shadow' over the town," said Kit.

Agent Mack cleared his throat and looked bored. "I thought we were past the haunted houses and conspiracy theories."

"Where's this going?" the sheriff asked as he adjusted his glasses.

Kit sighed. It was now or never. "Are you familiar with the name Melody Sellers?"

Sheriff Owens thought for a moment and glanced at Mack. "Girl went missing back in . . . what was it? The early part of the '80s?"

"The summer of 1981. She was last seen at the old arcade at the plaza. No one ever heard from her again as far as I know." Kit looked out the window as he plunged on. "Except the arcade *wasn't* the last time she was seen. I-I saw her later that day in the woods. With two of the Dunleys."

Ever since that day, Kit had wondered what it would feel like to finally let the secret out. He'd envisioned it bursting into flames like a vampire in sunlight. Now that it was done, he didn't feel any different.

The sheriff's eyes gleamed as he leaned forward. "*You* saw Melody Sellers after she went missing?"

Kit nodded. "I was twelve at the time. I'd been playing out in the woods." He decided to keep Troy out of it. His friend had a family here in town and would have to live with any repercussions that might arise. "I heard voices, so I hid. Greg and Jeff Dunley were with Melody. She was having difficulty walking as if she were drunk."

The sheriff motioned for Kit to wait and picked up the phone. "Blake, can you find me the file on a missing person? Melody Sellers, 1981." He replaced the receiver.

"Where'd they go?" Agent Mack asked. He took a legal pad off the desk and scribbled while Kit spoke. He was no longer bored.

Kit shrugged. "Honestly, I don't know. I followed them a little ways but got scared when I thought they'd seen me."

"Did they?" Agent Mack took a sip from his cup.

Kit shook his head. "They kept walking Melody up the side of the mountain. That's the last I saw of her."

"Which mountain?" Agent Mack kept writing.

"Blackpoint," replied Kit.

"Did you report this to the police?" Owens asked. "Did you tell your parents? Anyone?"

Kit shook his head again and didn't make eye contact. "No."

Agent Mack fixed a hard eye on Kit. "Why not?"

"I was scared shitless of the Dunleys! I was twelve, man. If the Dunleys had figured out I had been spying on them, they'd have killed me."

Mack looked at Owens for confirmation.

The sheriff sighed and nodded. "I've told you about that family. There was a bunch of them around back then too. He's right. If it got out that he'd told someone what he saw—"

"*That's* why I didn't say anything." Kit lowered his gaze to the bottom of the desk and the scuffed tiles beneath it. "And I guess I just wanted to believe the stories about her—that she ran away or became a prostitute."

"If I took you out there, could you find the spot again?" Sheriff Owens asked.

"Yeah, I think so. It wasn't far from a hideout we—*I* built." Prickly fear lanced through Kit's body. *I said "we."* He held his breath.

Agent Mack's eyes narrowed. He looked like an aggravated pit bull but remained silent. Sheriff Owens didn't appear to have noticed. He put his pen down and leaned back in his swivel chair. "Does anyone else know this?"

*Don't say a damn thing!*

Kit slowly took a breath. "No. This is the first time I've ever told anyone."

There was a quick knock on the door before it opened, and Deputy Blake handed Owens a file, then left.

"That's a hell of a burden to carry all these years," the sheriff acknowledged. He opened the file and scanned it before passing it to Agent Mack. "Well, I can tell you this, Kit. If anything you've said helps to reopen the case, you'll have made a big difference."

"There's . . . there's something else," Kit said softly.

*I've said too much already. If I tell him this, they'll throw my ass in a padded room at Vanderbilt Psychiatric Hospital!*

"About Melody Sellers?" Agent Mack tilted his head. "Or Walston and Collinsworth?"

Kit felt even more uncomfortable beneath the agent's unyielding stare, but he had to let someone know. It was too much to deal with, and it was eating him up inside. What happened couldn't just be brushed off as a prank. There was something going on around here. He cleared his throat. "No, it's . . . something I saw last night."

Sheriff Owens sat forward once more and picked up his pen.

Haltingly, Kit told them about the figures on the porch and the knocking on the door. He said that someone had been trying to get in his window on the second floor. He omitted the odor, the faces, and those words he had heard.

*Come out and play.*

This time he did shiver.

"Someone had a ladder to your window?" the sheriff asked.

"Maybe. I don't know. I didn't see one."

Sheriff Owens stopped writing and looked at him, perplexed.

"I know, I know," Kit said. "It's damned strange and makes no sense. I'll be the first to admit it, but that's what I saw."

The sheriff tapped the pen on the legal pad. He looked at Agent Mack but said to Kit, "I'll have some extra patrols run through your neighborhood. Probably just some kids flying a drone with Halloween decorations on it. If you see anything unusual tonight, call me."

"Yeah, I, uh . . . I'm not staying there anymore. Albert and I had a . . . disagreement."

Owens smiled. "I know Albert McNeil. He can be a hard-ass when he wants to be."

"You have no idea," Kit said. Now he *did* feel lighter. Freer. It was like finally taking off a pair of shoes that had been too small for years.

"Where are you staying?" Agent Mack asked.

"At the furniture store. I'm helping Vince out around the place. Hey, is it okay if I ask about Eleanor Davenport? You said she was murdered the other night. Do you have any leads?" asked Kit.

"What's your interest, Mr. McNeil?" Agent Mack crossed his arms, further emphasizing his broad frame.

"It's just that . . . I didn't know her all that well, but I did know her granddaughter, Allie. I connected the names after your visit the other day," said Kit. "She lived on the next block over from me growing up."

For a moment he remembered the games of Manhunt and flashlight tag they had played with the other kids on sultry summer nights. The parents of one of the kids (he couldn't remember who) always had boxes of colorful freezy pops. All the kids used their teeth to rip open the slim plastic tubes to get to the flavored ice inside, and after the ice was gone, they always drank the syrup that had collected at the bottom. Kit could almost taste the rough plastic edges.

According to Troy, Allie had died in 2000. Kit felt an emptiness inside him and hoped that her death had at least been normal and not like so many of the others.

The sheriff's voice brought him back to the present. "We've got some clues, but I can't say anything about an ongoing investigation."

"Sure, I understand. Just thought I'd ask," Kit said.

"Well, I think that's it for now," Sheriff Owens said. He stood and adjusted his belt.

But Kit had one question left. A crucial one. "Can I leave town?" *Please, please, please, let him say yes.* Kit felt like a seven-year-old asking for a puppy.

"Not just yet. I may need some more from you about the Sellers girl."

Kit couldn't hide his disappointment. He walked back to the furniture store, cursing his ruinous luck. He realized that if anything he had seen or said *did* lead to the Sellers case being reopened, he would be called on to testify in court *in front of the Dunleys.*

• • •

Shortly after 5:00 p.m., Troy walked in the furniture store. After greetings were exchanged, Kit took him aside and told him about the previous night.

Troy listened for ten minutes with a mixture of surprise, confusion, and uncertainty on his face. Kit needed his friend to believe him. He hoped Troy could see the sincerity—and fear—in his eyes and hear the anxiety in his voice. Of course, as Sheriff Owens had suggested, there could be a rational explanation for what he had seen, but this was still Black Rock. Many dark secrets lay beneath its surface.

"So Albert kicked you out," Troy said.

"Yeah. He thought I was strung out."

Troy thought for a moment. "Listen, I'd need to clear this with my wife, but I've got a storage area over my garage. It's a mess and hot as hell this time of year, but you're welcome to stay there. I don't have any spare bedrooms."

Kit shook his head. "No way. I appreciate the offer, I really do, but I won't put your family in danger."

"What danger? Like the sheriff said, it's just some punk kids up to no good. You know what this town is like when you're young and bored. Hell, we'd probably have done the same thing if we had drones when we were growing up."

"It's more than that, man. It's . . . hell, I don't know. It's fucked up and got me too scared to piss. Something is going on around here. Something very, very wrong."

"Please tell me you have a place to stay."

Kit nodded and pointed to the ceiling. "Vince is letting me use an old office, but there is one thing I was wondering."

"Anything, man. Name it."

"Could I borrow your bathroom? The store has a toilet and sink, but I need a hot shower."

Troy nodded. "Sure thing, no problem. Come by anytime."

"Would *now* be okay?"

"Yeah, of course. Why? You got a hot date tonight or something?" He winked at Kit and smiled.

With a confidence he hadn't felt in a long time, Kit grinned. "As a matter of fact, I do. With Courtney Shefford."

# 13

## CHANGE THE ENDING

*Friday, June 10, 2011*

True to her word, Courtney had texted Kit yesterday. He had intended to ask her to coffee but before he could, she invited him to dinner at a restaurant in Spring City.

"My treat!" she'd said. "Nothing formal. No strings attached."

He would not have to spend Friday evening alone in the furniture store. He could get a good meal, and most importantly, he would have a chance to go out with someone he never had the courage to ask out in high school. His lack of self-confidence remained, however, and he fretted over why she would want to be seen with him. She had suggested meeting at the restaurant since she already worked in the area, and he'd agreed. For some reason he felt self-conscious about picking her up as if they were teenagers going out. He had too many bad memories from that time in his life.

Throughout the salad and entrees, they shared about their lives and reminisced about teachers and friends. Kit found it easy to talk to her. She was a good listener and attentive to detail. That was unusual for him. Most of the women he had dated in the past had been focused on themselves. They had talked on and on about their families, work, stylists, friends, and bad relationships until he had felt his brain turn to oatmeal. It was nice to be with someone who didn't monopolize the conversation or try to always steer it back to herself. At one point he started to tell her about Troy's notebook of Black Rock oddities but decided there was no reason to ruin a perfectly good evening.

Courtney's light auburn hair ended just above the shoulders. Tonight she wore a short-sleeved pastel yellow dress with coordinated, tasteful jewelry. Her brown eyes, flecked with shards of green, were still as deep as Kit remembered, although he had been momentarily surprised when she'd donned a pair of reading glasses to study the menu. Neither of them were getting any younger, but Kit still pictured her as he remembered her from high school.

Over dessert they became candid about their former relationships.

"I told you that Doug and I were married," Courtney said between bites of cherry cheesecake, "and that things ended up not working out for us. Well, it was . . . a bit more complicated than that."

"Isn't it always?" He offered a sympathetic smile.

She put her fork down. "He was——" She put her fingers to her lips, as if to keep something from slipping out.

"You don't have to talk about it if you don't want to."

"No, it's okay. Even after all this time, some things are still just hard to process sometimes." She paused to gather her thoughts.

"We married in 1994, and for the first few years, everything was good. Then toward the end of '98 Doug became . . . withdrawn. Distant. It wasn't really noticeable at first, and when I did pick up on it, he'd just tell me it was stress from work. He was always good with the girls and a good husband, but I could tell that something was different. And then came 2001." She paused again and sipped her sweet tea.

"I-I found out Doug had been cheating on me. With a man from Nashville." Her voice dropped, and she lowered her head slightly as if she wanted to hide behind the tea glass.

"Oh, wow, I'm sorry to hear that."

Kit didn't have a judgmental bone in his body. In fact, his openness and acceptance were qualities that drew people to him. He was easy to talk to and never pretended to be better than anyone else. If Doug was gay or bisexual, that was his business. Kit had no stones to cast—no condemnation—considering his own laundry list of faults and failings, but he was sympathetic to the pain that the experience had caused Courtney.

"Yeah," she replied. "It had been going on since '99. I just . . . didn't know what to do at first. I was livid, of course. Not because he was gay, but because he'd lied to me. How many times had he been to Nashville on business, but he had actually been with the other guy?

"Well, we talked about it. I was confused and hurt. Angry. I tried to understand where he was coming from—and I do now—but at first it was just devastating. I went into a depression, wondering what I'd done wrong. Had I not met his needs? Was there something physically wrong with me that sent him elsewhere? That's when I started going to the gym. I thought maybe if I could get back to looking like I did in high school—"

Kit nodded. "You figured you could make it all go away, right? You could fix it."

"That was it exactly! I just knew it had to be my fault somehow. Do you know I even had a few people actually tell me that I had done something wrong and *turned* him gay? Yeah, unbelievable. But I soon came to realize that wasn't it at all. It really wasn't about me. He was working through his own identity."

"Was he— I didn't really know Doug. We didn't hang out with the same crowds in high school. Did he always know he was gay?" Kit took a bite of the steaming, gooey peach cobbler in his bowl.

Courtney shook her head. "He said he didn't know back then. I don't know if I believe him or not, but that doesn't really matter. I couldn't stay married to him, which was just as well because he wanted a divorce. My parents nearly fell apart when they found out. They've always been very conservative, and it was like having a piano dropped on their heads.

"Doug and I explained the situation to the girls as best we could. Jillian was six at the time, and Whitney was three. We told them just enough to explain but didn't go into detail. They were too young to try and process all of that. When they got older, I told them what had happened."

"Where's Doug now?"

Courtney lifted the last piece of cheesecake to her mouth. Before she ate it, she said, "He and Jacob are together in Nashville. Have been since we divorced in 2003."

Kit also polished off the remainder of his dessert. "Do you still see him?"

"Occasionally. Not as much now that the girls are getting older. They're both into so many things at school, but he does come to some of their events when he can. It's funny. They're a lot more tolerant than my folks."

"It's becoming more acceptable. I don't think it'll be long before they legalize gay marriage. The younger generation is growing up in a vastly different world than we did." Kit slid his dessert bowl to the side.

"That's the truth! What's the worst thing we had to deal with back in high school? Drugs? Our parents catching us sneaking out? Getting drunk? Now there's school shootings and cyberbullying. Kids can't play outside anymore because God only knows who might come by and snatch them."

Kit smiled. "Yeah, we used to play outside until—"

"Until the streetlights came on!" she said along with him.

"When those streetlights flickered, you'd better be hauling your butt home."

They laughed at the shared memory.

"Would you like a drink?" Kit asked. "A margarita or something?"

Courtney said yes, and Kit flagged down the waiter.

"So how did you adjust after the divorce?" he asked. "I just about went to pieces after my first. The second—that was a relief!"

"It was rough for the first two years. You know Black Rock. Most people expect you to be married and pregnant by the time you're twenty-two. There's still a lot of old cultural values that people can't let go of—divorce being a sin, a woman's place is in the home, things like that. I was suddenly a single mom of two who had somehow managed to turn the all-American high school heartthrob gay." She rolled her eyes. "I got a lot of sideways glances. I was a bit of a pariah for a while.

"I told you I started exercising before the divorce to try and hold on to Doug. By the time I realized it *wasn't* me, I'd already gotten into a workout routine. I've been doing it ever since but for me this time."

"That's terrific. I really need to do that too. I've let myself go for too long."

"To answer your question, after those first two years, I adapted pretty well. However, I did fall into the new divorcée trap. I started dating again too soon. Let's see, I found a clod, a player, and a liar before I realized I was pushing too hard. So I made some adjustments to my thinking and attitude. Since then, I've gone out a few times, but mostly those have been with coworkers or friends of friends."

"Blind dates, huh?" Kit grinned.

"Something like that, but I'm at the point now where it's going to take someone *really* special to get me to give up my independence."

Kit didn't know if that was meant as a warning or invitation.

Courtney's margarita arrived along with Kit's beer. He was delighted with Courtney's company and with how the evening was going.

*Sure wish I'd had the guts to ask her out in high school,* he thought for at least the fifth time.

Halfway through the margarita, she said the thing he'd been dreading. "So tell me everything about your music career."

Maybe it was the beer on top of all the rich food. Maybe it was the guilt gnawing at his soul. It could have been how comfortable he felt around her or the demure scent of her perfume. It could have been all of those or none of them, but whatever it was, he let his walls down and opened up.

"To be completely honest, I don't really have a music career. I've tried. Believe me, I've tried! But I can't get out of my own stupid way. There's been some . . . self-inflicted damage that I'm not proud of.

"I haven't met anyone famous. I haven't made an album or been on tour with anybody except for some regional honky-tonk bands. I've had some really good opportunities . . . " His voice dwindled as each one passed through his mind like models on a runway. He shook his head. "Somehow, I always find a way to screw them up. I'm a middle-aged, low-rent guitar player with no plan and no purpose."

The rawness shocked him. Kit waited for Courtney to grab her purse and flee the table, leaving him alone like John Travolta at the drive-in in *Grease.* But she didn't. She gazed at him, her eyes soft in the low light and a compassionate smile on her lips. She reached out and gently laid a hand on top of his.

A tingle raced up his arm.

"Chris, I'm sorry if I made you uncomfortable by asking that. It's really none of my business—"

He attempted to laugh it off, but it didn't work all that well. "No, no, it's okay. You didn't do anything. I'm just . . . disappointed that I've let so many chances get away."

"That's true for all of us. Nobody gets everything they dream about or takes advantage of every opportunity. We don't get the life we want. We get the life that's handed to us by millions of different decisions, and we do the best we can. It's what we make of that life that's important. But I do think you're selling yourself short."

Kit raised his eyebrows.

"Really," she continued. "All night I've heard you talk about how bad you think you are, how unimportant you think you are, and that's not true. You were immensely talented in high school, and I have no doubt you've grown even more so since then. You don't give yourself enough credit.

"We've all got things in our past we're not proud of—things we wish we could go back and do differently. So I try to look ahead instead of dwelling on past missteps. I think you should too.

"You've got a lot to offer. You're outgoing, approachable, kind. You've traveled. You make music. That sort of stuff interests people. They want to hear about places they've never been and experiences they've never had. You don't have to be some big country music act who gets to play the Super Bowl halftime show. Trust and believe that *you* are *enough*. No one has ever been exactly like you, and no one ever will be exactly like you. Instead of putting yourself down, I think you should celebrate how original and creative you are."

She paused to take a drink.

Kit swallowed hard. His eyes were wide. "Uh, wow . . . "

"I didn't ask you to dinner so I could brag on social media about dating a famous musician. I asked because I wanted to catch up with you."

Warmth flooded Kit's body. He wanted to say something poetic or profound, but all he said was, "Thank you."

"You're very welcome. You're quite a talent, Chris, and quite a guy."

They chatted for another hour before saying goodbye in the parking lot. There was no kiss—just a quick hug—but as Kit watched her drive off in her Subaru Outback, he didn't care. She had used the word *dating* during dinner. He smiled as he rolled the windows down to let in the warm evening breeze.

First Troy, now Courtney. Two people who had definitely made this trip worthwhile.

# 14

## STARING INTO THE FACE

*Saturday, June 11, 2011*

K it's cell phone rang as he swept the store. There hadn't been a customer all day. The store didn't receive shipments on the weekends, and there was nothing to assemble or deliver. Leaning the broom against the back of a sofa, he fished the phone out of his pocket. The caller ID said COURTNEY S. He smiled as he answered.

"Kit? Oh, thank God!"

Her voice sounded pinched. Harried. He thought she might have been crying.

"I'm sorry for bugging you at work, but I-I just had to talk to someone. You came to mind."

He smiled again, pleased to be the first one she'd thought of. "Are you okay? You sound upset. What's going on?"

"I am. I mean, I'm okay. Well, no, I'm not . . . I'm kind of freaked out. I think someone is following my daughters."

The uplifting feeling Kit had been experiencing vanished as quickly as a downpour washed away sidewalk chalk. He plopped down in a recliner that shifted under the impact. He had to lose some weight. "Do you have any idea who?"

"No. I didn't even know about it until just a little while ago."

"Yeah, you didn't mention anything last night," Kit said.

"The girls just told me. They think they've seen someone over the past two days in the bushes or the shadows."

Kit watched the occasional car drift by the front windows. "They have any idea who it is?"

"No, they haven't been able to get a good look. Jillian says it's just one person, but Whitney claims to have seen two. They're upset. I am too."

He nodded even though she couldn't see him. "Sure, who wouldn't be? Like we said last night, it's not safe for kids anymore." He paused. An image shot through his head, and he tried not to shudder. "Uh, what time of day have they been followed?" Kit tried to steel himself for the answer he knew was coming.

"Evenings and nights. Why? Does that mean something?"

Coldness settled in his stomach. Was it those *things* that had come for him?

*It could be the Dunleys.*

His stomach felt like a chunk of ice. After the altercation in the pharmacy parking lot, those degenerates would like nothing better than to get revenge. Courtney and her girls would make excellent targets.

"Have they . . . have the girls seen them anyplace special?" Kit asked. "Where have the girls noticed this happening?"

"Nowhere special. Except—" Her voice cracked.

He heard a soft sob followed by a few calming breaths. He waited.

"They . . . they saw them yesterday, not far from our house. In one of the homes still under construction in our neighborhood."

Fear surged through Kit. His tone dropped and became more insistent. "Courtney, listen to me. You need to take your girls and get out of Black Rock. You need to leave. Right now."

"Leave? But—"

"No buts. Don't waste any time. Get some things together. Is there someplace you could go for a few days?" He racked his brain, trying to remember if she had any relatives in the area.

"We can't just pack up and leave. I've got work—"

Kit took a deep breath and tried to mask his trepidation. "Courtney, I'm afraid it's the Dunleys. It's just the kind of shit they'd pull."

The line was silent for a moment.

"Then I'm calling the police," Courtney said with defiance.

He could almost hear her jaw tightening.

"I'm sick and tired of those inbred rednecks thinking they can do anything they like! If they so much as say something to Jillian or Whitney—"

Kit stood and started to pace. "I really think you should go. I know you don't want to, but don't risk it. Those bastards wouldn't think twice about—" He left the sentence unfinished. Both of them knew rape and assault were favorites of the sociopathic clan.

Courtney's voice hardened. There was no trace of distress, no sound of tears. "I'll call the sheriff. Thanks for talking to me."

"Of course, but I still think—"

She sighed. "When the girls told me, I just lost it. I'm really sorry for bothering you. I'm calling the police as soon as I hang up."

"Okay, you do what you think is best. And you're not bothering me. Please don't hesitate to call me if you need anything."

"Thanks, Kit. I appreciate it."

The call terminated.

*Why won't she leave? That'd be the best course of action. Just get away—*

But then he remembered. That was *his* standard operating procedure. When things got too hairy, too tough, too uncomfortable, he ran away. Like when he'd left Black Rock and his marriages and that band, Old Dirt Road. Every time he just picked up and ran when he didn't want to face the truth or the consequences. Courtney was a hell of a lot tougher than he was.

He pocketed the phone and picked up the broom. Shame burned in his gut. He hated it when the truth hit too close to home.

• • •

In addition to the offensive 1970s sofa with harvest-gold, avocado-green, and burnt-orange flower print fabric that he had wrestled out of storage, Kit had also discovered a television set that probably had last been used when *Starsky & Hutch* was on the air. He had bent and tweaked the antenna enough to get a cross between cheesecloth and a solarized snowstorm. Did stations even broadcast to antennas anymore?

The screen hissed and flickered, throwing spectral shadows around the office. He stretched out on the abomination of a sofa, its aged and prickly upholstery like sandpaper on his skin. It was after eleven on Saturday night. He stared at the yellowed ceiling tiles.

*Man, I sure know how to live.*

His cell buzzed. It was Courtney again. He thumbed the screen.

"Hey—"

"Kit! Help! They're here. Oh God—"

What sounded like a struggle in the background came through the cell. The shrill scream of a teenage girl catapulted him off the sofa. "Courtney, I'm here! What's happening?"

"Kit! We're trapped in the house! They—"

Something shattered. Two more screams in the background. "No! Get back! Get away from them!" Courtney screamed.

"Courtney, tell me what's going on! *Courtney!*"

Silence.

He looked at the screen. The words CALL ENDED mocked him in red letters.

Throwing on a shirt and shoes, he bolted out into the night. His tires churned gravel as he sped out of the back parking lot, nearly clipping a mailbox on the sidewalk. He was grateful that Courtney had told him during their date where she lived.

Sweat beaded on his forehead, and his heart refused to slow down. Images of the Dunleys, and what they were capable of, played through his mind. He drove faster, hands trembling on the wheel.

• • •

Courtney, Jillian, and Whitney Shefford lived in a brick split-level at the end of a cul-de-sac that abutted Blackpoint Mountain. Behind a privacy fence some fifty yards away, another house slept in the darkness. Three other houses around the circle were still in various stages of construction. The girls' stalker had been in one of them, even closer than Kit had imagined.

In the driveway Kit slammed on the brakes and jumped out of his car. The house was dark. He ran to the front door. Locked.

He pounded on the door. "Courtney! It's Kit! Can you hear me?"

There was no sound, not so much as a cricket, anywhere around the property. It was so silent he could have been on another planet. Blackpoint Mountain jutted into the sky, its surface a patchwork of impenetrable shadows.

He dashed to the garage and checked it. Also locked.

*Damn it!*

The house rested on a slope, and he jogged down the gentle hill beside the garage. Turning left, Kit found himself on a landing of grass that, after about ten feet, continued to slope down into the bowl-like backyard. He noticed a security light mounted at the corner of the house, but it wasn't working. A deck stood on pylons, and beneath it was a door.

With the house on his left and the backyard to the right, Kit eased forward. The night was inky black, and the streetlights didn't reach back here. He felt along the vinyl siding, unsure of his footing. That's all he needed—to step in a hole and break an ankle. There was still no sound from inside the house, and it was as silent as falling snow in the backyard too.

Kit stepped underneath the deck. Now there wasn't even the faintest tease of starlight. The darkness seemed to swell, a hungry, viscous thing. He could barely see the door. A pane of glass rested in the top half. He searched for the knob like a blind man. He wished he had a flash—

*My phone!*

Tugging the cell from his pocket, he punched the screen until he activated the flashlight feature.

Something moved in the window.

Terror engulfed him like a sudden downpour. His skin tingled. He gasped before realizing it was only his movement in the glass. He chastised himself for being so jumpy, but it didn't help calm him. It only raised his awareness that his back was exposed to the yard—to whatever might be lurking out there in the darkness, waiting to strike when he was most vulnerable.

Like now.

His body tensed. The tiny hairs on the back of his neck prickled. *What if those children are out there right now, creeping up behind—*

He spun around and thrust the cell phone forward as if warding off a vampire with a crucifix.

The blackness greeted him, silent as the grave and unfazed by the flashlight.

"Fucking hell," Kit whispered. His hands trembled nearly as bad as his heart.

He turned back to the door and saw the movement again. *Just my reflection.*

He gripped the doorknob, and a thought flashed through his mind. Wouldn't it be horrifying right now to see a face slowly emerging from the darkness of the basement? The hair on his arms stood up.

*Damned imagination! Of all the times to—*

Something moved in the window.

No way. He wasn't spooking himself again.

But icy apprehension gripped him. The movement was *inside* the basement! It drew closer, going from a dusky, shapeless blob to a larger, ashen oval—

*Get a grip. It's just Courtney or one of her daughters.*

Black pits appeared where the eyes were.

*What if it's one of the Dunleys? Oh shit!*

The face came into focus.

Kit screamed. He tried to jump back, but his hand wouldn't let go of the knob. The cell phone quivered as he held it toward the window. The milky flashlight beam played across the face.

Beneath a pallid, doughy brow, two eyeballs twitched as they held Kit in an unblinking stare. It was a child, a boy. His lipless mouth spread in a malefic grin, his teeth like awls jutted at different angles.

Kit shook so hard the knob rattled in his hand. He wanted to pull away, bolt from the house, and flush the image of that hideous grin from his mind. His feet acknowledged no such commands from his panic-stricken brain. A fetid, sour stench reached him through the door.

The boy slowly raised a hand and pressed it against the lower part of the glass. He withdrew it just as slowly, leaving behind a small, bloody print.

A scream from somewhere in the house nearly caused Kit's knees to buckle. The child drifted back into the darkness, his rictus grin unwavering.

Kit had never wanted to run so badly in all his life. Every fiber of his being screamed for him to move. What he had seen through the restaurant window—what had likely been watching *him* through Albert's living room window—waited somewhere on the other side of the door.

Kit was paralyzed. His mind refused to work. It ricocheted from image to idea and flight to fear, like a pinball that couldn't stop. Just like those eyeballs. Moving. Never blinking. Watching him from the blackness this very moment.

He heard another scream, followed by breaking glass.

Something in those two screams electrified his senses and broke his immobility. He had to get to Courtney!

Adrenaline boiled through him. Kit couldn't tell if the tremors in his arms and legs were from that or the fear. Clenching his jaw, he turned the knob he still held in his cramped, sweaty grip.

The door opened.

The faint odor of rank cottage cheese remained. Kit swept the cell phone back and forth, but the light was too weak to penetrate the blackness. Tentatively, he reached inside, fumbling for a light switch. He found it and flicked it up and down but nothing happened. From above he heard the sound of running feet and childish giggles. His blood froze.

*Come out and play.*

Fighting his instincts, Kit stepped into the basement.

# 15
## HIDE-AND-SEEK

*Saturday, June 11, 2011*

Inside the basement Kit saw a push mower, some tools hanging on the wall, plastic totes, boxes, and three bicycles—normal items found in every basement. A door stood open to his right.

Sweeping the phone from side to side, he edged over to the doorway and looked into the adjoining room. The size of it swallowed the tiny cell phone beam, so he could only focus on what was directly in front of him. Kit moved with caution into a family room. He noticed the foul smell was dissipating. With his eyes now better adjusted to the gloom, he saw a couch, two recliners, a coffee table, and a couple of lamps. There was a television placed on an entertainment center, and a set of stairs across the room disappeared into the darkness above.

He moved as quickly as he could around the furniture. At the stairs he heard another scream.

"Courtney!" He took the stairs two at a time, cognizant once again that his back was exposed to the darkness. An open doorway stood at the top. "Courtney!" he yelled again.

"Up here!" she replied faintly.

Kit emerged into a hallway. Two closed doors stood to his right at the end of the hall. He hurried the other way. The sounds of a struggle grew more pronounced overhead. He passed a bathroom and another closed door before entering the living room. Watery silver beams from the streetlights seeped through the curtains. To his left stood a sliding glass door that led onto the deck. On his right was a short flight of steps down to the front door, as well as open doorways to a dining room and kitchen. He surmised that the door on the other side of the kitchen led to the garage. Another set of carpeted stairs led to the upper floor.

A door opened behind him in the hall.

"Let's play hide-and-seek," a cruel voice said.

Kit spun around. His heart climbed into his throat. The mercurial light from his cell played across the approaching figure. The pale boy still had the fixed, toothy grin Kit had seen downstairs. Unblinking eyes reflected the light, and the foul stench increased.

"Better find a good spot!" the boy growled.

"St-stay back!" Kit shouted.

In the gauzy light, the boy looked to be no more than eleven or twelve, but everything else about him was disproportionate. His head tilted to the side too much, as if his neck wasn't strong enough to hold it upright. Arms longer than they should be caused his fingernails to reach to his knees. He seemed like a child's scribbly attempt to draw a body. Soiled rags that had once been pants and a shirt hung from his waxen form.

Choking back the urge to scream, Kit bolted for the stairs.

"One, two, three—" the child-thing rasped behind him.

Kit pounded up the steps as fast as he could. He glanced over his shoulder. No sign of the boy, although Kit could still hear him counting.

"Five, six—"

The struggle ahead of Kit grew louder.

So did the smell.

He was halfway up the stairs when a small figure appeared at the top, blocking his path. Kit stopped, unnerved by the sight of a toddler. It had the same hideous features as the boy, although it seemed to be wearing some sort of tattered dressing gown. Spiny teeth, like an inverted sea urchin, appeared gray as it grinned at him.

"Eight, nine, ten! Ready or not, here I come!"

The toddler stepped down. Kit heard soft footfalls behind him.

"Blood," the toddler growled, raising her arms. The universal sign to be picked up.

The footsteps came up the stairs. "I *know* you, know your *blood*," the boy said between giggles.

Kit's head snapped side to side. *Don't these fucking things ever stop grinning?* He could almost taste his own terror. His mouth felt like it was filled with ashes as he gauged his options.

There was no way he could leap over the toddler, not going up the steps. He was too old, too fat, and too slow. Even in his prime such a feat would have been all but impossible.

He would just have to do the one thing he couldn't stand thinking about.

The toddler waited with her arms out. The boy crept up the steps, and the putrid stench filled the stairway.

Gritting his teeth, Kit lurched forward. He seized the toddler-thing around the waist with both hands and lifted it off the floor.

"Yes! Blood!" she screeched.

Kit's fingers sank into the toddler's cold, spongy flesh. It was like holding a jellied chunk of ranch dressing. He gagged. The stench filled his nostrils and lay like a film across his teeth. His stomach convulsed.

One of the toddler's hands flicked out. Her nails raked Kit's arm, drawing thin lines of blood. He yelled and tried to throw the thing down the stairs, but she grasped his right wrist with both hands, refusing to be dislodged.

At her touch, Kit stiffened, and his left eye started twitching. The fetid odor oozed down his throat. Numbing cold settled into his hand and wrist. Then the world changed, and Kit was somewhere else.

• • •

Images raced through his mind. They flashed like the hyper-edits of an action movie trailer. Kit barely had time to register one before another took its place. They passed like rushing water around a rock. He was a participant in each one and yet watching it simultaneously.

There are First Nation people. Cherokee. This region belongs to them except for one part called the *Oolisihgee Ga'do'hi*—the Dark Lands. *Her* hunting grounds. An area dominated by a black-spired mountain where no Cherokee ever ventures. Within this land dwells Uyaga. The Cherokee call her *Nitib-pingwi Manitou*—the Black Earth Spirit.

On moonless nights, families huddle inside their sapling homes of mud and poplar bark. They whisper of *her*. Uyaga brings bad luck. Steals children. Spreads disease. Causes travelers to disappear. She roams the Dark Lands with her abhorrent children.

Kit gasped. Time seemed suspended. The pictures kept coming, forming and rolling, only to be replaced by more.

The Trail of Tears in 1838. The Cherokee are forced from this land. Uyaga isn't without playthings for long. The town of Black Rock is founded in 1862 at the base of the mountain the Cherokee called Blackpoint. It stands defiantly in the center of the Dark Lands. Strange accidents and bad luck abound in Black Rock. Blighted patches of ground testify to Uyaga's malign influence. Despite all this, the town grows.

Kit's head ached. He wanted to close his eyes, but he couldn't remember how. The images from history played out silently like pictures on a movie screen.

A man named Edgar comes among the untamed mountains and darkened glens. He possesses a hooked nose and wide-set eyes. He settles near Black Rock. Marries and fathers eleven children in fourteen years. He stumbles upon a cave and discovers Uyaga within. He comes forth changed. For ten years he does *her* bidding.

People in the twilight hollows visit Edgar. It is said he can heal the sick and see the future, raise storms and inflict curses with but a touch. He speaks to things that live in the spaces between the stars. The Warlock of Blackpoint. He is shunned by the townspeople. Twice a year he enters Black Rock for supplies. He rambles insanely about the Children of the Earth and of the Black Earth Spirit.

Kit thought there were tears running down his cheeks but wasn't sure. He felt so very little of his body now. *Am I dying? How long have I been like this?*

Edgar's firstborn son, Daniel, dying of tuberculosis. Edgar placing him in the cave. A year later Edgar's second child, Lena, who is beset by uncontrollable seizures, is put in the cave as well. Edgar spirals into madness. Degeneracy. He impregnates his third child, Janet. Two children result from their union. Edgar puts the second child, Lydia, into the cave. She is thirteen months old.

Now Kit knew he was crying. Tears were warm against his clammy flesh, and pressure built up behind his eyes. Were they going to burst from his skull because of what he was seeing? *Oh God! How much longer? How much more? Help me!*

The images refused to yield.

Edgar fills the pages of a book. His writing grows erratic. Crazed. An island of lucidity appears in his sea of delirium, and he knows what must be done. A gunpowder explosion seals him in the cave. He is never seen again. Yet the evil does not end.

Greg Dunley. Jeff Dunley. A teenage boy, a coed, a Hispanic man. A dark-haired girl wearing shorts and a blue halter top. All in a black, dead place.

*Oh God! Oh God! Oh God! It's Melody Sellers! They did kill her!*

Another wave of images rolled toward Kit. This time he felt them lodge in his chest. A frigid, dreadful awareness came over him.

Kit saw himself riding his bike. A summer night. Someone from the shadows touching him—

*My dream! Oh God, the dream!*

The scenes dissolve, shift, reform. Scotty Dunley discovers many bodies in a cave. Among them is an aged book bound with cracked leather straps and dingy clasps. He takes it. Uyaga, *Nitib-pingwi Manitou*, stirs. *She* craves blood again. Blood to break the seal.

Then it was over. The images spent at last. A part of Kit's brain recognized that the toddler still clung to his wrist.

*The toddler.*

Hot bile climbed Kit's throat. His stomach convulsed as he realized who he was holding.

*Jesus Christ, it's Lydia Dunley!*

Then that made the boy Daniel, Edgar's firstborn.

More tears fell. Kit tried to scream but couldn't.

• • •

The entire panorama had lasted less than five seconds, but Kit felt worse than a detoxing junkie with jet lag and the flu. It was all he could do to stay upright. Daniel and Lydia Dunley's stench in the enclosed stairwell stung his sinuses. With as much effort as he could muster, he slammed the toddler against the wall. Her grip loosened. He flung the writhing, creamy thing down the steps.

Lydia hit Daniel with a soppy thud, and they tumbled backward.

Nearly mad with fear, Kit scrambled upstairs. Saliva hung from the corner of his mouth.

The sounds of a struggle emanated from an open door at the end of the hall. When he reached it, he saw Courtney and her daughters in the far corner. They had squeezed between an armoire and the bed, and the girls screamed as they cowered behind their mother. Standing between him and Courtney was a girl who had to be Lena Dunley. The floor was littered with shards of glass, a busted lamp, an alarm clock, books, and a CPAP machine. Courtney had kept the thing at bay but was out of ammunition.

As Kit appeared in the doorway, the child turned in his direction with a look of familiarity, as if she knew him. She had the same unnerving grin and lidless eyes as her siblings.

"Good, good," she snarled. "You came. We knew you would." Lena started toward him.

"What? Why? What are you—" Kit stepped back, realizing his mistake too late.

Daniel grabbed him by the waist as Lydia seized his leg.

Kit had only worn a pair of gym shorts, a T-shirt, and shoes. His legs had no protection against the nails that raked his flesh. He screamed and felt blood running down his leg.

Kit managed to kick Lydia away.

"Blood!" she growled, getting up and toddling back for him.

Kit tried to pry Daniel loose, but his hands kept slipping on the boy's mucous-like flesh. With every touch, fresh images rocked Kit's mind.

Scotty Dunley. Gabe Beecher. Edgar in the woods. Blackouts. A hand on Kit's arm in the park. A pit.

Lena grabbed Kit's bleeding arm. She clamped her hand over the wound and stared at him, her expression ghastly yet serene. If not for the disfigurements of her body—the sparse hair, the elongated arms, the twisted facial features, the blanched complexion—she could have been any eleven-year-old girl.

He watched in horror as the flesh of her hand darkened and began to take on the normal coloration of human skin. Beneath her hand, Kit felt a gentle pull against his flesh like something was suckling.

Daniel released Kit's waist and started doing the same thing to the wounds on his leg.

They were leeching his blood away! As they did, their pigmentation changed. The children were sponges, absorbing his blood. Everything seemed to slow down, and Kit felt woozy and had trouble focusing. It was like being sedated in a hospital. He thought he staggered a bit but maybe it was just the room tilting.

She *craves blood again—blood to break the seal!*

Kit saw a blurry figure move across the room. Was it Courtney? He squinted. Yes, it was her. His vision turned gray as she opened a door. Was she pulling something from the closet?

His eyes snapped open at Courtney's scream of terror and rage. Everything still moved in slow motion, and he watched, disconnected, as Courtney brought a tennis racket down on Lena's head. The metal sank into flesh. The child-thing let go of Kit's arm. Courtney slammed the racket into Lena again and again. Lena's flesh squished, oozing a pearly substance that stank of vinegar and the blight.

Lena crumpled to the floor. Some of Kit's strength returned with a surge. It was like a stimulant kicking in. He found enough energy to boot the toddler away, but as soon as she landed down the hall she began crawling back.

Courtney stepped forward and swung the racket. It squelched against Daniel's back. He released Kit's leg.

Kit put his foot into the boy's chest and pinned him against the wall. He felt vigorous again, not drained. He pressed his shoe into Daniel, and something inside the boy's chest popped.

"Hit it again!" Kit yelled.

Daniel hissed and spit. He clawed at the air, at Kit's shoe and ankle. Daniel's legs kicked, but he couldn't escape.

With a growl of fury that ended as a scream, Courtney swung the racket with both hands. The edge collapsed Daniel's nose, burst one eyeball, and sliced into the other. Gooey, pungent fluid spurted like a lanced boil. Courtney hit him again. The front of Daniel's skull burst like a rotten melon.

Stringy, opaline liquid sprayed the wall, and the stench of putrefied vinegar filled the hallway.

Kit lowered his trembling leg. Daniel slid down the wall, leaving a slimy trail behind.

With aching limbs and sweat stinging his eyes, Kit grabbed Courtney and stumbled into the bedroom. He slammed the door and leaned against it. His brain felt numb and his wounds slowly wept blood. He looked at Courtney.

"A-are you okay?" he gasped. He pawed sweat from his face.

She nodded as she pushed hair behind one ear.

"And the girls?" He saw them huddled together, arms around each other. Terror filled their shell-shocked faces.

"N-not hurt. Sc-scared as hell. Like me," Courtney said. "What about you? My God, your leg—"

He waved her off. "It's nothing, just scratches."

The stench from the hallway seeped under the door. Kit paused as he tried to avoid breathing through his nose. "We've got to get out of here."

"H-how?" asked Courtney.

"The front door." Kit took the tennis racket from her limp hand.

Whitney shrieked and pointed at the door. "But what a-a-about *them*?"

"They . . . they're dead," Kit replied. "They can't hurt you."

Whitney shook her head and clung to her sister.

Courtney turned. "Jillian! Whitney! Come on, we're going."

Neither girl budged. Tears streaked their faces.

Kit thought he heard a noise on the other side of the door, and he tensed. His heart accelerated again. "Hurry! We've got to go *now*!"

With firm but tender encouragement, Courtney prompted the girls to their feet. She looked at Kit and nodded.

"Don't look down," he told them. "Walk as fast as you can." Gripping the racket, he slowly cracked the door.

He slammed and locked it.

"What? *What!*" Courtney yelled.

"Blood!" little Lydia growled from the hallway.

Kit shook his head, hopelessness creeping across his face. "They're getting up," he said softly, as if the sound of his voice might accelerate the resurrection process. "Daniel and Lena."

"Who?" Courtney asked.

"Never mind. We need—"

The door shuddered behind Kit as three sets of fists pounded on it.

Singsong voices and creepy giggles taunted them. "We're gonna get you! We're gonna get you!"

"We need a plan!" he shouted as his body jerked with each impact. The Dunley children were small but strong. He looked around the room.

The closet was not an option. They would tear the louvered doors apart in seconds. There were two windows, one facing the side of the house and the other the front. He knew the ground sloped along the sides, and a jump in the dark could result in a sprain or break.

He dashed to the front window, threw it up, and knocked out the screen. He looked down. Below him was a drop of about fifteen feet, but there was a row of boxwood shrubs to break the fall.

The door shook in its frame as the onslaught continued.

"We're gonna get you! We're gonna get you!"

"Don't they ever shut up?" Jillian wailed.

"This is our only chance," Kit said, pulling his head back inside.

"I can't . . . The girls can't—" Courtney said.

"Yes, you can! I'll lower you as far down as I can. You'll be fine. It's this or—"

As if on cue, the door shook again. Cracks appeared in the wood and lengthened with each blow.

"Girls, come on," Courtney said, her tone more determined than maternal.

When they hesitated, Courtney took Whitney by the shoulder. "It's going to be okay. Kit will help you down. Go on."

Reluctantly, Whitney stepped over to Kit. Her blonde hair lay plastered to her face and head. Kit smiled and held out his hand. He spoke as calmly and evenly as he could in spite of the machine gun in his chest. "I won't hurt you. It's okay. I'm going to get you out of here. Can you put your legs out the window?"

He lowered her as far as he could before releasing her. With a surprised yelp, Whitney crunched into a shrub.

"Blood!" the children cried.

Jillian took less convincing. Kit lowered her and waited for her to land and scramble out of the boxwood before helping Courtney. Grunting and groaning, she likewise thumped into the foliage. Her daughters hauled her out.

Kit threw one leg over the sill and flopped around onto his stomach, his hands gripping the sash.

The bedroom door burst open.

Kit wiggled his legs, trying to move his center of gravity back.

Daniel, Lena, and Lydia charged him, arms outstretched as fury twisted their faces.

*How the hell are those two still alive?*

Kit thrust himself backward. His fingertips raked the top of the sill, and he was falling. He landed with a grunt in the partially flattened bush. He rolled out and onto the ground just as Courtney took him by the arm.

"Call 911!" he said, panting.

"Our phones are inside!" Jillian yelled.

Kit fished in his pocket and pitched his cell to Courtney. He had put it away just before he grabbed little Lydia on the stairs.

As Courtney made the call, three blanched faces watched from the window. From this distance they seemed like three children who could've been watching it snow or waiting on friends to arrive. Then they were gone.

Jillian and Whitney were hysterical. Courtney comforted them as Kit struggled to his feet. After a moment, Courtney collapsed into his arms, sobbing. He held her as she convulsed the adrenaline, fear, and shock from her system.

Kit was exhausted. His body ached. Blood squelched in his sock.

"Oh God, Kit! I saw . . . *I saw.*"

"Saw what?" His voice was tight and nervous. "Did one of them touch you?"

"Y-yes. I-I saw things. Images—" She buried her head against his shoulder.

"It . . . it'll be okay." He wanted to believe that as much as he wanted her to believe it. But where had those things gone? How were they still alive? He and Courtney had to have killed the boy, yet the children were all in the room at the window after Kit had escaped.

*What are they?*

But he knew. At least, he knew who they had once been.

Now they were the Children of Uyaga.

He helped Jillian and Whitney into the back seat of his CR-V. He and Courtney stood outside.

*Blackouts. A touch on my arm. What's the connection?*

He held Courtney as the sirens drew near.

# 16

## IN THE AFTERMATH

*Sunday, June 12, 2011*

A police SUV pulled into the cul-de-sac. Its lights threw blue smears across the front of the house. Two doors opened when it stopped. Kit remembered being part of a similar scene on County Road 501. The deputy who had taken his statement the day after that incident and Sheriff Owens stepped out. Both held flashlights.

"Courtney?" the deputy asked. He aimed the light on her torso so as not to blind her.

"Oh, Paul, I'm so glad to see you!" she told him.

"Ms. Shefford," Sheriff Owens greeted her. "And Mr. McNeil. Why am I not surprised to find you here?"

Kit couldn't miss the sarcasm in the sheriff's voice.

"You're bleeding," Owens said. "Paul, get a paramedic over here."

Kit glanced down. Rivulets of blood caked his leg. "No, that's okay. It's not as bad as it looks."

"Call it in," Sheriff Owens ordered, and Deputy Mitchell complied.

"Are you hurt?" the sheriff asked Courtney. He flicked his flashlight into the CR-V and saw Jillian and Whitney. "Are they okay?"

Courtney put her hand on her upper left arm. "Just a few scratches. Nothing serious. The girls are fine—just terrified."

Satisfied that no immediate medical aid was needed, Sheriff Owens sharpened his tone. "Now what the hell is going on here?" He planted a hand on his hip. The flashlight beam formed an elongated oval on the driveway between them.

Kit and Courtney exchanged confused looks. Kit didn't know what to do, and he could tell she didn't either. They couldn't pretend everything was okay, but could they tell the truth? Kit was struggling to compose a coherent story when Courtney spoke.

"Ben, I—" She lost the words in a sob.

The sheriff motioned for Deputy Mitchell to look around as he waited for Courtney to relax.

*What can we say that wouldn't make us seem like raving lunatics?* Kit wondered. *Hi officer, we were just attacked by three dead kids. I threw one down the stairs. Don't worry, we killed two of them, but they aren't really dead. They got back up. They were trying to suck our blood.* Kit looked at his feet.

Courtney wiped her cheeks and took a deep breath. She explained about calling the police earlier to report the potential stalker.

Sheriff Owens eyed Kit. "*You* had problems with unwanted persons around your father's house the other day." He sounded suspicious.

"Uh, yeah. Earlier this week," Kit agreed.

"Ben, we've known each other for a long time," Courtney said. "I used to live across the street from you when Doug and I were still married. You know I'm not prone to hysterics."

Owens scratched the back of his head. "No, you're not."

"You know I don't lie." Courtney glanced at Kit.

Did she want validation for this course of action? Kit merely stared back, perplexed.

"Ben, I was attacked in my home tonight," Courtney said.

Sheriff Owens narrowed his eyes. "Is the person still here? Do you know who it was?" He pulled a notepad from his pocket. "What time did this happen?" He keyed his body mic to alert Deputy Mitchell, who had disappeared around the side of the house.

"I-I don't think they're still here—" said Courtney.

"They? There was more than one?" Sheriff Owens wrote something on his notepad.

Courtney dropped her head and put a hand over her eyes. Kit knew she was struggling with how to say the impossible. "Yes," she continued, "there were three of them. They were small. I don't know who they were."

"When was this?" Owens asked.

She answered, "Less than an hour ago."

The sheriff's radio buzzed. Deputy Mitchell's disembodied voice sounded metallic. "Ben, this is Paul. I'm around back. There're definite signs of forced entry—a window into the downstairs den has been broken and there's a bloody handprint on the exterior door."

"Affirmative. Don't go in yet." Sheriff Owens pressed the button a second time. "Dispatch, this is Owens. Request backup to 2335 Basset Drive."

"Copy that."

Sheriff Owens stepped forward. "Now Ms. Shefford, Mr. McNeil, let's go through this very slowly."

• • •

Fifteen minutes later the ambulance and backup unit arrived. Deputy Ellis joined Deputy Mitchell at the rear of the house. Tom, the paramedic Kit had met earlier, eyed Kit with doubt as he dressed his wounds. Kit could certainly understand why.

Kit and Courtney fumbled through a vague explanation of events, but both knew Sheriff Owens wasn't satisfied. The sheriff paused from time to time to answer his deputies as they continued to investigate. With Kit's and Courtney's injuries addressed, the paramedics checked Jillian and Whitney before departing.

In the short time he had known Sheriff Owens, Kit had come to like him. Maybe it was because he was from Atlanta, but Sheriff Owens was open-minded—something Kit found unusual for a small-town cop. In Kit's experience, most cops had their minds already made up and wouldn't budge in their thinking. Owens seemed fair and was genuinely likable, but he *was* a transplant. He hadn't grown up here and didn't know the subtle peculiarities of the town.

The bottom line was could Sheriff Owens be trusted enough for Kit to risk sounding like a madman? Would the sheriff be willing to accept what had happened tonight? Kit had told him about the children at Albert's but hadn't given any details.

Again, from Kit's own experience, cops were not known for their broad imaginations and willingness to entertain flights of fantasy, but he had already trusted Sheriff Owens with two things, one of which Kit had thought he would never tell another soul. Based on what Lena had said about how they'd known he would come, this had all been a setup. They were after him and had no qualms about who got in the way.

Kit put his hand on Courtney's shoulder and looked at the sheriff.

"Do you remember the other day in your office when you and the TBI agent were there? You remember I told you about the . . . kids at my father's house, and how they tried to get in? I mentioned that Black Rock has always had a reputation for peculiar things." He didn't wait for the sheriff to reply. "This is one of those things. It was the same kids here tonight."

Courtney shivered despite the humid night air. "They weren't . . . *normal* kids, Ben. They were . . . I-I don't know what they were."

"You say you hit them, these kids?" Sheriff Owens asked.

They nodded. "They were attacking us." Courtney pointed to the cuts on her arm, and Kit lifted his leg in case Owens had forgotten.

"And you hit these 'kids' with a tennis racket?" Sheriff Owens said.

They nodded again.

The radio squawked and Courtney jumped. "Ben, we've done a complete sweep of the house. There's nobody here."

"What about the lights?" the sheriff said into the mic on his shoulder.

"Working on it now. Power was shut off. Ah, there we go."

A couple of lights popped on in the upstairs windows, as did a light at the end of the sidewalk.

"Smart kids," Owens murmured. "Cut the power before going in. Courtney, do you know if anything was taken?"

She shrugged. "No idea. We were too worried about getting out."

Before he could hold it back, Kit said, "They weren't burglars. They weren't after *stuff*. They wanted blood."

Sheriff Owens raised his eyebrows. "How do you know that?"

"Because they told me," Kit said.

"Wanted blood?" Owens questioned as he wrote it down.

Kit glanced at Courtney, then back to Sheriff Owens. "Your deputy out on 501? Wasn't she missing nearly all her blood?"

The sheriff chewed his lip for a moment before going back to the mic. "Paul, get the county forensics unit down here. Whoever was in there apparently didn't take any steps to hide their identity, so there are probably prints all over the place."

"You got it."

With the lights on, Kit felt a little more at ease, but as he looked around, he saw dozens of places where Daniel Dunley could have attacked him from the shadows when Kit had arrived. He shivered, remembering the face that had stared at him from the basement.

"Come on," Sheriff Owens said, striding past them. "Walk me through what you did, Mr. McNeil. Courtney, you stay here with your girls." Owens followed Kit as he retraced his steps through the family room and up the stairs.

"One of them, the boy, came from back there." Kit pointed down the hall. All the doors were open in the wake of the search. "I don't know which room."

*Let's play hide-and-seek.*

"He followed me up the steps."

Footsteps sounded overhead and Kit tensed. When he saw Deputy Mitchell come down the stairs, Kit relaxed.

"There's definitely been a struggle upstairs, Ben, like the lady said. Blood too, but not very much. There's splintering of the bedroom door and frame, so entry was forced. And take a look at these." He held up two small evidence bags.

Sheriff Owens took them and turned them from side to side. "What is it?"

"A scrap of fabric. Seems pretty old and it smells," the deputy said.

Sheriff Owens opened the bag and lifted it to his nose. He recoiled. "I've smelled that before." He looked over at Kit. "The blight smells like this."

"I thought there was something familiar about it but couldn't place it," Deputy Mitchell said.

Kit remembered his fingers sinking into Lydia's mushy body.

The sheriff studied the second bag. "And this?"

Deputy Mitchell shrugged. "That I'm not too sure of. It looks like somebody blew their nose and wiped it on the wall. There's quite a bit of it in a splatter pattern."

As Sheriff Owens held the bag up to the light, Kit saw the milky, glutinous matter that had erupted from Daniel's mashed skull and looked away.

"Do I need to smell this one too?" Owens deadpanned.

"It's nasty. Vinegar-like," said Deputy Mitchell.

Kit cleared his throat. "It's . . . fluid . . . from one of the ki—" He stopped.

The deputy stared at him, confused. Deputy Mitchell didn't know about the children yet. Better let Owens be the one to tell him. Kit smiled. "It's from one of the *people* who were here tonight."

Deputy Mitchell looked at the sheriff for confirmation, but Sheriff Owens ignored Kit's comment. "Okay, I want pictures of everything, top to bottom. *Something* happened here tonight, but I'll be damned if I know what right now." The sheriff turned to Kit. "Show me the upstairs. After that, we're going to the station. I want a description of these—*people*."

*Oh shit.*

# 17

## WITH ONE BLIGHTED TOUCH

*Sunday, June 12, 2011*

K it had been more than ready to get out of Courtney's house. Even with all the lights on he still found himself flinching at every movement out of the corner of his eye. Everywhere he looked he saw the Dunley children.

*Why* my *blood? What's so special about it?*

Children of the Earth. Children of Uyaga. What did all that mean?

The sheriff had given Courtney permission to take her daughters to Crossville, where her parents lived. It was an hour there and back. She promised to meet him and Kit at the station.

Kit used the bathroom at the station while Sheriff Owens fixed a pot of coffee and fielded calls from the crime scene. Then they sat down in the sheriff's office.

"Tell me about these attackers, the children," Sheriff Owens said. He opened a file folder and prepared to take notes.

"Well, there are three of them—two girls, one boy. I'd say the biggest girl and the boy are both about twelve years old. The other girl is little like a toddler."

Sheriff Owens looked at Kit like he couldn't believe what he was hearing but encouraged him to continue.

*How much do I tell him? How far do I go?*

Kit knew he had to provide a physical description, but should he say anything about the visions? That might just make things worse. Would the sheriff be less inclined to take him seriously if Kit told him about the evil Cherokee spirit and the curses and the Dunleys or how Kit knew things from hundreds of years ago that he shouldn't know? Kit decided to say nothing about all that for the moment. Maybe later it would make more sense.

*Yeah, right.*

"What do they look like? Do they have any identifying characteristics?" Sheriff Owens asked.

*Oh yeah, you could say that.* Kit nodded. "They're really white—like albino white. They have big eyes and sharp teeth." This was sounding more ridiculous by the minute even to him.

"Sharp teeth?" Owens kept a straight face and wrote it down.

"I'm sorry, man, I know how this sounds, but I swear to you it's true. They're like . . . I don't even know how to say it. They're not normal."

"Uh-huh."

"Listen, I picked one of them up. The toddler. It was like . . . picking up a sponge filled with mayonnaise. Their bodies are—" He sighed miserably. "All I know is they're ghost white, they stink like the blight, they seem to be immune to pain, and they're fucking creepy to look at."

Sheriff Owens finished writing it down. He closed the folder and looked at Kit. "Thank you. Why don't you try to get some rest until Ms. Shefford gets back? You can use my couch over there."

"Do you believe me?"

The sheriff stood up. "Right now, the only thing I believe is that there's something unnatural going on in my town. It's almost one in the morning. Get some rest, Kit."

At 2:45 a.m., the sheriff sat down at his desk across from Kit and Courtney. He took a sip from his TOWN OF BLACK ROCK mug and grimaced. Kit had to smile. In all the stations he had been in during his bar fight days, there seemed to be only two types of police station coffee: dishwater or industrial sludge. Obviously, municipal budgets didn't extend to Keurigs for police departments.

Sheriff Owens looked at Kit and Courtney over the rim of his mug as he took a drink. "I won't make you go through everything again, although that's standard procedure. I think we *all* need to hit the hay."

Kit agreed. He knew he looked awful. Hell, he felt awful. He hadn't gotten any rest on the couch, because his mind had been unable to relax. Just
sitting in the chair now took tremendous effort.

The sheriff adjusted his glasses. "There wasn't enough blood at the house."

Courtney looked lost. "What do you mean?"

"From your wounds. Kit's mostly. Based on the lacerations, there
should've been more blood in the upstairs hallway. Are you sure neither of
you cleaned anything up?"

Courtney shook her head. "We didn't have time."

"So it was like what happened out on the highway?" Kit asked.

Sheriff Owens nodded. "There wasn't enough blood there either." He
tapped a gray file on his desk. "Same with Eleanor Davenport."

Kit held a Styrofoam cup of hot coffee in his hand, but he didn't feel
it. His whole body was numb. He remembered Lena's hand against his arm,
Daniel's hand on his leg. Suckling. They had been taking his blood.

*Are they vampires?*

It sounded ridiculous because there was no such thing as a vampire. Of
course, two days ago Kit would have thought the same thing about creepy,
deformed children who show bizarre shit in your head and want to kill you.

Sheriff Owens was talking to Courtney, but Kit wasn't listening. His
thoughts were too loud. *I saw Melody Sellers in one of those . . . visions. I know
what happened to her, or at least I know how she ended up. And the missing people—Collinsworth and Walston—were there too.*

He tried to remember where he had seen their bodies. They were not in
coffins or graves. As best he could tell, they were just lying in a dark, dead
place. Like broken, forgotten toys children had tossed aside.

*Children.*

Surely, they weren't used as *playthings* for Daniel, Lena, and Lydia?
Chilly fingers worked their way up Kit's spine. Were the missing people in
some mass grave? The place where they were was not wet, so that ruled out
being underwater.

The basement or cellar of a house maybe? But what house? Where?

His head still hurt and the longer he sat, the drowsier he became. It was
all he could do to keep his eyes open.

"Kit?" Courtney asked.

He jumped, nearly spilling his now lukewarm coffee. He looked at Courtney and Sheriff Owens. "What?"

She laid a hand on his arm. "You dozed off. Are you okay?"

Kit yawned. "Shit. Yeah, just . . . exhausted. What time is it?"

"Nearly three thirty," Sheriff Owens said. He looked at Courtney. "Is there any place you can stay? I'm afraid you can't go back to your house until we've finished."

"That's fine. I don't want to go back there." She looked at Kit, her eyes imploring him for refuge.

Kit felt miserable. Courtney needed his help—needed a place to stay, and he could offer nothing better than a night upstairs in an old furniture store. He dropped his eyes so she wouldn't see his shame. "You, uh . . . you could get a hotel room. Over in Spring City." He couldn't be sure if he saw a hint of rejection or disappointment in her eyes. That made him feel worse.

"That'll work," the sheriff said. "You can pick up anything you need from the house. We've still got people there. Thanks for your help. Courtney, I'm sorry this has happened to you, but we'll put it right."

• • •

Courtney returned home, and Deputy Ellis escorted her upstairs where she threw together an overnight bag. "Stay with me," she said to Kit when she met him in the driveway. "I-I don't want to be alone."

The suddenness of the request caught him off guard. "Huh? Are you sure?"

She nodded. "I just . . . After all this . . . With my girls gone, I just need to be around someone."

"Sure, absolutely."

Kit wondered how many times he'd fantasized about something like this with someone like Courtney when he was younger, but there was nothing sexual about her request. She was just a traumatized woman who needed company. He was only too happy to oblige. He didn't want to go back to that cavernous, shadowy furniture store either. Would they come for him there too? The thought petrified him. He left his CR-V at the police station, and they talked about the night's events as Courtney drove them to Spring City.

By four thirty in the morning, Kit—still in his bloodied T-shirt, shorts, and sneakers—sat on one bed, while Courtney lay across the foot of the other, staring at the ceiling. Despite their fatigue, neither could sleep.

"Did . . . did any of them touch you?" she asked, her voice just above a whisper.

"Yeah, they clawed my arms and legs—"

"No, not that. Did they *touch* you?"

He would never forget Lydia Dunley's tiny fingers grasping his wrist as he tried to throw her down the stairs. He rubbed his wrist. "Yeah, they did."

Courtney rolled over onto her stomach and propped herself up on her elbows. Dark circles were forming around her eyes. "Did you . . . see anything . . . when that happened?" She must have read the answer in his expression because she nodded. A moment of silence passed.

"I saw—" He dragged a hand down his face and felt the stubby prickle of hair on his jaw. *Better than feeling Lydia's flesh.* "There were . . . images. Visions. They flashed through my mind, but it's like I was physically there, watching it as it happened."

"Me too," she replied in a forlorn voice. "The bigger girl . . . She grabbed me, clawed me . . . just before you got there."

Kit swallowed hard and leaned forward. "Wh-what did you see?"

Courtney looked at her hands for a minute. When she spoke, her gaze drifted to the floor. "I saw Indians. They lived in the area where Black Rock is now, but there was something else—some kind of beast or *thing*. The Black Earth Spirit."

"Pale, bony. Lots of mouths that kept appearing and disappearing."

She shivered. "Don't remind me."

"I saw a man named Edgar, although I've got no idea how I could know something like that. And I saw Greg and Jeff Dunley with—" He stopped, unsure how to or if he should say the name.

Courtney bit her lip. "Melody. They killed her. Why, Kit? Why would they do that? Melody never hurt anyone!"

"The Dunleys are cruel. There's something rotten inside them. They've been that way as far back as anyone—" He stopped and stared at her. Realization dawned.

"What?"

"*We* know when it all began. With Edgar finding Uyaga's cave."

"Did you see him writing things?"

"Yeah, in some kind of book."

She sat up on the bed. "What I don't understand is, if the land belonged to Uyaga, why was *she* in the cave? Why didn't she come out when Edgar found her?"

Kit shrugged and tried to sort through the images in his head, but there had been many he had only seen for a second or two. It had been too much to process at one time. He shook his head. "Maybe she couldn't or maybe she didn't want to. What I want to know is, why does she want my blood?" He rubbed his bandaged leg.

"And what did Scotty do with the book?"

He jerked his head up. "What?"

"Didn't you see? Scotty found the cave and took the book. Edgar's journal."

Kit concentrated but couldn't find an image that corresponded. "We must've seen different things—some of the same things but different ones too. What was in that book?"

"I never saw what he wrote, but Scotty found a way to contact Uyaga." She said it so simply, so straightforwardly, that Kit nearly fell off the bed.

"Wh-what? What for? Why?"

Courtney yawned. "Who knows? All those Dunley bastards have been tainted by that *thing* in the cave. Who's to say what they think or why they do the things they do?"

"But why me? Why *my* blood?"

Courtney looked at him with bloodshot eyes. "I was going to tell you a minute ago when you asked. The children—they're feeding the blood to Uyaga. The deputy's. Eleanor Davenport's. Yours."

"But why *mine*?"

"You were at the Sweet Spot, and the Children of Uyaga were watching you. After you left, they found your blood."

Kit tensed. The memory hummed through his mind. *The crushed beer can!* He'd nicked his finger on the aluminum edge. He stared at the finger as if it had suddenly become leprous. "Holy shit," he whispered. "So Black Rock really is cursed. If not by Edgar Dunley, then by Uyaga's presence. Jesus, all that bad luck, all those deaths—they're all connected. I guess that explains my own bad luck, as well as all the deaths in our graduating—"

He could almost feel the color draining from his face.

Courtney certainly noticed. "What's wrong? Are you going to be sick?"

From the dark recesses of his mind, something *laughed*. It was vile and sinister and clung to the inside of his skull like black mold. He began to tremble violently.

Courtney was on her feet, holding his shoulders. "Kit! What's wrong?"

The laughter showed him everything again.

*It was after one in the morning. He rode through downtown and cut across the park. Something small came out of the shadows and touched his arm. He fell off his bike. His head hit the ground. He almost passed out.*

He wished now that he had.

*Someone bent over him, watching, grinning.*

He had convinced himself that he was alone that night—that it had just been a tree limb that touched him. That it was just the wind whispering in the trees. Only all of that was a lie. The laughter revealed the truth.

*A Child of Uyaga bent over him and whispered the spoiled words that had cursed him:*

*"With this touch, from this moment on, you are my conduit. Whenever you stand upon this land, this Black Earth, anyone you touch will be marked by my curse. They will become my victims, suffering for my pleasure. Every time you fall unconscious, I will take one victim from among those you have touched. Nothing shall stay this death when it comes for them—not distance, not time, not pleas of mercy, nor bargains offered. Even if they are no longer on my land, they will die, and in their dying, each shall know it was your hand that made it possible.*

*"Henceforth, you will not remember this meeting or these words. In this state of ignorant unknowing, you will spread my evil and destruction from one to the next whenever you set foot upon this blighted ground. I use you to carry out my insensate cruelty. Now rise, vassal, and scurry into the light. For I have marked you and will always be waiting for you in the darkness."*

Kit fell sideways on the bed and curled into a fetal position. Courtney held him to keep him from shaking, yet still the whole bed quivered. All the while he murmured, "It's my fault, I killed them. It's my fault, I killed them."

# 18

## DARKNESS IN THE DARK LANDS

*Sunday, June 12, 2011*

**K**it finally fell asleep just before six in the morning, his body drenched in sweat. If he dreamed, he did not remember it and for that he was thankful. He awoke to the sound of running water. It took him a moment to get his bearings, and the events of the previous night rushed back to him. It was like a black tidal wave, inescapable and overpowering.

*It's my fault. I killed them.*

He groaned and rolled over.

The water stopped, and after a few minutes, Courtney came out of the bathroom. Steam curled out after her. "Hey, you're awake," she said when she saw him lying on his side, staring off into space. "How are you feeling?"

He did not respond.

"The housekeeper woke me up a little before nine, but I was able to get back to sleep." She brushed her hair in front of the mirror. "Then I got up about around twelve thirty, feeling like I was starved to death. I still feel like I've been dragged along two miles of bad road, but the shower helped a little."

Kit could see her watching him in the mirror, and he saw the concern on her face. He did not like seeing her that way. She was pretty and intelligent and should not be worried about someone like him. All he had to offer was death.

Courtney turned to face him. "Come on, let's go get something to eat," she said in a positive, uplifting voice.

Kit climbed out of bed and shuffled to the bathroom. It smelled like warmth and shampoo and soap. He closed the door and looked at himself in the defogging mirror. Dark circles lay under his eyes, and his face was scruffy with stubble. He looked haunted.

*And why shouldn't I? After what I've seen. After what I've learned.*

He stepped under the hot shower and realized Courtney was right. It did feel good. It stung the wounds on his leg and arm, reminding him that he was still alive. Unlike so many others. He had no clean clothes, so he put his dirty, bloody ones back on. While his body was clean, his heart lay buried under layers of black guilt. His thoughts repeated like a stuck record.

*It's my fault. I killed them.*

He didn't remember much about lunch. He ate little and said even less. Courtney tried to get him to open up, but he was too scared. What if his words carried the same curse as his touch?

On their way to the car, Courtney said, "Kit, you told me that you've struggled with depression before. I have too. After my divorce. I know what the signs are . . . and I know it's got a tight grip on you right now. I'd . . . like to help if you'll let me."

"Thanks," he mumbled as they got into her Subaru Outback.

"Just know that I'm here if you need me—if you want to talk or anything." She started the vehicle. "I'm going to call Troy. He's your friend, and I think he'd want to know what's happened."

Kit shrugged and stared out the window as she drove back to Black Rock.

Now he truly mirrored the town. As the derelict buildings and empty storefronts slipped by, Kit saw the reflection of his own soul in their dingy windows. Crumbling corners reminded him of the broken pieces of his life. Faded signs were like his hopes and dreams. Even the green trees, the red stop signs, and the blue sky seemed dull and washed out. Uyaga's words perched in his mind like vultures eyeing a carcass. *He* was to blame. All those deaths—all that suffering and tragedy—were on him. He sighed. It was the only way to express his melancholy that didn't require effort.

*Was Mom's death my fault too?*

That thought nearly crippled him completely. He closed his eyes and leaned his head against the passenger window—as much to try and blot out the idea as to keep from puking at the possibility. Had his grandparents died because of his touch? Who would be next? Troy? Courtney?

He had doomed them all.

All the bad luck he had experienced was Uyaga's fault as well. Ever since that night in the park, his life really hadn't been his own. Oh, he had lived it sure enough, but it had been manipulated by something else. He was nothing more than a pawn in his own existence.

Maybe it was finally time to just end it all. He had never attempted suicide before, but the idea had surfaced on more than one occasion. But if it wasn't really *his* life—and if it was the only way to save people from Uyaga's curse—then why not? His spirit sank lower. The void it left filled quickly with depressive guilt. He would wish the Outback would run into a tree right now, but only if it would not hurt Courtney. Maybe he could do that when he got back to his CR-V.

He was out of drugs, so an overdose was not an option. With a few phone calls, he could scrounge up enough to do the job, but that would require going back to Nashville.

*So much for staying clean and turning my life around.*

He tried to remember what medications Albert was taking. Was there something there he could use?

What about just slitting his wrists? He did not have a gun and was not keen on the idea of shooting himself, although that would get it over with quickly. He did not like to consider hanging either. He had read somewhere that people who hanged themselves lost control of their bodily functions. He was not comfortable with anyone finding him like that.

"What're you thinking about?" Courtney asked.

He saw a patch of blight in someone's yard.

*That's part of* her *too. Or a side effect of her presence.* "Nothing," he lied and turned his head farther to the right. His chin was almost on top of his shoulder.

"Kit, I need to know. What did you mean last night when you said, 'It's my fault, I killed them'?"

He sighed again. There was no use trying to hide it or pretend like she didn't know about it. "It's something that happened to me in the park when I was a kid." He told her about that night, the mysterious touch, and the awareness he had received in the vision that he was responsible for the deaths of those he touched.

The fact of the matter was that as long as he was on *her* land, he was a walking death sentence to anyone he came in physical contact with, and the only way to stop that from happening was to stop living. For a moment he felt sad. He had just gotten to know Courtney, and now that was all over. He would miss Troy too. At least he could be with his mother again, although that did little to assuage the bleakness he felt.

Courtney called Troy on the way. He agreed to meet them when they got back in town. She drove to a fast-food restaurant where he waited in his truck. Troy and Courtney got out, but Kit didn't move.

"What's going on?" Kit heard Troy ask. Troy studied him through the windshield.

"I'll tell you in a minute. Grab us a table, preferably away from every-body else," Courtney replied.

Troy went inside with a look of consternation on his face. Courtney came around and opened the passenger door. Kit got out and stood beside the Outback, his eyes downcast. His body felt like it was about to collapse in on itself. He plodded behind Courtney, saying nothing.

The after-church crowd had thinned out, so there were plenty of emp-ty tables. Troy had picked a corner booth farthest from the counter. He drummed his fingers as he waited for Courtney and Kit to be seated.

"Hey, buddy," Troy said with a worried smile.

Kit nodded and stared at the tabletop.

Troy looked at Courtney with a questioning gaze. She explained every-thing that had happened at her house. She showed Troy the scratches on her arm and pointed out Kit's T-shirt and shorts with dried blood on them. When she attempted to lift Kit's arm so Troy could see the claw marks, Kit jerked it away.

Then she told Troy what had happened to Kit in the hotel.

Time passed in a haze as Kit heard Courtney talking and saw Troy lis-tening, but it seemed like it was happening far away, as if he were witnessing it through the wrong end of binoculars.

After twenty minutes, Troy sat back, and the cushion he sat on squeaked like a fart. He looked at Kit and Courtney in silence, eyebrows working up and down as he fumbled with all he had just been told.

"Jesus Christ," Troy said. "You're not joking, are you?"

Courtney shook her head. Her face was lined with worry, her tone solemn and flat. Kit said nothing. He stared out the window at the cars going by on the road.

"I just . . . I can't believe this," Troy said. "I mean, I *believe* you, but—" He hesitated. "What you're saying is that this *thing*, this Uyaga . . . put some sort of curse on him, and when he touches anyone—"

Courtney nodded. "That person becomes susceptible to Uyaga. Becomes a target for *her*, I guess you'd say."

Troy rubbed his beard and told her about his binder of oddities.

"You think the deaths of our classmates are a result of this curse?" Courtney asked.

"Kit and I were talking about it the other day. I found a . . . pattern between our classmates and his blackouts. Every time he passed out there was a—"

Kit glanced up at him and saw the struggle on his friend's face.

"At the time I just thought it was strange. But now—"

Courtney nodded. "There's a connection all right." She told Troy about the message Kit had received when he was twelve.

Troy sighed. "Shit . . . No wonder the doctors couldn't ever find a neurological cause. There wasn't one. This Uyaga-thing touched him, which gave him the curse. He touches anyone, and they get entered into some infernal lottery, is that it?"

"Yes," Courtney replied, "but only when Kit is here. On *her* land."

"So if he's in Nashville and touches someone—"

"I don't fucking kill them," Kit said, his voice a lifeless monotone. He looked at Troy. "You remember when the deputies came into Marty's Joint to break up the fight? Deputy Richie touched me on the shoulder when she went by. Soon after, she turns up dead. When I'm on Uyaga's land, anyone I touch or who touches me gets marked. They die because of me."

"I told you before," Courtney said. "*You* haven't killed anyone. It's Uyaga's doing. *She's* the killer."

Troy pursed his lips as he shook a finger in the air. "Wait a minute. Did you black out when Deputy Richie died?"

Kit shook his head. "No, I was driving back from Melvine when she was killed."

"What about when Eleanor Davenport died? Did you black out then?" Troy asked.

"Not that I can recall."

"Then why not? Every other time someone has died, you've blacked out," Courtney said to Kit.

"What's so different about those two?" Troy asked. "Why no blackouts all of a sudden?"

Kit shrugged, frowning as he stared out the window.

Courtney looked at Troy. "So, Kit can touch anyone, anywhere—with no consequences—unless he's here in Black Rock."

"In Scarburn County," Kit said to the window.

"How do you—" Troy said.

"I just do."

"But when he's in the county anyone he touches gets marked with the curse. And then it follows them wherever they go," Courtney continued. Now it was her turn to frown. "But that still doesn't explain why Kit didn't black out recently." Her frown deepened.

Troy watched her. "What's wrong?"

"Kit, you told me that in your vision Uyaga needs blood to break a seal."

"Yeah, so?"

Courtney stared at the center of the table. "What if you didn't black out because these recent deaths are related to that blood? If she's gathering it or collecting it or whatever . . . Maybe that explains the difference?"

Kit sighed. "That makes sense, I guess. Better than anything I can come up with."

"You're not blacking out now because it's not so much about the curse—"

"As it is about needing the blood," Troy finished. He remained silent for a moment before adding, "What do we do about this then? What *can* we do?"

"I've been thinking about that," Courtney said, "and I've got an idea. It's a long shot though."

"Go on," Troy said.

"Kit and I both saw a book—a journal—when those things touched us. Maybe there's something in it that can help?"

Troy crossed his arms on the edge of the table. "Like what?"

"I don't know. A way to undo the curse? Something that might help fix all this?"

"Where's the book? And how would we get it?"

"I don't know!" Courtney snapped. She rubbed her eyes. "I'm sorry, Troy. I didn't mean to yell at you. It's just—"

"No, it's okay. I get it. Kit, you got any thoughts on all this?" Kit turned to face them again.

"Yeah. I've been thinking about what to do. I figure if I kill myself, this all goes away," Kit said in the most matter-of-fact way.

"What? No!" Courtney exclaimed. She started to put a hand on Kit's slumped shoulder, but he pulled away. "Don't even think that!"

"Don't go there, buddy," Troy said.

Kit shook his head. "It makes sense though, doesn't it? If I'm not around, I can't touch anyone, and that fucking thing can't use me anymore." His voice remained flat and emotionless. "It's the only way."

"No, it isn't!" Troy said. "I'll be damned if I'm gonna let you do something like that."

"That goes for me too," Courtney added.

Kit didn't feel like trying to convince them. He sighed and stared at the tabletop.

"What do we know about this Uyaga?" Troy asked.

Courtney shrugged. "Did you bring your laptop like I asked?"

"It's in the truck."

While Troy stepped outside, Courtney went to the counter and ordered drinks. Kit sat with his gloom and guilt. Courtney returned to the table with filled cups. Troy opened the laptop and pushed it toward her. "I'm not great with these things. I can find my way around them, but it takes a while. I mostly use it to pay bills."

Courtney connected to the restaurant's Wi-Fi and opened a search engine. Kit watched her type in UYAGA. "Got a couple of hits. Hold on"

Troy sipped his drink and stared at his friend. Kit remained lost in the dark channels of his mind.

Courtney's fingers flicked across the keys. She typed in CHEROKEE EVIL SPIRITS and followed the links. After a few minutes, she sat back and shook her head. "Well, that was less than helpful. There's practically nothing about it. All I found is that Uyaga was an evil earth spirit that roamed Cherokee lands, always in conflict with the forces of good. *She* could appear and disappear at will."

"That's it?" Troy asked, raising his eyebrows. "Talk about a waste of time."

"Let me check a few more things," Courtney said and went back to the keyboard.

While she did, Troy excused himself and disappeared into the restroom. He returned to find her still staring at the laptop screen.

"Anything?" Troy asked.

"Maybe. Bits and pieces. I decided to look up Black Rock. Got a long list of links—mostly chamber of commerce, businesses, tourism, civic stuff like that. Some news articles about the missing coed and boy, but I did come across this. The land the town is built on was originally considered taboo by the Chiaha Cherokees that lived in the region. They referred to it as *Oolisihgee Ga'do'hi*—the Dark Lands."

Troy smirked. "Well, that sure as hell explains a lot."

"Doesn't it? Hmm, this looks interesting. It's a social media site. It looks like someone else has been putting together their own binder of oddities online."

"Yeah, I found that too and pulled some stuff from it," Troy said.

"Says here it was updated recently. When was the last time you checked it?"

Troy pursed his lips. "Three or four months ago."

"Here's a . . . Oh my! I'd forgotten all about that." She looked across the table at Troy, then over at Kit. "Do either of you remember the train accidents back in the '80s?"

Troy shook his head, but Kit nodded.

"This says in late July 1981, a train collided with a van that was sitting on the tracks. The engineer—oh. *Oh my.* The engineer claimed to have seen a small child walking away from the van just moments before impact."

Kit turned and stared at her.

"Did any of the passengers get out?" Troy asked.

Courtney shook her head. "The Richardson family—father, mother, and baby—all died. Based on the testimony of family and friends, there was no one else in the van."

"A child," Kit murmured. He absently rubbed the wound on his arm.

"Here's another one. Now I *do* remember this. In 1983, a man named Edmund Garland committed suicide by standing between the couplers of a train as it was hooking up."

Troy's eyes widened. "Say what? Wow, that's a creative way to go."

"Railroad employees tried to get to him but couldn't. They claim to have . . . seen a child running from the scene."

Troy scratched his beard. "What'd the cops find?"

"According to this, nothing. The police never connected a child or children to either event. And here's something else from 1985—"

"Our senior year," Troy said to Kit.

"Police responded to a domestic violence call. It ended . . . badly. The husband ignited the gas line in the kitchen and blew up his entire family. Five people total. The Kieldorfs. No mention of any children who shouldn't have been there."

Troy shifted in his seat and looked at Kit. "Did you know any of those people? Think hard. Richardson. Garland. Kieldorf."

Kit let the names float through his mind. He remembered the tragedies, but only because they had been the topic of conversation for weeks. He shook his head as if it weighed a hundred pounds. "Nothing comes to mind, but I did work in the furniture store part time. It's possible I could've run into them that way. The kids would've just been babies back then."

"Then that's great!" Troy exclaimed, sitting forward. "This proves that you're *not* the cause of all the weird shit in Black Rock! You didn't know any of those people, yet they all died mysteriously. You had nothing to do with that, man."

"Maybe, maybe not. If I touched them, even in passing . . . or if they touched me, they could've been marked," Kit said.

"But you didn't touch them!" Troy replied. "You just said—"

Kit shrugged and sighed. "I said I *might've* run into them. I can't remember every single person I've touched in my life. Those people could easily have picked up the curse just by bumping into me in a crowd."

"So who's to say that our classmates died because you touched them? I've already told you about some of the more puzzling deaths over the years. Just like those." Troy pointed to the laptop. "Just because we've lost a lot of class-mates, that doesn't automatically mean it's connected. Maybe there isn't any curse on you. Maybe Uyaga's just fucking with your head. Maybe the curse has always been this town."

"This *land*," Courtney added. "The Dark Lands."

"Exactly!" Troy grinned.

Kit sat up and listened more intently.

"That would explain a lot of things," Courtney said.

"Let me ask you this," Troy said, changing tacks. "You said that you both saw Melody Sellers in your . . . visions. What about the two missing kids, Collinsworth and Walston? Did you see either of them?"

They nodded.

"Then why don't we go to the police with all this and let them handle it?" Troy asked.

Kit put his elbow on the table and rested his chin in his hand. He stared at his friend with somber eyes.

"There's no evidence," Courtney said. "The police wouldn't take us seri-ously unless we had something solid for them to build a case around. Sheriff Owens knows what happened to us, but I think he's borderline skeptical. Be-sides, Kit is the only one who saw where they were, and all he saw were the bodies, not a location."

"They were in a cold, dead place," Kit said.

"Like a cemetery?" Troy asked.

Chin still in hand, Kit shook his head. "I couldn't tell where it was. It wasn't a grave. It was too big, too open."

Courtney took a drink from her straw. "Open how?"

Kit sighed. "It was a wide space, not cramped like a grave or mausoleum. It was dark."

"Did you recognize anything?" Troy asked. "Signs, landmarks?"

Kit shook his head again. Courtney pushed a strand of hair behind her ear.

"You could talk to Scotty Dunley," Kit said, turning to look out the window.

Troy and Courtney must not have known if Kit was serious. When they didn't respond, Kit looked at them. "What? We know he's involved. We saw it. And he's got the journal. Maybe he knows something about the curse."

Troy was incredulous. "You're serious?"

Kit folded his arms across his chest and slumped back in the booth. He looked at the edge of the table.

"Actually . . . that's not a bad idea," Courtney said. "It's not as if we're swamped with options at this point."

Troy shook his head. "There's no way. Scotty wouldn't talk to either of you. Half the town knows what happened at the pharmacy. Nice tag team, by the way."

Kit offered a half smile for the first time. "Just like the Wild Samoans back in the day."

"But what if we—" Courtney said.

"No chance," Troy interrupted her. "You know how the Dunleys are. They're not going to open up to anyone. About anything."

Courtney threw her hands up. "We need to find some way to put an end to this! Kit's life is at stake."

"Hey, I know. I agree." Troy's eyes roamed around the restaurant as he thought about it. "Talking to a Dunley is out," he repeated, "but what if you could talk to somebody who knows them *really* well?"

Courtney looked puzzled. "Who?"

"Gabe Beecher. He's close to Scotty and some of the others. He *might* be a way in."

"I saw him in the vision," Kit said.

"He works at a garage down in Duskin Corners, off Highway 248, just before you get to Luminary," said Troy.

"Where's he live?" Courtney asked.

"Here in Black Rock—just off of Motes Road."

She took another drink. "Will he talk to us?"

Troy shrugged. "That depends on what's in it for him."

Courtney smirked. "So what does he want?"

"Gabe is a show-off. He thinks that because he hangs around with the Dunleys, he's a badass. Truth be told, he's pretty much a wimp, but he does like his booze, his cars, and his music," said Troy.

Kit looked up. "What kind of music?"

Troy grinned. "Country. What else? And if I know my local rednecks, he'll be at Marty's Joint tonight. Something tells me he'd *love* to meet country music's newest superstar."

"Who the hell is that?" Kit asked, furrowing his brow.

"Oh, that'd be *you*—assuming you can still lie like a Persian rug."

Kit let the good-natured jab pass. He sighed heavily. "I-I don't know, man. I feel—"

Courtney squeezed his arm. "I know this is hard for you. I can't imagine how you must feel. But if there's any way we can do something about this curse, we need to try." She stared hard into his eyes. "Killing yourself is not an option, mister. We need to see that journal."

# 19

## LOOSE LIPS

*Sunday, June 12, 2011*

O n weeknights, Marty's Joint was a laid-back place to grab a beer, enjoy some wings, watch a ball game, or shoot pool. But on weekends it became raucous and electric, packed with rowdy folks looking to blow off steam. Friday and Saturday nights featured local bands. People came to drink, dance, and drink some more.

The fact that Sunday was the Lord's Day didn't deter folks from Marty's Joint. It was the last opportunity for a good time before going back to work. Most Sundays were quieter, the crowd sparse and relaxed, but Reggie had booked The Volunteer Outlaws, a fan favorite from Knoxville, for three shows. They were setting up their gear for their final performance of the weekend while Kenny Chesney's "She Thinks My Tractor's Sexy" played over the PA system.

The air was already heavy with smoke and boisterous laughter when Kit and Troy stepped inside at 8:30 p.m. The pool tables and dartboard were busy. Several couples two-stepped on the dance floor. Patrons bunched around tables, their collections of beer bottles like miniature brown bowling pins.

Kit and Troy had decided earlier that it would be best if Courtney left this part of the plan to them. She fit with Marty's Joint about as well as caviar did with cornflakes. It wasn't that the women who frequented the bar were homely or undignified. Some weren't. Most, however, looked like weather-beaten barn doors. Within the first two minutes, Kit had already seen more tramp stamps, bleached hair, and fat hanging out from under tight halter tops since . . . well, the last time he had played somewhere like this.

Troy squinted through the smoke. He nudged Kit, nodded, and slipped into the crowd of cowboy boots and Harley-Davidson T-shirts.

The plan they had worked out was simple. Troy would find Gabe, and after a few moments of banal conversation, he would pretend to notice Kit by the door. It all hinged on two things: Gabe being here and being willing to talk.

Kit watched Troy's progress past the bar to a booth on the darkest side of the room—the same booth Gabe and Scotty Dunley had used when the brawl broke out. Kit could barely make out the mealy mustache, goatee, and black, gelled hair of their quarry. Kit sighed in relief. That took care of the first part of the plan.

And what do you know, Gabe was sitting alone. Kit and Troy knew that if any of the Dunleys showed up and noticed Kit, the whole thing would go to hell. Kit would not be surprised by that given his luck.

The black shroud of depression closed in around Kit, but he did his best to ignore it. Now wasn't the time. He needed to focus and play his part—not get swept under by the darkness again. He watched the far booth discreetly, waiting for the signal and praying that no Dunleys walked through the door.

As it turned out, Gabe wasn't alone.

A lanky redhead with too much makeup and hooker boots exited the restroom and stopped at the booth. Troy stepped aside. Kit saw them exchanging pleasantries. Troy played it well—just another dude hanging out and chatting with whomever he bumped into. The woman sat down beside Gabe. Troy ordered them another round of drinks.

Fifteen minutes passed, and Kit's depression grew heavier. He didn't stand out from anyone else in the bar but nevertheless felt like he was in the spotlight. Every time the door opened, he expected to see the Dunleys.

As the band tuned their instruments, Alan Jackson's "Chattahoochee" brought a few more couples to their feet for some line dancing. Kit saw Troy look in his direction, put on a big grin, and start waving.

*Showtime.*

Kit worked his way through the crowd, careful not to touch anyone. Thoughts tumbled through his mind like boulders caught in an avalanche.

*How should I be walking? Tall, proud, and confident? Casual? How do big-name artists walk?*

He had always dreamed of making it big but had never given a second thought about how he should walk. If his guts weren't so cold and his spirit so black right now, he would have laughed at the absurdity of it.

"Chris! Over here!" Troy called.

They had decided to use his given name since there might be someone in the bar who could remember his nickname. They had also decided on a fake last name.

"Rambo! I want you to meet somebody." Okay, Troy had decided on the last name.

Kit groaned internally but he kept his fake smile in place as he reached the booth.

"Gabe, Misty, I'd like you to meet one of Nashville's hottest new stars! This is Chris Rambo."

The booth reeked of beer, perfume, and the kind of cologne men get from bathroom dispensers. Kit didn't shake hands but nodded and smiled before sitting down beside his friend.

Troy ordered more beers and kept the banter going. "Chris is passing through. He was shooting a music video down in Chattanooga and decided to take the scenic route on his way back to Nashville. His first album comes out in September."

"You really got an album comin' out?" Misty gushed. Up close, her makeup was so heavy that her face resembled a topographical map. Large gold hoop earrings glinted in the smoky light. She had large, expressive blue eyes, but her skin had the leathery look of too much time in a tanning salon. She wore a blue T-shirt with a design that said DIXIE CUPS above a screen-printed bra with Confederate flags on them. Kit guessed she was in her midtwenties.

Beside her, Gabe wore a black T-shirt with the names WILLIE WAYLON MERLE HANK JOHNNY in bold white letters down the front. His mustache and goatee had the patchiness of a thrift store couch cushion. He was probably in his early twenties. A simple silver chain hung around his neck. Gabe tapped a lighter against the pack of cigarettes lying on the table.

Kit smiled in his best gosh darn Peyton Manning sort of way. "Yes, ma'am, I do. It's called *Tennessee Sunrise*."

She squealed and squeezed Gabe's arm. "Gabe, darlin', we're sittin' here with a real Nashville star!"

Kit could tell that Gabe was impressed but needed to downplay it in order to be cool.

"Yeah, okay. How come I ain't never heard of you before?" Gabe asked.

"I've been playing a lot of bars and doing some smaller shows between Nashville and Memphis. Just trying to stir up some buzz. You know the shows that Tim McGraw did last year—the Southern Voice tour? Lady Antebellum opened. The shows in the summer also had Love And Theft opening, but I was *supposed* to be on the bill for those summer gigs. Love And Theft took my place when I got sick and couldn't do it," Kit said.

Misty's eyes widened.

Gabe's expression was softening. "So what're you doing in this dump?" He took a drink of beer.

"Just passing through like Troy said. Going back to Nashville. I really like hitting up places like this. It's important to support local talent, and honestly"—he leaned conspiratorially across the table—"these are much better venues to play. Keeps you close to the fans." The thicker he laid it on, the more Gabe ate it up.

As Troy ordered shots and another round of beers—Reggie thankfully paid for waitresses on the weekends—cheering and clapping almost lifted the roof. The Volunteer Outlaws, in their matching orange-and-white plaid shirts, launched into their first song. People danced shoulder to shoulder.

Gabe quizzed Kit on the Nashville music scene, his favorite artists, and stories of the road. The questions were not profound. They were surface level, but Kit knew Gabe was trying to appear more knowledgeable than he actually was to impress Misty. For Kit, this was as simple as picking low-hanging fruit.

As they talked, Kit snuck glances at the door. So far, no Dunleys. This reprieve in his bad luck would not hold forever though. Gabe was on his fourth cigarette and had amassed seven bottles in front of him, along with three empty shot glasses. He flicked ashes into one of them.

"You know, just before I got here, I was reading some really interesting stuff about this town," Kit said, transitioning to the ruse they had devised. "Saw your welcome sign coming in too."

Gabe nodded. "Yeah, it's a fucked-up kinda town." His eyes were beginning to show the droopy slowness of inebriation.

*This is it.* Kit leaned back and took a drink of his beer. "I heard there's a curse on the town. I thought that was strange. I mean, I've heard of a cursed house, but a whole town? That's a new one for me."

Gabe finished another bottle with a belch. "Go get me another beer, bitch," he ordered Misty. She started to say something but stopped. Hurt and angry, she left the booth.

"I'm collecting stories like that," Kit said. "I have a friend who wants to turn them into songs for an album he's planning."

"Yeah? What kinda album?" Gabe's speech began to slur.

Kit smiled and leaned across the table once more. "Oh, it's sort of a concept album that will center around myths and legends of the Tennessee mountains."

Gabe frowned. "What's a con-shept album?"

"Oh, don't worry about that. It's the stories that're important, Gabe. And"—Kit paused and made a show of glancing around—"they'll pay well for the stories that get used." He leaned back, nodded, and took another drink.

"They pay people for the shtories?" Gabe asked.

"Absolute truth. It's $5,000 for a story that makes it onto the album—plus credit, of course," Kit said.

Gabe's eyes widened slowly, as if it took extra effort to raise his eyelids. He looked from Troy to Kit. "For one shtory?" he asked in disbelief.

Kit and Troy nodded.

Misty returned with two more bottles of beer. "Can I get you two another drink?" she asked with excessive charm. She posed beside the table.

"None for me, thanks," Troy said. He had been nursing the same beer since he sat down.

"I haven't finished this one," Kit replied with his best performer's smile, "but thank you."

She began to step from side to side. "Honey darlin', I jus' gotta go pee."

"Well, go on then," Gabe replied with a dismissive flick of his hand.

"So are you interested?" Troy asked after she left.

"Inner'sted in what?"

"Making some money. The stories of Black Rock. For the album," Kit prompted.

Gabe lit another cigarette and exhaled. "Sure, but it's not like I know a lot."

*Amen to that.*

The band segued into another cover tune, the slide guitar reverberating through the building.

"Okay, how about I just toss out some questions? They're the kinds of things my friend will ask you when you come to Nashville," Kit said.

Gabe stopped the cigarette halfway to his lips. "Come to Nashvull?"

"Oh yeah, Chris forgot to mention that," Troy said. "They'll want you to come to their offices so they can get it all down."

A twinkle appeared in Gabe's glazed eyes.

"For example," Troy continued, "they might ask something like, 'What sort of odd or unusual things have you personally experienced in Black Rock?'"

Kit nodded. "Or what do you know about the blight?"

"The blight?" Gabe hesitated. "Nothin'. Just some dead spots onna ground."

"Okay, let's try this one," Kit continued. "Do you know of any strange deaths that have occurred in Black Rock?"

Gabe scowled. Kit could not tell if he was opposed to the question or just thinking hard.

"I don't know nothin' about . . . Say, wait a minnit." Gabe scowled again.

*That's definitely his thinking face.*

"Carter Billups fell inna his combine. Kilt im," Gabe said as if he had just solved the mystery of the universe. "An' Paula Finnsetter dropped dead on her way t' fill up her bird feeder."

*This isn't working,* Kit thought as he shot Troy a we're-running-out-of-time look. *These are just normal, if unexpected, tragedies.* He needed to get to the real questions. Refitting his best smile, Kit said, "This is great stuff, Gabe. How about—"

"Hi!" Misty exclaimed as she reappeared at the table. Before she could sit down, Gabe held up a grease-stained hand.

"Git on over there with your friends for a bit," Gabe slurred, "or fuckin' go dance with shumbuddy. We're talkin'."

"Fuck you, Gabe!" she snapped. "I didn't come here t'night to dance with nobody else." Her tone softened a little. "Let's you and me go dance, hmm?"

"Bitch, I said we're talkin'. It might even git me onna Nashvull record album. Now go on. I'll catch up with you inna minute." He slapped her butt as she turned away.

Struggling to focus, Gabe looked across the table. "Now what was you sayin'?"

"Gabe, have you ever seen any old books around? Diaries or notebooks, that sort of thing?" Kit asked.

Gabe smoked his cigarette and scowled. "My uncle's got a purdy nice collection of old *Hustler*s an' *Playboy*s."

"No, older than that. Something like an old account register—or a journal?" Kit held his breath.

"Sure. My buddy, Scotty, he's got one of them," Gabe said.

"Have you ever looked at it?" Troy asked.

Gabe nodded and dropped his cigarette butt down the neck of a bottle. "Scotty showed me some stuff in it. It was written by his kin a long ways back."

"Do you know where he got it?" Kit glanced toward the door. Still no Dunleys. He felt the urge to rush the conversation with Gabe but knew he had to take it easy. It was a delicate balancing act.

"Sure. He found it inna cave," said Gabe.

*A cold, dark place.*

"A cave? Where?" Kit asked. His heart beat faster. What he had seen in the visions could've been a cave.

Gabe yawned. "Up onna mountain."

"Which mountain?" Troy asked.

Gabe frowned at them. "What the fuck diff'rence does it make? I thought you wanted to hear about weird shit inna town."

"Oh, I do. I do," Kit replied, smiling like a used-car salesman. "But old books like that usually have some great stories in them too. What did you see when you looked at it?"

Gabe relaxed a little. He stared at the shapes gyrating to the music, belched, and looked back. "Crazy shit. Stuff about Indians and the ground and how all of this"—he swept his arms wide to include everything around him—"belongs to 'Yaga."

Kit's skin prickled at the name. "That's amazing, Gabe. What's Uyaga?"

Gabe sat up a little straighter and grinned. "Well, accordin' to the book, Scotty's ancest'r, Edgar, stumbled upon 'er inna cave. He started feedin' her with folks he kilt, but after a while, Edgar had a strike of cons . . . conshensas . . . con—"

"Conscience?" Troy suggested.

Gabe snapped his fingers. "Yeah, that's it. Edgar decided he wasn't gonna feed 'er or serve 'er no more. So he took some gunpowder and sealed hisself and the book up in that cave." He paused to light another cigarette and blew smoke into the dull, red, glassed light over the table. "Edgar wrote all kinda shit down in it—stories and curses and crazy shit about 'er."

Kit shivered despite the stuffy air. "Wow."

"Edgar's old book said that 'Yaga's always been here. Cherokees feared 'er. She causes all kinda bad shit to happen."

"Like the blight?" Troy asked.

Gabe paused, squinted, and tapped ashes into the shot glass. "Yeah, I guess so."

"Did the journal say anything about where this Uyaga is . . . or where the cave is located?" Kit hoped that Gabe did not pick up on his return to the former topic.

"Nope. But me and Scotty know."

"You do?" Troy tried to hide his surprise.

"Sure. We took a couple of animals to it. Scotty kilt 'em. Said the blood would feed 'Yaga."

Kit and Troy faced each other with frozen expressions.

"Have you heard about the people missing from this area? Tyson Collinsworth or Meredith Walston?" Troy asked.

Gabe's eyes narrowed. He set his mouth in a straight line. "Don't know. Ain't sayin'."

"Do you think Uyaga took them?" Kit asked.

Gabe's body language changed. He shrunk like a crumpled paper bag, elbows tight to his sides. His gaze flitted across the tabletop. His face was flushed from the alcohol, and his fingers trembled slightly. He finished his cigarette in silence and gulped his bottle dry. "Lishen, I think I done said about enough." He eyed them warily.

Kit did his best to put Gabe at ease. "You've been a great help. This'll probably be one of the best tracks on the album. I'll even talk to a couple of people and see if I can get that fee raised a little for you." He winked.

"Gabe, you said that you and your friend took some animals to Uyaga. Can you tell us where that is?" Troy tried one last time.

Gabe shook his head. "Scotty had me blindfolded onna the way there. Said it was a secret place—a *special* place. He took the blindfold off when we got there so I could help kill the dog and deer."

*Blindfolded. Just like Melody Sellers.*

"Was it out in the woods?" Troy asked.

Gabe blinked like he was moving in slow motion. "Yeah, but I don't know where'bouts. Didn't recognize it."

Kit knew that last beer was working through Gabe's inebriated system. He guessed they had only a handful of minutes before Gabe became incoherent.

Troy glanced at Kit. "Gabe, did the book say anything about how to . . . stop Uyaga?"

Gabe shook his head.

"Did it say anything about children—three children?" Kit needed to know.

Again, the head shake. This time it was accompanied by another belch.

Kit finished his beer. "Do you think I could see the journal, Gabe?"

Troy stared at Kit in shock. "What're you doing?" he asked from the side of a plastered-on smile.

Kit shrugged. "It's worth a try."

Gabe's head lay against the back of the booth. His mouth hung open.

"Gabe. Gabe?" Kit asked.

Gabe stirred and slurped at the saliva that had collected in his mouth. "Whuut—"

Kit knew he was pressing his luck but couldn't stop now. "The journal. Where is it?"

Gabe's head lolled to the side. He jerked half-awake in order to straighten it. "Where was we?"

"You were about to tell us where Scotty keeps the journal," Kit said and glanced at Troy.

"Journal? Oh yeah, Shhcotty's got it . . . "

"You told us that. Where does he keep it?" Troy asked, growing anxious.

Gabe stared across the table as if he were trying to see them from a distance. He licked his lips. "Unner the front seat of 'is truck. Keeps it there."

"You're sure, Gabe?" Troy said. "In his truck?"

"S-sure." Gabe sounded like a leaky basketball. His head dropped forward on his chest, and he slumped sideways, oozing down the wall like a slug.

Kit turned to his friend. "Do you know the truck?"

Troy nodded. "It's a black Chevy Silverado, a dually."

"Good, come on. Let's get the hell out of here."

# 20

## AN UNEXPECTED GIFT

*Monday, June 13, 2011*

**C**ourtney checked her phone for messages as she left the building. Sheriff Owens had called to tell her that she could go back to her house. She welcomed this return to normalcy but felt apprehensive. What if those things came back? They had used her to get to Kit once. Would they use the same tactic a second time?

But she really needed to get home. Jillian and Whitney were safe at her parents' house, but she didn't want to leave them there indefinitely. She decided to pick them up after work. With their company and noise—and the increased police patrols in the area—everything would be all right.

The sun shone fierce in its summer glory. She unlocked her Outback and opened the door to let some of the accumulated heat escape, then she climbed in. It was like entering a sauna. She started the car and turned on the air conditioner.

Digging through her folio, she pulled out the legal pad she had been using during the interview. She had recorded everything per protocol, but the law firm also required written documentation—personal observations, body language, tone of voice, and other cues that would aid in the preparation of the case. She was glad to be back at work. After the events of the weekend, she needed something predictable and dull and orderly.

With her notes completed, she fastened the seat belt and was ready to leave when she spotted it across the parking lot. Her heart sped up and she gripped the steering wheel.

The black Chevy Silverado with dual rear tires sat like a great spider among the surrounding vehicles. Scotty Dunley's truck.

She couldn't tell if it was running or if anyone was in it. Her eyes darted around the parking lot, but she saw no one. An idea leaped into her mind, and guilt began to stir in the pit of her stomach in its wake. She tried to justify the thought by reminding herself that what she was thinking about doing would save a life.

*I must be crazy, out-of-my-gourd insane to even consider this! But I like Kit.*

Like him? She didn't even know him, not really. She couldn't say they were getting reacquainted since that implied some sort of previous relationship. It would only be a week tomorrow since they had met at the pharmacy. It was way too early to be *liking* him. She chewed her lower lip and watched the truck. The cool air moved her hair.

She felt sorry for Kit. That had to be it. The poor guy had been through so much in his life, and now this mess on top of it. Maybe what she felt was pity, not love. She frowned.

*It could . . . become love,* she allowed herself to think.

Right. Like she was going to chuck eight years of independence for a guy who was working and living in the same furniture store he'd worked at during high school. From what he had told her, his life was a train wreck. She did not need that kind of baggage right now.

*So why am I still sitting here?*

That was simple. Because Kit had said that he would kill himself, and she knew he hadn't been joking. It wasn't a ploy for attention. She had seen the dead, haunted look in his eyes yesterday. If she didn't do something to help him, she would never forgive herself.

She put the Outback in reverse, released the emergency brake, and backed out of the parking space.

*Good! There you go making the smart decision.* Her conscience applauded.

Courtney drove toward the parking lot exit, but instead of turning onto the street, she veered down another aisle. Her heartbeat quickened as she saw an empty space in the perfect location. She pulled in, a Nissan Altima to her right and Scotty Dunley's truck to the left. Her skin tingled and she forced herself to calm down.

Scotty's truck didn't have tinted windows. She saw no one inside.

*Just do it quickly.*

*You do this, and you're going to get fired! Stop and think!*

She opened the door, got out, and looked around the parking lot as inconspicuously as possible. No one was in sight. There were no surveillance cameras on light poles or building corners.

*Do it. Do it quick!*

*Get your fat ass back in the car!* her mind bellowed.

Kit had called her late last night after he and Troy had left Marty's Joint. She had been anxious to hear what had happened. After giving her the details, Kit had told her that he was going to try and steal the journal tonight.

Now she was thinking about doing it for him. She was not only breaking the law. The truck—and the journal—belonged to a Dunley. What would she do if one or more of them came after her? What if they came after her daughters?

Courtney stood like a statue between the two vehicles. Every indecisive moment increased the risk of getting caught, but her conscience was right. If Scotty found out, Jillian and Whitney would be in serious trouble and so would she. There was no telling what the Dunleys might do in retaliation.

*Let Kit do it! He's the one who wants it. Let him take it!*

But Kit might not be able to locate the truck tonight, or he might not have a chance to get the journal. She was here right now. Should she risk it or follow what her instincts screamed for her to do?

Courtney made her decision. She turned.

Her hand grasped the truck's door handle. To her surprise, the door opened smoothly. The pungent and distinctive odor of wintergreen-flavored dip wafted out with the interior heat, causing her to recoil.

He had not even bothered to lock it! Of course not. Who would be stupid enough to steal from the Dunleys?

*Oh, wait—*

Crouching down, she scanned the inside of the cab. A naked-woman air freshener hung from the rearview mirror. Several plastic Mountain Dew bottles on the passenger floorboard were half-filled with a brackish liquid.

She saw a crumpled fast-food bag, a screwdriver, and a pair of work boots. In the seat were several CDs, a pack of cigarettes with a lighter, and a phone charging cable.

No journal.

She steeled herself to reach back under the passenger seat.

Her fingertips brushed the smooth metal of a coin and the textured rubber of the mat. She felt a wrinkled napkin, the grit of dirt and crumbs, and a condom wrapper. She grimaced and prayed the condom was not under there too.

Courtney stuck her hand farther under the seat, and her fingers brushed against something thick and flat. She extracted it easily, and for a moment, she was surprised to see the book in her hand. It was about the size of a phone book and no thicker than her thumbnail. Courtney turned it over. The binding was broken brown leather. Two straps held it shut, and their buckles were covered with a patina resembling diseased lichen. Even the trapped heat and wintergreen could not mask its smell of antiquity. It reminded her of old people—not grandparents whose homes are like sugar cookies and warm blankets, but those left alone in nursing homes, unwanted. The binding felt like their wrinkled hands.

Her inner voice still raged, but it was too late. Carefully closing the door, she rushed to get into her vehicle. It felt as if every eye in the world were on her. She crammed the journal into her folio, fastened her seat belt with trembling hands, and backed up. She could not have felt more exposed if her car had flashing neon signs and a loudspeaker blaring, "Look at me, I'm a thief!" Pulling out of the parking lot, she realized her clothes were stuck to her.

• • •

"Hey, Courtney," Kit said as he answered his cell.

"Can you meet me in a few minutes?" she asked. "Just for a minute. I've got something for you."

"Oh?" He glanced around the showroom floor, empty except for the chairs, sofas, and tables in need of rescue. "Yeah, I can slip away for a few. Where are you?"

She told him, and they arranged to meet in front of the furniture store.

"W-why there?" he asked as he tried to keep the surprise out of his voice.

"Because you're working there."

Kit swallowed hard. "How'd you—"

She giggled. "Don't even pretend like you don't know how fast word spreads in this town."

He conceded but tossed up a silent prayer that she didn't know about his current accommodations. Living in Black Rock was like being in a fishbowl.

"I'll be there in about ten minutes," she said. "Bye!"

Kit ended the call. Had there been a tremor in her voice, or had he imagined it? Had something else happened? His mind lurched into overdrive. It could be the Dunleys, catching up with her about the incident last week.

*Please don't let it be those children again.*

He found himself thinking of ways to protect Courtney. He realized he was more concerned about her than he had been about anyone since his first wife. It was more than just the thrill of a girl from high school paying attention to me. He wouldn't classify it as love, at least not yet, but he did feel something for her. Of course, he still had a broken, aimless life which was nothing to offer someone like Courtney.

Kit forced the thoughts from his mind and occupied himself with breaking down cardboard boxes. He drifted to the showroom floor every few minutes to scan the street like a soldier waiting for a message from home. When he saw her pull in across the street, he told Vince that he was stepping outside for a moment.

Air-conditioning gave way to a wall of smothering heat. He jogged across the street before Courtney had a chance to get out. He smiled as he went to the driver's side.

"Hey," he said when she rolled the window down. He put his hands on top of the Outback but yanked them away immediately. The metal felt like a blast furnace.

She smiled in reply and pulled the folio into her lap.

"A surprise, huh? Been a while since I had one of those. But really, you didn't have to," Kit said.

"I know," she replied while she rummaged through the satchel. "But I couldn't pass up this . . . opportunity." She withdrew the journal and handed it to him.

Kit looked at it, turning it over. "What's this?"

She grinned. "Edgar Dunley's journal."

At first Kit thought it was a joke. He even gave a short laugh to show he was a good sport. When she did not reply with any humor, he stared at her. The sun warmed his hair and prickled his scalp.

"No, seriously, what is this?" he asked again.

"It's the journal you told me about last night—the one you said you needed."

He looked at the book as if it were giving off radiation. "You're serious."

She nodded.

Again, he flipped the journal back to front, running his fingers across the buckles. "Wh-where'd you get this?"

She told him about Scotty's truck in the parking lot. "It wasn't locked. Nobody saw me."

Kit's heart caught in his chest. "Jesus, Courtney, you shouldn't have done this. I was going to get it tonight."

"I know. But like I said, it was right there in front of me. I thought I'd be saving you some time." Her tone took on a defensive edge.

"Damn. You realize what'll happen if Scotty—or any of them—finds out it was you?"

"Of course, I do." The edge in her voice became harder. "I also realize I could lose my job if anyone finds out. Do you want me to take the damned thing back?"

"I— No, no. It's just—"

"What?" she demanded.

"I just don't want anything to happen to you is all," he replied, disheartened.

His reaction must have gotten to her. She sighed. "Listen, I'm sorry. I didn't mean to take your head off."

Kit smiled, trying to lighten her guilt. "It's okay, I get it. I don't mean to come across as ungrateful, believe me. It just—it took me by surprise. I've been thinking all day about how I was going to find Scotty and get into his truck. I definitely wasn't expecting you to show up and hand it to me in broad daylight!" His tone softened once more. "But seriously, you shouldn't have jeopardized your job on my account."

She returned his smile. "It'll be fine. No one saw me. I made sure of that. You just find something—anything—in there that'll help. I won't let you kill yourself because of whatever is going on." She reached over and laid her hand on top of where his rested in the open window

Kit tensed.

"What's wrong?" she asked, pulling her hand back.

He shook his head and gripped the journal with both hands. "It's the curse. Anyone I touch, or anyone who touches me . . . Well, I don't want you to get it." He talked as if it were a virus.

"I think it's a little too late for that," she replied with a weak smile. "You helped me out of my window, held me in the driveway . . . "

"Oh, God, Courtney! I-I didn't think! I . . . "

"It's okay. Really. It couldn't be helped. And it was bound to happen sooner or later. I just want you to know that there's nothing wrong with *you*."

He'd been thinking a lot about the curse. Troy was right. Every time Kit blacked out, Uyaga killed someone that he'd touched at some point after receiving *her* curse. That had been her voice speaking to him that night in the park. She'd told him what she was going to do. He guessed his mind had blocked that part out or stuffed it away somewhere in his subconscious. That's why he didn't remember it except when bits floated to the surface in his dreams.

He still couldn't understand why Uyaga had linked the blackouts to the deaths. Was that just another aspect of *her* evil—another way to torture him? If all she wanted to do was kill people, why bother to curse him at all? Why didn't she just kill them?

*It has to be some sort of twisted game to her. Maybe that's how she gets her kicks.*

The connection was there. They'd become bonded somehow. It made him sick whenever he thought about it. Since there wasn't anything medically wrong with him, *she* was the cause. It really was all a sick, perverse manipulation. She'd toyed with him almost all his life. He'd been nothing more than a puppet, an extension of her poisonous cruelty. His stomach soured. He tasted bile.

"I'm really sorry," Kit said. He hated himself for dragging her into his misery. If she died, he didn't know what he would do.

Courtney smiled and nodded. "I know. And like I said, it's okay. A part of me still has trouble believing that some ancient Indian legend can hurt people just because they came in contact with you, but . . . after this past weekend . . . I'm ready to believe just about anything. So, since I'm in this too, I couldn't just stand by and do nothing when it was in my power to act."

Kit watched her, absorbing the details of her face. The tiny mole on the left side of her forehead near the hairline. The slight curve of the tip of her nose. The shortness of her eyelashes. He hadn't noticed any of that before.

How was it that she cared about his aimless, unlucky life? He had nothing to offer, yet she'd risked a lot to get the journal for him. Could it be possible that she saw him as more than just damaged goods? Could someone like her see beyond his failures and find something to redeem? What had she said a moment ago?

*I just want you to know that there's nothing wrong with you.*

"I've got to go," she said, pulling him from his thoughts.

"Sure. Thank you for this. I mean it. I'd never have imagined anyone would do something like this for me."

"Well, like I said, just find something useful in there."

He stepped back as the window hummed shut. She offered a quick wave and drove off. Kit carried the journal under his arm as he hurried back inside the store. Upstairs in his room, he slid it beneath the ugly sofa.

• • •

Scotty Dunley looked up as Gabe Beecher pulled into the parking lot of the vacant grocery store. The building lurked behind him like a set from a postapocalyptic movie. The late afternoon sun on the asphalt made the cracks look like black veins from which tall weeds sprouted.

Gabe stopped his mud-splattered Ford F-250 beside Scotty's truck and rolled the window down so they were face-to-face. "What's up?" he asked before spitting into a soda bottle.

"It's gone," Scotty said, as if that told Gabe everything he needed to know.

"What's gone?"

Scotty's wide-set blue eyes narrowed and glinted like ice on a razor. "My journal, asshole! It's been stolen."

"Say what? Ain't nobody who'd steal from you. You must've misplaced it."

"I didn't lose it!" Scotty bellowed. Gabe flinched.

"The fuckin' thing was right *here* in the truck!" Scotty dragged a battered camouflage cap off his head. The front said IF YOU DON'T KNOW WHETHER TO SHIT OR GO BLIND, CLOSE ONE EYE AND FART. Running a hand through his long brown hair, he growled, "Some motherfucker is gonna pay!"

"Any idea who took it?" Gabe asked, spitting in the bottle again.

"If I did, you think I'd be here asking you? Speakin' of which—who you been mouthin' off to about it?"

Gabe shook his head. "Me? I ain't said shit to nobody!"

"You had to! Ain't but the two of us who knows about it, and I sure as hell didn't tell anybody!" Scotty replaced his cap and rubbed the mustache that drooped into a goatee beneath his hooked nose. "Who you been talking to?"

Gabe looked through the windshield to avoid Scotty's baleful gaze. He had told no one about it. The journal, the cave, everything they had done—that was strictly between them. Nobody else knew. Nobody else *could* know. They would spend the rest of their lives in prison—if they didn't fry in the electric chair first.

"I can't think of nobody, Scotty," Gabe said with an earnest shake of his head. "Seriously. I was just with Misty last night at Marty's Jo—" His face froze, mouth open.

Scotty watched Gabe's eyes widen. "What is it?"

Gabe grimaced. "Oh fuck."

"What the hell is it? Who'd you talk to, asshole?"

"Aw, shit, Scotty. Last night . . . last night I—"

"Spit it out!" Scotty roared, leaning out of the window of his truck.

Gabe winced and offered a scalded expression. "There were these two guys. Last night at Marty's Joint. I got wasted."

"What guys?"

"I don't remember. They bought a lotta drinks though. One was from Nashville, I remember that. He's some kind of musician, I think."

Scotty's eyes were slits of blue fire. "Why the *fuck* were they talkin' to *you?*"

Gabe shrugged. "I dunno. They was just asking about local legends an' shit."

"Damn it, Gabe! They got you shit-faced and pumped you for information! And you told 'em about the journal," Scotty snarled through clenched teeth.

"No! I didn't say nothing about the book—" He stopped, then added mournfully, "Least I don't think I did."

Scotty flung himself back in the seat. He hammered the steering wheel with both fists as he glared through the windshield. "You stupid, ignorant fuck! You got any idea what you've done!" It wasn't a question.

"Shit, Scotty, I wasn't . . . I just thought—"

"You didn't think about nothin' except gettin' wasted like you always do! You asshole! If you fuck this up for us—"

Gabe threw up his hands as if to ward off an invisible enemy. "Hey, chill out. We can find out who took it."

Scotty arched an eyebrow. "You can't even find your dick with both hands and a set of directions."

Gabe fumed as he turned away and stared out the passenger window.

"I'll find it," Scotty stated. "I'll . . . contact *her*. Uyaga will tell me who took it. And you"—Gabe glanced over at him—"*you're* going to get it back."

# 21

## DIARY OF A MADMAN

*Monday, June 13, 2011*

**K**it went to check on his father after work. He hadn't heard anything from Albert since he'd left the house. That wasn't surprising. As a teenager, he and Albert had often gone weeks without speaking.

Albert was fine, and Kit did not linger. He picked up a fried chicken dinner and a six-pack on the way back to the store. He had been tempted to go by the liquor store for a bottle of tequila and had almost given in. His brief visit with Albert had resuscitated all the old feelings. They had gone at each other without missing a beat. Kit's frustration had segued into self-pity and from there to depression. He should've gone to the liquor store—hell, he *would* have any other time—but not now. Maybe Courtney was having a positive effect on him.

He still found it hard to believe that she had risked so much on his behalf. There were few people in his life willing to go to such lengths. His mom. Troy. And now Courtney. Yet his feelings seesawed. He felt good knowing that Courtney saw him differently than others did, but Albert had reminded him yet again of how disappointing his life choices had been. Kit wondered if he was destined to be miserable. Guilt and shame poured back in, drowning the glimmer of Courtney's influence.

He returned to the furniture store, pouty and morose. He let himself in the back door with the key Vince had given him and climbed the creaky wooden stairs to the office. He fiddled with the old television antenna while he ate, trying to bring in a signal. Occasionally, there would be snippets of conversation through the hissing snow, but he could never manage a picture. Kit browsed through social media on his cell, grateful for at least a few inches of video, but his gaze repeatedly drifted to the sofa.

It was just after 7:30 p.m. The sun's rays poked over the tops of the western mountains as if desperate to cling to their claim on the day. Kit cracked a second beer and shut off the television. He reached beneath the sofa, pulled out the journal, and sat down beside the lone window he had opened. An oscillating fan circulated the air in the office, and birds chirped in the distance as dusk approached. Cars drove by in front, making a *ssshhhwwmmm* sound that drifted between the buildings. He heard laughter from somewhere, and a horn honked. The evening breeze crept over the sill and nudged his hands. Taking a drink, he pushed the remains of his dinner aside and sat the journal on the table.

The discolored buckles came undone smoothly, no doubt because of Scotty's recent usage. Kit undid the straps and opened the cover. His eyes wandered down the page.

The Journal of Edgar Dunley<br>October 5, 1894

It was written in a loose, angled script, not quite a doctor's chicken scratch, but neither was it calligraphy. The ink had dulled to sepia, worse in some places than others. The book smelled of wintergreen and dirt, but beneath those scents, Kit detected the singular odor of rot. Of blight. He found himself repeatedly wiping his fingers on his pants.

The initial entries told of Edgar's discovery of a cave on October 3, and his subsequent explorations in the days thereafter. There seemed to have been little of interest in the cave, crushing Edgar's hope of hidden treasure. He wrote of Louise, his wife, who was seventeen to his twenty years when they married in 1881. Children quickly followed, and Edgar had recorded their names: Daniel Dunley, born January 24, 1883—

Kit shivered. *That's who wanted to play hide-and-seek!*

Twins Lena and Janet—Lena was the girl who had tried to leech the blood from Kit's arm—arrived on February 12, 1884. Virgil Dunley, April 2, 1885. Alfred Dunley, September 17, 1887. Penelope Dunley, August 25,

1888. A second set of twins, Stanley and Glen, arrived on April 14, 1890. Alan Dunley, December 6, 1892. Leroy Dunley, October 30, 1893.

As Kit read, an image formed in his mind of an uneducated, cruel, duplicitous man who drank profusely and whose handwriting grew larger and sloppier when enraged. Edgar had worked at various times as a trapper, logger, grave digger, railroad repairman, and general day laborer. Judging by the entries, he seemed to care for his wife in his own peculiar way, although Kit shuddered at the vivid entries that recorded his abusiveness.

Nov. 1, 1894
Strange dreams last nite. *She* called to me. Shewed me things. Didnt wanna look but couldnt help it. Promussd me powr. Sed I could be a god like her. Woke with a fever.

Nov. 2, 1894
I dun woke *her* up when I went in the cave. More dreams last night. Injuns runnin from her. Fightin her. They put her in there in the pit.

Nov. 17, 1894
*She* ken come out with blud. Wants me to bring sum. I ken do that.

Nov. 25, 1894
DAMN THEM KIDS. THEY BROKE TH

Dec. 12, 1894
*She* gose way back. Long time. The land is hers. Injuns tride to take it. Stoopid thing to do. Shes a god, lotsa powr. She shews me things at nite, things she sez I ken do with her powr. All I have to do is bring the blud.

Kit finished off the beer and opened another. He switched on the jade-glassed lamp on the desk. He heard fewer cars out front. Insects replaced birdcalls as he continued to read.

Edgar had not written every day. Sometimes there were long intervals between entries, and Kit tried to piece together people, places, and events as best he could.

Mar. 21, 1895
Got anuther gurl. Named her Viola. Louise feels puny after burth.
Daniel still coffn.

May 3, 1895
Daniels got the consumpshun. Coffn up blud. Aint enuff for *her*
tho. Animals blud dont work neether. Needs to be humun. Lots
of it.

June 7, 1895
WHY DONT IT WURK? I TUCHED THE VARGAS GIRL
AND SHE GOT BETER! WHYS WONT IT WURK ON DAN-
IEL?

June 20, 1895
*Shes* the Black Urth Spirit.
Hen'yehmoak taan! Uyaga! Uyaga!
The fools in Black Rock talk, say I struk a deel with the Devil.
Wont come neer to me when I go for things. I heer them whisper
thet Im a warlok. Yet the mountn peeple bring their sick and ailin.
I fix them.
Hen'yehmoak taan! Uyaga! Uyaga!

July 6, 1895
Daniel getting wurse. Tomorrow I'll put him in the cave. Best thing
fur him.

July 17, 1895
Uyaga! Uyaga! Why cant I heel Louise? She aint well. What do I do?
Furst its Daniel, now my wife. Why wont you help me? I bring you
blud. I do what you sez. DONT YOU CARE?

Sept. 1, 1895
I see now. Beter than before. What crossd the span of nite brung
slivers of understandin and the open places reech for signs. In dim
ways without the songs of the Injuns, Bastershurn-Kal screems in
silence. I go into squares that peel and cry and when I see that long

black medvor'alblaso I laff and laff and laff. Hen'yehmoak taan! Uyaga! Uyaga!

Throughout the autumn and early winter of 1895, Edgar's ramblings grew lengthier as he attempted to explain the things that were taking place in his family and on the mountain. Some of the words Kit had never seen before. Those made him feel fuzzy and cold when he read them, as if he were lost in a foggy, frost-covered field of glass. It had to be the third beer and the strain of deciphering Edgar's pale scrawls and atrocious spelling. The more pages Kit turned, the more ragged the writing was. Strange symbols and horrific drawings began to appear in the margins. Random sepia blobs, where Edgar had apparently started to write or draw something and then scratched it out, became prevalent. It mirrored Edgar's mental state.

Christmas Day, 1895
Louise died yesterday.

Tragedy struck again in the new year. Edgar raged about Lena's "fits." Epileptic seizures, obviously, but a frightening thing to witness without the benefit of medical knowledge. Not knowing what else to do—his unique ability to cure others by touching them denied to his own family—Edgar put Lena in the cave with the corpse of her brother and covered the entrance.

For two-and-a-half years, Edgar's entries ranged from maniacal ravings that made no sense to placid reports about his livestock, the weather, and family happenings. He had developed an utter loathing for the town and eventually stopped going there altogether.

Kit's eyes burned from the low light and from squinting at the rangy words. He went to the bathroom and walked around for a few minutes to stretch his legs and get the blood flowing again.

*Blood. For* her.

How was any of this possible? It was unbelievable—like a low-budget horror movie that shows up in the Walmart discount bin. Caves and curses, dead children, and draining blood to feed a Cherokee myth. It had to have been the extreme isolation. Edgar's family lived on the slopes of Blackpoint Mountain and had minimal contact with the outside world. Given their over-all lack of education, the legends and tales that thrived in the twilight hollows, and what had to have been a complete mental breakdown, it was no wonder Edgar had written what he did. Yet Kit had the unmistakable sense that Edgar had believed every bit of it.

*Scotty had this journal. He's read it. Maybe he believes it too.*

Fourth beer in hand, Kit returned to the journal and immediately wished he hadn't. In 1899, Edgar's other twin daughter, Janet, who was fifteen at the time, became the subject of his deranged fancy. The more Kit read, the more his stomach soured. He wanted to take a drink of beer to flush the threat of bile back down, but suddenly, its smell sickened him. As Kit's eyes passed back and forth across the page, he put his hand over his mouth.

The entries grew explicit. Vulgar. Debased. Kit thought about skipping a few pages but was afraid he might miss a vital piece of information. So he gutted it out as Janet gave birth to Jack Dunley on June 22, 1899, and to Lydia Dunley on November 9, 1902. For reasons unexplained, Edgar put thirteen-month-old Lydia into the cave as well in late 1903.

Jan. 1, 1905
Uyaga bids, I do. Sounds come from everything yellow. The sun screems all day. Hen'yehmoak taan! Uyaga! Uyaga! Carbak en dideyaw as is rite and tru. When all is black, stars shew colors and *she* calls in my dreems. My children R in there. To much, the mind, fells, a'barha

Feb. 23, 1905
IS IT WHY—LOOSE—THERE IS A WAY I HAVE SAW IT! SHEDON'TKNOWSHEDONTKNOWSHEDONTKNOW! No, no, no. I am seed by all among that evul conclave. I will write it, but not heer. Ill keep it on me. dont look please let it be why. is no come the shapes I for that empty. a key for the lok.

Apr. 27, 1905
who does I am
*She* looks over my sholdur
i dont know where i was last nite. did he do it? take me somewhere what i have saw black urth spirit dwellin dwellin
Ub'sekketh Uyaga—blud—deth in the stars. talk to me Louise

Mustmustmust destroy cave
Gunpowdr. i got sum. enuff to blow up the cave. blow it to hell.
seel it off forever

June 11, 1905
Last chance. mind sum beter. cLear. musT do lok. MUST! No 1
else no 1 else shuld see or kno about ANY of ThIs. ends it all. got
Key got Lok got Gunpowdr. blow it all to hell. SINS! SINS! By
God I am judged eternal n doomed, for this is rite and just. sEEl it
all off. how? HOw? did I let it come to this

July 20, 1905
time is runnin OuT—mUSt act soon. there is no forgivnuss for
such like me—only sufferinpaindeth. *SHe* brung—made me do
aweful things Uyaga! Uyaga! dam be you dam be you dam be you!
oNlY 1 way—only way—the keY is here.

Aug. 4, 1905
tmorrow. i ends it. i goes away. sorry. forGiVE fORgIvE. pleese god
dont let no 1 else find *her*. got to seeL the cave. nObOdy neVernev-
Er go in the black beeyond furst cave WhERe i put them kidS. LEt
this LaNd fall on me wIth the BOOM. i am wrong, deserv deth.
sEeL iT ofF. END
TMoRro w

Kit closed the journal. It felt like spiders were skittering across the backs
of his eyeballs.

He shoved the journal across the desk, knocking over the half-finished
sixth beer, and ground his fists into his eyes.

It was not just the words. It was also those deranged pictures in the margins. They were like doodles at first, spirals and geometric shapes and what
might have been a cave, but as Edgar had degenerated, so too did the images.
Circles within circles, filled by strange symbols. Solid black blotches, like ink
spills, from which Edgar had written words in a language Kit had never seen
before. They weren't Latin or Arabic or even Chinese, but some bizarre merg-
er of all three that made Kit's eyes feel like they were being peeled from the inside. Edgar had also drawn mouths with sharp teeth. Dozens upon dozens of

mouths, different shapes and sizes, in every margin and sometimes over top of the entries. There were drawings of a cabin—presumably Edgar's—animals, and intricate mazes of interlocking chains. Kit guessed those alone must've taken days to complete.

Then there was the cave. Always drawings of the cave. And within it, something malevolent and ancient and wrong. Peculiar sigils that meant nothing to Kit stood in tall, thin columns all around it. Even scribblings that looked a lot like algebraic formulas—*there's no way Edgar knew anything about advanced mathematics*—offered little in the way of interpretation or purpose.

Some margins had been smeared with black ink, making it seem as if the words were being birthed from the gulfs of space. Kit couldn't be sure, but he thought he saw figures in the black, writhing and screaming with silent voices. Those pages he skimmed quickly because he had an uneasy feeling of being watched, although when he glanced at the open window or through the door at the blackness beyond, he saw nothing. His ears must have been playing tricks on him too. There was no one else here, so there could not be footsteps outside his door.

Kit trembled. He focused on the black rectangle of the doorframe. He should've closed the damn thing when he came in.

*I did close it. Didn't I?*

Suddenly his feet and fingers were cold. His heart bucked. He imagined an albino-like face leering out of the darkness, then a second and a third with their gray grins, coming toward the door and trapping him inside this tiny office.

*Blood for* her.

*Let's play hide-and-seek.*

*We're gonna get you.*

There were lots of places to hide in a dark furniture store.

Kit forced himself to move, but instead of leaping to the door, he felt like he was running through water. He willed his legs to move faster. His eyes never left the doorway. He was halfway across the office—which suddenly seemed as long as a football field—when he saw movement out in the storage room.

He screamed and, in his panic, almost fell into the door. From the darkness outside a shape flopped toward him, growing larger. He grabbed the door. The movement continued.

Then he saw it. A human shape. He almost screamed again.

Until he realized what it was.

Propped against an overstuffed chair out in the storage area was a large mirror. Kit's quivering reflection stared back. Cursing himself, Kit slammed the door shut and leaned against it. Sweat trickled down the side of his face.

He staggered to the window and stuck his head into the night air. Breathing deeply to calm himself, he closed his eyes, afraid of what he might see in the parking lot below. When his pulse settled, Kit lowered himself into the desk chair. He wanted to be outside, away from these claustrophobic walls. At least out there he had places to run and hide. Here, he was a sitting duck.

But he couldn't convince himself to make the journey. His imagination taunted him. Maybe that *hadn't* been his reflection.

*No, it was!*

Maybe it was Daniel or Lena or Lydia. Waiting for him in the darkness.

*No!*

He needed some cocaine and cursed himself again, this time for not getting the tequila. At least if he was blasted out of his skull when they came for him, he wouldn't give a damn.

The journal lay before him on the desk next to the spilled beer. Using some paper towels he had taken from the cleaning closet, Kit sopped up the mess, half-tempted to squeeze the contents down his throat.

He lifted the journal off the desk, but it slipped out of his trembling hands. It hit the corner of the desk and landed facedown on the dingy, buckled linoleum. He was about to pitch it back onto the table when he noticed a loose page near the back. Turning there, Kit saw a different set of entries written in blue ink. The print was narrow, the impressions hard, and the margins clean.

The first entry was dated January 26, 1981.

Me and Jeff finally got in the damn cave. Took us a month. Not easy with all this snow.

That's where we found this book. And the bodies.

*She* gave us strange dreams. Showed us stuff.

Promised us power in exchange for our loyalty and service.

I feel drawn to her for some reason.

I don't like writing. To much like school. But she says to write it down, says it'll help those in the family who come after. I can't wait for this power. So many fuckers are gonna pay.

She says we can be immortal like her. I like it! Me and Jeff can be like gods.

But first she needs blood.

Kit rifled through several pages, pausing only to scan the dates. He found what he was looking for amid the entry on June 28, 1981.

Tomorrow it's Melody Sellers's turn.

# 22

## AN ULTIMATUM

*Tuesday, June 14, 2011*

Courtney pulled into her driveway and pressed the button on the garage door opener. As she got out, the suffocating heat trapped inside the garage bowled into her. She unlocked the door, walked through the utility room, and flipped on the kitchen lights.

The mail was not on the counter like usual. Yesterday's dirty dishes still cluttered the sink. The trash had not been emptied, and nothing had been put away. She growled in her throat as she set her purse and folio on the table.

"Jill! Whitney! I'm home! Why haven't you done your chores?" She was not in the mood to spend the evening cleaning up, and it was already nearing eight o'clock. She wanted a glass of wine, a hot bath, and her bed.

"Girls!" she yelled again.

Courtney thought she heard faint mumbling. Or was it whimpering? The sound was coming from the girls' room upstairs or was it from down in the den? Exiting the kitchen, she discovered it was neither. Her eyes widened as the rest of her body froze. Courtney gasped.

Across the room, Scotty Dunley and Gabe Beecher stood behind the matching armchairs. Jillian occupied one, Whitney the other. Both girls were gagged, and their wrists bound with zip ties. Jillian's and Whitney's eyes bugged above their gags and were red from crying.

"Oh my God!" Courtney screamed and started into the living room.

202 • J. TODD KINGREA

"That's far enough, lady," Scotty growled, pulling a hunting knife from behind his back. He pressed the edge against Jillian's throat. She squeezed her eyes shut, spilling fresh tears.

Gabe did the same to Whitney.

"You got somethin' of mine an' I want it back," Scotty said as if talking about a borrowed lawn mower or extension cord.

Courtney tried to speak, but the words couldn't climb past where her heart stuck in her throat.

"Yeah, give it back," Gabe said. He leaned over the back of the chair and laid his knife horizontally beneath Whitney's chin.

"I-I-I don't know—" Courtney stammered.

"Don't lie to me, bitch!" Scotty shouted. "You got my journal. Give it back or the next cut"—he slid the blade down Jillian's cheek, leaving a crimson trail in its wake—"goes across her throat." Jillian screamed and cried through her gag. The wound oozed blood. It was not deep, just enough to prove he meant business.

"I-I don't h-have it," Courtney cried.

"Fuck it, I warned you." Scotty's knife dropped across Jillian's throat.

"NO!" Courtney shrieked. She stepped forward, hands out as she pleaded with them. "I gave it to someone! I gave it away!"

"Who's got it?" Gabe demanded.

Courtney's heart tore in half. She didn't want to give Kit up, but she couldn't let these lunatics hurt her girls. She wrestled only for an instant. With her hands still out, shaking so much it appeared as if she were playing an invisible piano, she said, "K-Kit McNeil. I-I gave it to Kit McNeil. Please let my daughters go!"

Scotty and Gabe exchanged a glance that meant nothing to Courtney. She whispered to the girls that everything was going to be okay and to remain calm, but she knew they could hear the terror in her voice.

"Sit down," Scotty ordered, pointing the knife at the sofa.

Courtney complied, shaking and wiping away tears.

"Please, *please*, don't hurt them. I'll do anything you want. J-just let them go."

"Tie her up," Scotty told Gabe.

The skinny man in work boots, grease-stained pants, and a Lynyrd Sky-nyrd T-shirt zipped a plastic tie around her wrists. He smelled of oil and gasoline as he bent down over her.

"Here's what's gonna happen," Scotty said. He rested one arm across the back of the chair while keeping the knife in place with the other. "You three are comin' with us. Soon as I get back what's mine, you can go."

"Wh-where are you taking us?" Courtney asked.

"Don't fuckin' worry about it! You best be thinkin' about what's gonna happen if I don't get my property back!" Scotty let the knife down slowly, so the point rested between Jillian's breasts.

"Okay, okay. Please, don't hurt them," Courtney said.

"Gag her and blindfold all of 'em," Scotty said, pulling several strips of cloth from his pocket and tossing them to Gabe.

• • •

Courtney's back ached from the metal ridges of the truck bed. She had no idea how long she had been lying here, but to her spine and shoulder blades, it felt like forever. Jillian and Whitney were beside her. Once she had been blindfolded and gagged like her daughters, the pair of men had led them out of the house. They were manhandled into the back of the pickup Scotty had parked behind one of the unfinished houses on the street. Gabe had climbed in after them. He covered them with a tarp and used tie-downs across their bodies to keep them from sitting up. Whitney continued to whimper.

Finally, the truck stopped. Both doors opened, then closed. Scotty and Gabe went to work in silence. The tailgate lowered, the straps were removed, and one by one Courtney and her daughters were dragged out and forced to stand. Their wrists were still bound in front of them, and a rope was tied around their waists.

Courtney could hear insects but no cars or voices. The ground was soft beneath her feet, not like asphalt, and she smelled bark, honeysuckle, and pine.

"Let's go, ladies," Scotty said. "We're goin' on a little hike." He jerked the rope. Whitney and Jillian were in front of Courtney, and she heard them mew and moan as they stumbled forward. The rope tugged at Courtney's waist, and she started walking.

Courtney lost all sense of time. She knew they were in a forest and were going up. They had to be on a mountain, but which one? And why?

Scotty and Gabe said little. Scotty occasionally gave them orders or warned them of obstacles in their path. They stopped twice to give the women brief gulps of lukewarm water. Then they were marching upward again.

Courtney hated what she had done to Kit, but she had no choice. She would not sacrifice her daughters over some old book. However, as she walked, a numbing reality settled over her. Even if Scotty got the journal back, there was no way he would let them go. They knew his and Gabe's identities. No matter how hard she tried, Courtney couldn't envision a scenario in which she and the girls got out of this alive.

Heart racing from this realization and the forced hike, Courtney began to consider their options for escape. They had to try. She wasn't going to leave her daughters at the mercy of these two. Even if she perished in the attempt, Courtney needed to ensure that Jillian and Whitney had a chance to escape.

Just how she was going to do that—blindfolded, gagged, and her hands tied—she had no idea.

• • •

*What time did I get home? Was it eight o'clock? Eight-thirty?*

If she had finished those depositions sooner, maybe she could've gotten there before Scotty and Gabe. She'd ask them what time they had arrived, but she couldn't talk. And she didn't really want to know. That would only give her more to feel guilty about.

Even though she worked out regularly, Courtney's legs burned from the climb. The two men kept them moving at a stern pace. Jillian and Whitney had both fallen but were yanked to their feet and pressed forward. All Courtney could hear was the crunching of feet through leaves and underbrush. The air cooled the higher they went.

It became monotonous. *Right, left, right, left.* She breathed harder as the incline increased, and her hands clutched the rough rope that led to her daughters up ahead. It was like being trapped in quicksand in a nightmare. Courtney thought she heard thunder in the distance.

After an indeterminate time, the ground leveled somewhat, and Scotty said, "You gotta crawl over some rocks, but it ain't too hard. Go slow." Once more the women were tugged forward. Courtney cracked her knee against a boulder and groaned through the gag. With her hands out and fingers splayed, she fumbled and crawled ahead. *This would be much easier without a zip tie around my wrists.* Stone scraped her knees and tore her skirt. She lost her balance several times and flopped against moss-covered stones. She was grateful she had worn flats instead of pumps today, an observation that made her question her sanity because she was thinking about shoes at a time like this. She could hear the girls grunting and moaning as they navigated the rocks.

Once they were past the rocks, the ground angled down. Now it was more dirt than rock. They scooted down until the ground flattened, and Scotty told them they could stand. The air still felt cool but now smelled odd— stale and old and earthy. Courtney also smelled something rotten that became more pungent the farther they went.

"All right, that's enough," Scotty said. His words echoed slightly. He and Gabe pushed the ladies against a stone wall. "Sit down."

Courtney and her girls slid to the ground. The heavy stench that surrounded them was punctuated with the same sour aroma that had come from the children who had broken into their house. Jillian and Whitney huddled against their mother, whimpering. Since Courtney could not put her arms around them, they all held hands. She heard Scotty and Gabe talking.

"I want you to go to my cousin, Jimmy Earl, and tell him I said it's time to deliver the message," Scotty said.

"Huh? You want me to hike all the way back down *and* all the way back up again?"

"Did I fuckin' stutter, Gabe?"

"N-no . . . it's just . . . That's a long walk, man."

"Then you best move your sorry ass."

"Why don't you just call him?"

"Because there's no fuckin' signal up here! You know that. Now go tell Jimmy Earl to deliver the message. Then the two of you escort McNeil up here."

"Why don't I just bring the book back?"

"Do what I fuckin' tell you an' quit askin' questions!" Scotty snapped. "This is all your fault, remember?"

A moment of silence followed. Scotty said something else, but it was too soft—or too far away—for Courtney to understand. They continued talking in the same low tone. Courtney strained to make out what they were saying but had no luck. Then she heard Gabe.

"You're gonna do *what*?"

Scotty's response was impossible to make out. Courtney leaned forward, hoping to pick up more of their conversation. She needed to know what they were planning. She needed to get the girls out of here.

"Aww, come on, Scotty," Gabe pleaded. "This ain't like that, and you know it. Those others were drifters, hitchhikers. Nobody was gonna miss 'em."

A mumbled reply.

"Shit, man, these are people who *will* be missed! We can't just—"

"Gabe, I swear to God, if you don't do what I tell you right now, I'll cut your fuckin' nuts off! Stop bitchin' and go. Tell Jimmy Earl what I said." He paused. "Just think, we do this and Uyaga will give us even more power once she's free."

"Yeah, Scotty, but—"

"No buts. This is for runnin' your fuckin' mouth too much. You're in this just as much as I am. We're gonna see it through."

Another moment of whispered conversation was followed by the sound of footsteps receding.

"Try to make yourselves comfortable, ladies," Scotty said. "We're gonna be here awhile."

• • •

*Wednesday, June 15, 2011*

Kit woke, dressed, and went to Troy's house to clean up. He returned to the furniture store just as Vince was opening up. Kit was rearranging the window display shortly after nine when the door opened.

"Good morning, welcome to—" The words locked in Kit's throat as he looked up.

"What's up, motherfucker?"

Buzz Cut, the Dunley whom Kit had throat-punched in the pharma-cy parking lot, displayed a cocky smile. He glanced around the showroom, probably to make sure they were alone, and stepped closer.

Kit took a step back, bumping into a table.

"Lemme tell *you* what's up, fat ass. You got something that belongs to my cousin, Scotty. He wants it back."

"I, uh—" Kit was unsure of how to reply.

Buzz Cut stepped closer until he was only an arm's length away. His breath smelled of bacon, and his eyes held all the warmth of a rattlesnake. "Scotty got something you'll want in exchange."

"Something I . . . What're you talking about?"

Buzz Cut kept grinning as he reached into his pocket. The sudden move-ment made Kit flinch.

"Oh, don't worry none. I ain't gonna kick your ass right now. But lat-er on, shithead? I'm gonna fuck you up *real* bad." Buzz Cut pulled out a cell phone and punched several buttons. A triumphant smirk spread across his face as he showed Kit the screen.

It was a picture of Courtney and her daughters. They were restrained and sitting on the ground. The lighting was poor, and he couldn't tell where they were. He saw no blood or apparent injuries.

*Thank God!* "Wh-what is this?" Kit asked. "What's going on?"

"They're with Scotty. Safe for *now*. And they'll stay that way if you do *exactly* what I tell you. Bring Scotty's journal to the old burned-out school at noon today. You don't say a word to no-fuckin'-body, especially the cops. If the cops show up, all three of 'em die. If anybody but *you* shows up, all three of 'em die. Bring the journal, do as you're told—and they might just make it out of this."

Kit's shock turned to outrage. "What've you done to them? If you've hurt any of them—"

Buzz Cut leaned forward, eyes hard and jaw set. "*Shut* the *fuck* up." He brandished the phone. "I make one call and they die. So you'd best keep your igner'nt mouth shut." The leering, hateful grin returned. "I told you that day in the parking lot that this wasn't over."

208 • J. TODD KINGREA

Kit didn't know whether to scream or stay silent, to lash out or remain motionless. The sun brightened the sidewalk and street outside. Cars drove by. Soft adult contemporary music drifted from the PA system.

"Noon. The old school. Come alone and bring the journal. We clear?"

Kit wanted to say something, but the cotton in his mouth prevented it. He nodded instead.

Buzz Cut whirled around and waltzed out the door as if he had just paid off a five-piece living room set.

Trembling, Kit collapsed into a plush recliner. His head swam. It seemed ridiculous. This was the sort of thing that happened on television shows and in the movies. What was he going to do? He had no doubt that Buzz Cut or Scotty would make good on the threat.

It was his damn luck again. No matter what Kit did, no matter how hard he tried, nothing ever fell into place for him. If he had left the journal alone, none of this would be happening. Like everything else, this was his fault. Courtney had only taken it because he thought he had to have it. And what good had it done him? It wasn't like he had learned anything helpful.

Was there a way out of this—a way to work around the instructions? No, he couldn't risk alerting anyone. Too much chance of Scotty doing something to Courtney and the girls.

What about Sheriff Owens? Absolutely not. If the Dunleys so much as *suspected* a cop—

Troy? No way in hell was he going to drag his best friend into this.

Beyond that, there really was no one else. Kit was on his own.

*One thing is for sure,* he told himself. *I'm not going to risk Courtney or her daughters over an old journal. Scotty can have it! Maybe . . . maybe he'll keep his word.* God, how he hated Black Rock! He walked to the office to tell Vince that he'd be leaving today. What Kit didn't tell him was that he had the distinct feeling he'd never be coming back to the store again.

# 23

## ON THE SLOPES OF BLACKPOINT

*Wednesday, June 15, 2011*

**K**it arrived early at the old Black Rock school. He wasn't going to take any chances. The day had turned cloudy, and a misty rain covered the windshield as he stared out at the blackened walls. He'd parked so he could see the weed-choked road. His dashboard clock read 11:58 a.m.

He'd been surprised by how quickly the idea had come to him and how easily he'd accepted it. It wasn't fancy, but maybe it would go a long way toward resolving this mess. If nothing else, it was sure to resolve his troubles.

A sense of peace settled over him. He closed his eyes and let the serenity enfold him. *It has to be done. There's no other way. It's not what I would've expected and certainly not the place. But nobody gets everything they want, do they?*

Through the blurry windshield Kit saw someone moving among the walls of the school and coming toward him. Gabe Beecher. Before getting out—and while Gabe could not see him clearly—Kit set his plan in motion. Then he got out and closed the door.

"You got it?" Gabe asked. He was out of breath and seemed irritated.

Kit held up the journal. "Now let Courtney and her daughters go," he said with hardened resolve.

Gabe shrugged and held out his hands. "They ain't here. I'll take you to 'em."

"Yeah, I figured as much."

Gabe walked up and patted the front of Kit's shirt several times. "No wire. Good. Did you tell anybody?"

Kit shook his head. "I'm not stupid."

"But you ain't real fuckin' smart, are you?" a familiar voice said. Kit's stomach knotted as Buzz Cut stepped out from behind a wall. He was dressed as he had been this morning. He also wore a cap with a rebel flag on it, and the bill had a large fishhook clipped to it.

Kit had put on a black T-shirt with a picture of Johnny Cash giving the middle finger on it. It was a silly, passive-aggressive response to the situation, but it had made him smile. Kit turned so the picture faced Buzz Cut.

"Come on, let's go," Gabe groused and started off through the damp weeds. He picked up a backpack when they reached the back wall of the school. As they walked by, Buzz Cut kicked Kit in the butt. Kit gritted his teeth and let it go. This was not the time. Not yet.

"Knock it off, Jimmy Earl," Gabe said. "We got a long way to go an' I ain't in the mood."

Buzz Cut—Jimmy Earl—fell in behind Kit, which made him anxious. If Jimmy Earl happened to notice the bottom of Kit's shirt—

"What's wrong with you?" Jimmy Earl asked as they plodded through the scrub brush and weeds. "Gabe! I'm talkin' to you!"

"Nothin', man. I'm fine."

"You look like you swallowed a used condom." Jimmy Earl laughed.

"I'm tired of runnin' up and down this goddamned mountain," Gabe snapped.

Jimmy Earl spit into the weeds. "You some kinda pussy or somethin'? Scotty says you act like one."

"Just shut the fuck up and walk!"

After a quarter mile of walking, the ground started sloping up. Kit saw the side of Blackpoint Mountain thrusting out of the treetops, its summit almost hidden by ashen, low-hanging clouds. Gabe said little but walked at a brisk pace. It wasn't long before Kit had trouble matching it. He noticed with wicked delight that the same was true for Jimmy Earl.

Gabe and Jimmy Earl had basically confirmed Kit's fears. They weren't planning to let Courtney and her girls go. If they did, they were bigger idiots than Kit had ever imagined. Of course, that also meant that he wasn't getting off this mountain alive either, but that was okay. He had a plan.

There was no rain beneath the trees, only the soft tromping of feet and heavy breathing. Kit didn't see a trail of any kind, but Gabe seemed to know where he was going. Behind him, Jimmy Earl huffed like a teenager with an aerosol can.

Gabe halted them after an hour. He took out bottles of water and pitched them around. "Good to know you don't want me to die on you," Kit said sarcastically after he took a drink.

"Shut up," Gabe ordered.

Kit glared at him. "What am I here for? You've got the journal." He held it up. "Why not just take it back at the school?"

"Because Scotty wants it done this way!" Gabe said, looking away.

Kit studied the young man. He didn't see the cockiness from Marty's Joint nor the antagonistic attitude that had led to the bar brawl. Gabe seemed distant, preoccupied. Kit sipped his water and stared at the pine needles and leaves at his feet. He pulled out his cell phone to check the time. Almost one o'clock.

*If they took me seriously, they should be there by now.*

"What the fuck?" Jimmy Earl shouted. He leaped up and knocked the cell out of Kit's hands. He turned on Gabe. "You didn't think to get his fuckin' cell phone? Jesus, you really are some kinda fuckup!"

Gabe curled his lip. "I told you once before, Jimmy Earl. Get off my back!"

"Shit, what else is this fat ass carryin'? Did you even search him?"

Kit stiffened. His pulse sped up.

"He ain't wired if that's what you mean."

"Stand up, fat ass," Jimmy Earl demanded, "and raise your hands."

Kit felt adrenaline kicking through his system. This was not how he had planned it, but when had any of his plans ever worked out? He prepared to make his move.

"Goddamn it, Jimmy Earl!" Gabe bellowed, disturbing the birds in the surrounding trees. His eyes blazed as they bore into Jimmy Earl. "Enough! I'm sick of your shit!"

212 · J. TODD KINGREA

A demonic light glinted in Gabe's eyes. His jaw tightened, and one hand repeatedly flexed into a fist just like Kit had seen him do at Marty's Joint after the brawl. While Gabe was tall, he was not muscular. Yet Kit saw a tension in his arms, the muscles visible beneath the skin in a way that did not seem natural.

Jimmy Earl sneered. "Like I give two shits what a pussy like you thinks."

With an explosive lunge, Gabe grabbed Jimmy Earl by the throat. He lifted him off the ground and slammed him into a tree trunk. Jimmy Earl gasped in shock. He beat at Gabe's bony arms to no avail. His feet raked against the bark, unable to find purchase. Jimmy Earl was more compact and probably outweighed Gabe by forty or fifty pounds, yet he hung in the air, face reddening, while Gabe snarled at him.

*I could do it now.*

The pistol Kit had smuggled out of Albert's house pressed into his spine. He could drop both of them right now, then find Courtney and the girls. Kit hesitated. He had no idea where they were. He could wander for days without ever locating them. In the time it took him to stumble upon them by accident, there was no telling what Scotty might do. Kit opted to wait although he hated to watch this opportunity pass.

Gabe let go, and Jimmy Earl dropped like a bag of cement and fell over, clutching his throat. Gabe knelt in front of him and said something. Kit could not make out what it was, but Jimmy Earl quickly nodded.

"Get up. We've wasted enough time," Gabe ordered. When he turned to start up the mountain, Kit noticed the fire was gone from his eyes. Gabe's body language reverted to the slumped shoulders and downcast gaze he'd had before.

Jimmy Earl climbed to his feet, coughing and rubbing his neck.

Kit caught up with Gabe. After a few steps he realized how quickly they were walking, yet Gabe was not winded.

"Listen, about the other night at the bar," Kit said. "I wasn't trying to make a fool of you. I just . . . I needed this journal."

To Kit's surprise Gabe said, "What for?"

They walked in silence for a moment.

"Have . . . have you read it?" Kit asked.

Gabe shook his head. "Bits and pieces, like I told you. Scotty told me some of what's in it."

Kit hesitated but decided he had little to lose by remaining quiet. "I read it last night. Gabe, did you and Scotty bring Uyaga any . . . blood?"

"Yeah, we did." He paused. "But I didn't do nothin' to them. Scotty is the one who did it. All of it."

"Did what?"

"Sacrificed 'em to Uyaga."

Kit had to catch his breath before continuing. "W-who did he sacrifice?"

When Gabe looked at Kit, his eyes were haunted and filled with doubt—something Kit had not seen from him before. Gabe's tone dropped an octave, making it harder for Kit to hear. "Those two missin' people—the guy and that college girl—and there was also a migrant worker. Santiago somethin'. I forget his name."

"Is Scotty planning to sacrifice Courtney? Or her daughters?" Kit dreaded the reply.

Gabe didn't say anything, but his shoulders slumped even more.

The light dimmed as clouds continued to bunch together. Thunder rolled behind the mountain. Jimmy Earl trailed behind like a whipped puppy.

Kit's stomach was a block of ice as he imagined Scotty's plans. He didn't know how long they had until they reached their destination, but another idea was beginning to form in his mind.

After several minutes, Kit said, "I take it that means yes."

"I didn't do nothin' to them," Gabe said. "Scotty killed 'em." He looked at Kit. "Uyaga gave us power. As long as we do what *she* says."

"Gabe, Uyaga is evil. She can't do anything good. No matter what you got from her, it's corrupted in some way or it'll corrupt you. Why do you think the Cherokee imprisoned her? Look what happened to Edgar. All she knows how to do is hurt and destroy. She manipulates and lies. All the bad shit in Black Rock comes from her."

They climbed another hundred yards before Gabe said, "Maybe."

"It's all right here in the journal. She caused Edgar to go mad. I'll bet you've noticed something different about Scotty too, haven't you? That's *her* influence. She destroys everything she comes in contact with—and she doesn't care."

Gabe started to speak, then stopped. He sighed. When he spoke again, his voice was even lower. "Scotty plans to kill 'em. I told him it was a bad idea. They'll be missed. That migrant worker? He won't be missed, least not for a good while."

Kit's legs burned and ached. Sweat poured down his face and back. "The Collinsworth boy and the Walston girl—*they've* been missed. You know the cops and the TBI are looking all over for them."

"Of course, I know," Gabe said. "That's what I was *tryin'* to tell Scotty. We can't keep takin' people who're noticeable. We were supposed to stick to the hitchhikers and runaways. That's the mistake Scotty's kinfolk made back in the 1980s. He told me all about it, yet he's doin' the same damned thing."

"What happened in the '80s?"

"Greg and Jeff Dunley found the cave and the journal. They started out bringin' people who wouldn't be missed, but then they got greedy. Or stupid. Or both. They tried to kidnap some girl in Knoxville while her parents were home. Got caught, of course, and went to jail. Not long after there was a riot or somethin' in their cell block—both of 'em were killed."

Kit remembered the newer entries at the back of the journal. "Were they responsible for the disappearance of Melody Sellers? Did they kill her too?"

"Don't know."

"Greg mentions her in one of his journal entries."

Gabe shrugged.

"Gabe, listen, I know this *power* you've got—I'm sure it's intoxicating. I know you feel invincible. I can only imagine what having something like that means in a place like Black Rock. Kind of makes you king of the mountain so to speak. I grew up here. I know what a shitty place this is—how hard it is to get out of and how hard it is to get people to take you seriously if you're not from a high-class neighborhood. What you've gotten from Uyaga makes you special—different from anybody else around—but please, *please*, listen to me. *She'll* mess you up just like she did Edgar. Like she's done to Scotty. You're nothing but a plaything to her."

The thought stabbed Kit's heart. He heard the echo of insidious laughter in his mind, remembered the dream of being chased through town.

"I am too," Kit said. He told Gabe about his encounter in the park when he was twelve, and the curse Uyaga had placed on him. "*She* picked me at random so she could fuck up my life for her enjoyment." Kit grew livid talking about it.

"Yeah, maybe," Gabe said.

• • •

Jimmy Earl had confiscated his cell, so Kit had no idea of the time. He figured it had to be around two or three in the afternoon. The air was cooler and still dreary thanks to the thunderheads above the trees. The wind had picked up. It was going to be a strong storm when it hit.

Kit prayed that help was on the way. He needed all of it he could get.

They weren't far from Blackpoint's summit. The rocks were blackish gray, while the soil looked like volcanic dust. As they had climbed, Kit had noticed fewer patches of blight. Now, as they neared their destination, there was none to be seen. He remembered hearing that the blight never appeared on the summit.

"This is it," Gabe said. He indicated a pile of rubble on a flattened shelf of rock just above them. The stones had probably been brought down by a lightning strike or rockslide.

*Or an explosion,* Kit thought. *Edgar's gunpowder explosion.*

Kit saw Scotty Dunley standing on the rubble, watching them.

Gabe directed Kit up the pile of rocks. Kit had to crawl on his hands and knees before he could squeeze through an opening. He could understand why no one had ever discovered the cave on purpose. Unless someone was standing right beside it, there was no way to see the entrance. He skidded down a pebbly incline with Gabe and Jimmy Earl right behind.

The cave was larger than he'd expected, and Scotty had it lit with battery-operated camping lanterns. In their garish white glow, Kit guessed the cave to be about 150 feet at its widest point, probably a little less than that in height. The ceiling had a few stalactites. The floor was uneven, dotted with boulders and a couple of stalagmites. Far in the back was what appeared to be another cave or a tunnel. The stench of death lingered in the temperate air.

What was it that Edgar's journal had said? *nObOdy neVernevEr go in the black beeyond furst cave WhERe i put them kidS.*

Kit stood up and spotted Courtney and the girls on the left side of the cave. Their hands were bound, and they clung to each other. Scotty had removed their blindfolds but not the gags. Courtney started crying when she saw Kit.

To his right, human bodies lay scattered across the floor like scraps of garbage. Kit saw several skeletons dressed in little more than rags. Three corpses were in increasing stages of decay. One appeared to have been Hispanic. Flies buzzed around the putrefying corpses. Kit's eyes roved over the deceased. In front of a stalagmite lay a skeleton wearing what had once been shorts and a blue halter top.

*Melody Sellers.*

Kit's stomach flipped. The urge to run—to scramble back through the opening and breathe clean air again—overwhelmed him. He tried to contain his mounting panic.

Daniel, Lena, and Lydia appeared from the rear of the cave. The Children of Uyaga stood in front of the tunnel opening. Their own spoiled scent added to the miasma.

"My journal," Scotty said as he stepped toward Kit. His face was a mask of icy contempt.

Kit gestured toward the women and held the journal close to his side. "L-let them go."

Scotty stuck his arm out, palm open.

"You get it when they're out of here," Kit said with more courage than he felt.

"Yeah, I had an idea you'd say something stupid like that." Scotty sighed and turned to Gabe. "Slit the youngest one's throat," he ordered in the most mundane manner as if he were responding to survey questions from an automated phone system.

"No!" Kit exclaimed. "Don't!"

Gabe didn't move.

Courtney squealed and struggled against the zip ties.

"Gabe!" Scotty barked. "Get going!"

Gabe shot Kit a confused look.

"Give me the fucking journal or Gabe starts killing them until you do." Scotty's tone was pitiless, hard as the stone that entombed them.

"Scotty, listen to me," Kit urged. "Uyaga isn't what you think. *She* doesn't care about you. She'll destroy you!"

Scotty threw his head back and laughed. "I *serve* Uyaga, you ignorant son of a bitch! I ain't afraid of nothing!"

"Well, you should be! She'll chew you up and spit you out. What happened to Edgar will happen to you."

Scotty stopped laughing. His eyes turned cold. "Edgar was stupid, a waste of Uyaga's power. He sealed himself in here to try an' stop *her*, but she can't be stopped! She's the ground itself! The land belongs to her!" His voice rose with each exclamation.

Scotty stopped and turned as if just remembering Gabe was there. "What the fuck are you waiting for, asshole? Kill her!"

"C-c'mon, Scotty, you don't really want me to . . . to kill 'em, right? J-just scare 'em a little." Gabe's tone was pleading, desperate.

Scotty slid a hunting knife from the sheath on his hip. He walked toward Courtney and her daughters, eyes locked on Kit, Gabe, and Jimmy Earl. He stopped less than a foot from Whitney.

"Wait, wait!" Kit begged. "Don't do it!"

With his back to the captives, Scotty glared at Gabe. "Now pay attention, Gabe."

# 24
## FAMILY LOYALTY

*Wednesday, June 15, 2011*

Scotty spun around, screaming at the top of his lungs and waving the knife in Whitney's face. All three women shrieked and recoiled.

Scotty burst out laughing. "There you go, Gabe. They're scared. Now get your ass over here!"

Eyes downcast, Gabe shuffled across the cave and took the knife from Scotty's hand. He forced the women away from the wall and stood behind them, deflated as a week-old balloon. The knife hung loosely in his hand.

"Okay, okay, stop!" Kit yelled. "Here! Here's your damn journal!" He flung it into the middle of the cave. "Now please, let them go."

Scotty grinned in triumph as he picked up the book. "What do you think, Gabe? Should you kill one or let them all live a little while longer?"

The gangly youth swallowed hard and did not reply.

"Jimmy Earl! How the fuck are you?" Scotty shouted as if this were the first time he had seen his cousin in years. His voice echoed through the cave. "What do *you* think we should do?"

Jimmy Earl stood motionless; his bravado neutered.

When he did not reply, Scotty spat on the floor. "Assholes and cowards."

"Scotty Dunley," a voice said from the back of the cave. Daniel Dunley came forward, his eyes protuberant within their black sockets. "You have a problem."

"Huh? What problem? What're you talkin' about?" Scotty asked.

Daniel's head swiveled toward Gabe. "*Him.* He is planning to betray you."

"What?" Gabe gasped. "Huh? No! *No!* That's bullshit, Scotty!"

"I have seen this," Daniel said. "He is weak, spineless. He wants to be like you, but he is incapable of serving me. He is shackled to his morality and will betray you."

Gabe extended supplicating hands to Scotty. "C'mon, man, we're friends! I wouldn't sell you out!" He attempted a laugh that sounded more like choking.

Daniel pointed. "You see how he hesitates to kill? His spirit is unwilling. He does not have the strength to do what must be done. He is *unworthy* of me."

"What've you done, Gabe?" Scotty demanded, scowling at his friend whose presence wilted by the minute.

Gabe's eyes were wide. "Man, I ain't done nothin'! I swear to Christ. I'm on your side."

"Then why does the Black Earth Spirit say you're plotting against me? Why don't you do what I tell you?" asked Scotty.

Gabe was close to tears. "Scotty, please, man. This lady and her kids—people know them. If we kill 'em, the cops will nail us for sure. They already suspect us in those disappearances."

"You see?" Daniel said, goading Scotty. "Weak."

"Shut the fuck up!" Gabe yelled at Daniel. "Quit lyin'!"

Jimmy Earl hooked a thumb in Kit's direction. His bluster had returned. "Scotty? I think ya oughta know—Gabe *was* talkin' to him on the way up here. A *lot.* They were whisperin' back and forth."

"Go to hell, Jimmy Earl!" Gabe shouted. He did his best to hide the tremor in his voice, but the panic on his face was clear as a movie on a screen.

Scotty looked sideways at Gabe. "Did you, Gabe? Were you gettin' chatty with McNeil?"

"No, I—"

"Bullshit," Jimmy Earl said. "I heard you talkin' about the journal an' somethin' called Uyaga. Fat ass over there was tryin' to get him to turn on you."

Gabe stepped around the women and started toward Scotty, shaking his head. "That ain't so, Scotty. I did just what you told me. Jimmy Earl is just pissed 'cause we got into an argument."

"Weren't no argument," Jimmy Earl said with a sly smile. "He tried to kill me."

Scotty's eyes narrowed to icy slits. "Gabe, what's happened to you? I thought you had my back. We were gonna rule this place with the power Uyaga gave us. Maybe I oughta give Jimmy Earl that power instead."

"Did I not tell you?" Daniel asked. "His disloyalty cannot be excused. He is unreliable." He paused while his snaillike tongue slid across his lips. "You have no need of him. Your cousin is here. He is family—just as *we* are your family. We are of the Dunley blood. But Gabe Beecher? He is an outsider."

Gabe started to sob. He retreated two steps from Scotty.

"Give me his blood," Daniel said in an emotionless voice. "Show me *your* worthiness, Scotty Dunley. Show me your family loyalty."

Scotty reached under his shirt. He tugged a gun from the waistband of his pants. Without hesitation, he sighted on Gabe and pulled the trigger.

Even though Kit saw it happen, the deafening boom rocked him back on his heels. Within the womb of stone, the sound almost shattered his eardrums. He slammed his palms against his ears, but it was too late. The sound ricocheted like an angry yellow jacket inside his skull.

Kit saw Courtney and the girls screaming but heard nothing except a muffled roar. He watched Gabe's head jerk back as if someone had pulled his hair. Blood and shards of skull splattered the cave wall.

Scotty held his pose, arm extended with a black Taurus .357 in his hand.

Gabe's body collapsed in front of Courtney, Jillian, and Whitney. Splattered with blood, they scrambled backward until they were against the wall once more.

Kit watched Jimmy Earl scream. He almost looked comical with his fingers stuck in his ears, the color draining from his face, and his eyes bulging.

Lena and Lydia joined their brother and together they crept forward, kneeling around Gabe's body as if about to partake in some unholy sacrament. Daniel cradled Gabe's head. The two girls raked their talons along his arms and immediately clamped their hands over the wounds. Just as Kit had seen before, their pasty complexions began to darken as they leeched the blood. He had to look away to keep from being sick. The memory of those small hands against his own skin roared back.

Kit's hearing returned in fragments. Scotty was saying something. "Ji . . . Earl, take . . . gir . . . dow . . . tunnel."

Jimmy Earl moved to carry out the order. He grabbed Courtney by the shoulder and forced her to stand.

Kit yelled, but his voice sounded like the buzz of an angry yellow jacket swaddled in cotton. Jimmy Earl paid him no attention. Kit started to move to help the women, but Scotty leveled the Taurus at him.

Kit froze with his hands up, heart hammering.

"Where do . . . thi . . . you're going?" Scotty asked.

Kit could do nothing but watch Jimmy Earl yank Jillian and Whitney to their feet. Grabbing a lantern—which sent shadows squirming around the cave—Jimmy Earl herded the women toward the black opening.

*Help isn't coming,* Kit told himself with resigned disappointment. Such was his luck. He knew he shouldn't have expected it, yet a part of him had held on to the faintest glimmer of hope.

*I also didn't count on Scotty having a gun. So much for my great plan. Now what the hell do I do?*

But Kit knew the answer to that. He'd do whatever was necessary to get Courtney and her daughters out of here. He just had to think on his feet—something he'd never done well.

"You're next," Scotty said. He motioned Kit toward the back of the cave.

*nObOdy neVernevEr go in the black beeyond furst cave.*

Kit walked slowly past Scotty. At least his hearing was better.

Thunder boomed, and Kit felt it inside the cave. The storm must have been right on top of the mountain.

"Hurry, Scotty Dunley," Daniel said. He stood up, releasing Gabe's head. It sounded like a mushy tomato when it hit the floor. "It is almost time."

Scotty turned to say something. Kit saw him do it and closed the distance between them in one and a half steps.

Scotty turned back after the first step, realizing his mistake. He brought the Taurus around, but it would take another full step for him to aim and fire. Kit's half step brought him within reach of Scotty.

Kit grabbed Scotty's arm. He forced Scotty's gun down as he plowed into him. The suddenness of the attack caused Scotty to drop the pistol as he reacted on instinct and tried to protect himself. Scotty tumbled backward, and

Kit went down with him. The momentum carried Kit over and off Scotty's body. Kit scrambled to his hands and knees, but Scotty was already looming over him.

"Son of a bitch!" Scotty snarled. His boot slammed into Kit's ribs.

Kit wheezed and curled into a fetal position.

The Children of Uyaga lurched toward Kit. Scotty waved them off. "He's mine. Take your blood to the pit," he growled.

From the brawl in Marty's Joint, Kit knew Scotty was stronger than he looked. He now realized just how strong. Scotty grabbed Kit by the throat with one hand and lifted him off the floor, like Gabe had done to Jimmy Earl earlier. Kit kicked as hard as he could. He made solid contact, but Scotty showed no sign of pain or injury. He almost seemed to enjoy it.

Scotty hurled Kit across the cave where he crashed into the pile of corpses and skeletons. Kit's hand squelched into something cold and jellied. He gagged, rolled onto his side, and spit blood.

• • •

Jimmy Earl must have heard the commotion because he spun around.

Courtney took advantage of Jimmy Earl's lack of attention and drove her heel into his kneecap. An ugly *pop* followed. He crumpled to the ground and bellowed like a dying moose.

Courtney ripped off her gag. "Jillian! Whitney! Run! Get out of here!"

Both girls stood transfixed. They held each other's hands; their faces were streaked with dirt and Gabe's blood.

*"Go! Now!"* Courtney screamed. This time the severity of their mother's tone galvanized them into action. Crying and screaming, the girls dashed for the entrance.

Courtney advanced on Jimmy Earl and kicked him in the crotch. He rolled over, crying and gasping. As he shielded his ribs, her foot connected with his skull. His head cracked against a boulder, and he groaned. His movement slowed, and she saw the wooziness in his eyes.

Courtney sidestepped him and moved toward Scotty.

• • •

"No, don't!" Kit managed to yell when he saw what Courtney was doing.

Scotty motioned to the Children of Uyaga. "She's yours. Take her."

"No!" Kit screamed again. As he attempted to stand, his foot slipped in one of the fresher bodies. Cursing, he fell back into the pile of bones, dusty clothing, and putrefying flesh. The stench caused him to vomit.

Jillian was helping her sister up the incline toward the cave opening.

"Daniel!" Scotty shouted. "Stop them!"

"You do not give *me* orders, Scotty Dunley," Daniel said in a guttural voice.

Lena and Lydia advanced on Courtney, forcing her to back up.

Kit got to his knees and stood on quivering legs. Broken and splintered bones surrounded his feet, but he noticed something among them. Another piece of oddly discolored ragged clothing.

Scotty leaped for his gun.

Kit reached behind his back and pulled out his father's Smith & Wesson .38 revolver. He leveled it at Scotty.

Albert had taken him hunting a few times when he was younger, one of his ways of teaching his son "how to be a man." Kit didn't care for the sport but was comfortable enough around firearms.

Kit was a bit more prepared for the boom this time since he was the one pulling the trigger, but it still made his ears ring. The .38 didn't have the kind of stopping power a .357 did, but it was sufficient in these close quarters. The round caught Scotty in the left shoulder, spinning him out of reach of his own firearm.

Whitney had disappeared outside. Jillian was halfway there.

Scotty stood up, touched his shoulder, and looked at the blood on his fingers. He leered at Kit. "Didn't think you had it in you, McNeil."

Kit clenched his teeth and fired again. The shot went wide, pinging into the cave wall. Cursing his luck, he squeezed off another. This one slammed into Scotty's chest, knocking him off his feet.

Outside, thunder continued to assault the mountain. It vibrated the floor as Kit watched, dumbfounded, while Scotty pushed himself back up. Kit extended his arm again and squeezed the trigger.

Another miss. *Damn it!*

Scotty threw himself behind the cover of a boulder.

"Kit!" Courtney screamed.

He saw her struggling to get up. Jimmy Earl, pale and sneering, gripped her ankle. Lena and Lydia closed in on her, their fingers clawing the air.

Kit closed one eye and sighted Lena. He fired and the shot blasted her aside.

He was aiming for Lydia when something like thunder boomed so loud it seemed to shake the cave. It deafened Kit again. He staggered back. He hadn't fired another round just now, right? For some reason, he couldn't remember. His leg was burning. Kit cried out when he saw his pants darken as blood spilled from his thigh.

*Oh Jesus, my artery!*

Kit looked up, panicked, and saw Scotty pointing the Taurus at him.

Kit needed cover, but his leg wouldn't cooperate. Instead, his leg surrendered, causing Kit to collapse to the cave floor. He fired the .38 in Scotty's general direction. How many shots did he have left? One? Two? How many had he started with?

A chilly wind erupted from the tunnel. It reeked of the blight and smeared against his skin, ancient and repulsive. Lena and Lydia stopped. Daniel did too after he slid back down the incline into the cave. Kit, sweating profusely, dragged himself behind a stalagmite. Jimmy Earl gawked as he remained sprawled in the dirt.

"It's time! It's time!" Scotty exclaimed. He walked into the middle of the cave, seeming unconcerned by the threat of Kit's weapon.

The wind continued to stream from the tunnel. Thunder cracked around the mountain.

Kit steadied his arm and aimed carefully. Scotty stood enraptured, his head in Kit's sights.

*See if you can get up from this, you white trash son of a bitch!* Kit smiled grimly as he pulled the trigger.

Click.

*No! Shit!*

He tried again. Click.

Screams of unbridled terror erupted outside, outlasting the thunder.

"Jillian, Whitney!" Courtney shouted. She started toward the cave entrance. "Something's happened to them!"

# 25

## NITIB-PINGWI MANITOU

*Wednesday, June 15, 2011*

"**C**ourtney, wait!" Kit yelled. "Watch out for—"

With a speed that belied his injuries, Scotty intercepted her. His forearm closed around her throat. He pulled her close as she struggled to break free. An elbow to the stomach didn't faze him.

Kit moved toward her, but Scotty pressed the barrel of the Taurus to her head.

"Don't," Scotty ordered. "Jimmy Earl, get his gun."

Scooping it off the floor, Jimmy Earl checked the cylinder. "It's empty."

"Give it to me." Scotty stuffed the .38 in the waistband of his jeans. "Now let's go." Scotty turned Courtney toward the tunnel, and Jimmy Earl limped along behind. "You too, McNeil. You got something Uyaga wants."

For a second, Kit thought about trying to rationalize with Scotty again, but the gleam he had seen in Scotty's eyes after Gabe had died told him that if Scotty wasn't already insane, it wouldn't be much longer. The time for talking was over. Survival was all that mattered now.

Courtney's survival. Kit knew he wasn't going to get off this mountain alive. He'd known that when he'd received the message this morning. This had always been a one-way trip for him.

Only days ago, he'd contemplated suicide as a way to protect his friends and end the curse. He didn't *want* to die. It was just the most logical choice. Now that he knew what the curse was and how it was transmitted, he had no desire to go through the rest of his life unable to touch people or being terrified that someone might touch him. Uyaga claimed that he had to be standing on *her* land for the curse to work, but this spirit was deceptive, ancient as the brooding hills, and capable of anything. Kit couldn't risk touching anyone, anywhere, as long as there was the tiniest chance that they could be affected.

Kit didn't have a lot to go back to anyway. He'd been struggling for a long time, and there were moments when it all seemed so pointless. If he could do something good and meaningful, maybe that would help make up for his mistakes. If not, at least he knew that he'd done the best he could.

Edgar Dunley had imprisoned himself in this cave to keep Uyaga in check. To hold her. To weaken her. Kit didn't understand how dying inside a cave could do that, but Edgar had found a way.

There was only one wrinkle in Kit's plan, something he'd been unable to account for. How was he going to seal off the cave? Edgar had used gunpowder to bring down part of the mountainside, but Kit didn't have anything like that. He had no dynamite either. Contrary to television shows and movies, it was hard to come by. So exactly *how* he was going to complete his plan was still up in the air.

The shuffling of small feet intruded upon his thoughts. Daniel, Lena, and Lydia gathered around him. They blocked any attempt at escape. Kit turned and limped after Scotty, Courtney, and Jimmy Earl.

The floor sloped down at a gradual angle and leveled out as it entered the tunnel. It was not man-made, and they had to pick their way around rocky outcroppings. The temperature remained moderate, but Kit noticed that the stench grew stronger the farther they went.

Jimmy Earl carried two lanterns. The chalky light helped them avoid crevices that could break ankles and stalactites that hung low in the passageway.

Kit was conscious of the Children of Uyaga behind him and kept telling himself that they weren't going to kill him. Not yet anyway.

After forty or fifty yards, the tunnel opened into another cave, larger than the first. The walls disappeared up into the darkness.

"There's lanterns around the walls," Scotty told Jimmy Earl. "Go turn 'em on."

Jimmy Earl looked at his cousin, a mixture of uncertainty and barely concealed fright on his face. "Uh, why me, Scotty? I think that bitch broke my fuckin' knee! It's big as a set of bull's balls and hurts like shit."

"You've already got a lantern to see by, numbnuts. Leave one here and take the other."

"But my knee—"

"Go, damn it! Stop wasting time!"

They waited, the only sounds the scuffing of Jimmy Earl's footsteps and his angry cursing. Scotty kept the gun against Courtney's temple. They watched Jimmy Earl work his way around the perimeter of the cave, lighting the lanterns as he went. With each fluorescent corona of light that appeared, more of the floor was exposed. There was the pit in the center. Kit estimated it was at least thirty feet in diameter. The noxious stink originated from its depths.

"Wh-what is this place?" Jimmy Earl asked when he rejoined the group.

Scotty didn't reply. He shoved Courtney forward, the pistol at the back of her skull. "Get over there on the other side."

Kit heard the Children of Uyaga creeping up behind him. He expected to feel razor-sharp nails slice his back open at any moment. His leg burned like it was filled with acid, and his sock was sticky with blood. His shoe squelched when he tried to put weight on it.

Kit was no med student, but if he was still alive, then the bullet must have missed his femoral artery. *For once luck is with me!* He also recognized how lucky he was that the bullet had not hit his femur. The hole in his jeans was over the outer part of the thigh where it was all muscle. Kit limped as best he could and used the cave wall for support as Daniel, Lena, and Lydia herded him around the side of the pit.

Scotty pressed Courtney and Kit against the back wall of the cave. There was enough room between them and the pit to park a Cadillac.

Daniel, Lena, and Lydia turned in unison and walked to the edge of the pit. They got down on their hands and knees and opened their mouths. A torrent of blood, like three crimson waterfalls, cascaded into the pit. As they expelled the blood, their coloration faded; their flesh once more resembled the starchy, polypore fungi found on tree trunks.

A tremor moved through the cave, rattling loose bits of rock and dust from the walls.

Their expulsion completed, the Children of Uyaga stood, turned, and stared at Kit.

"Your turn, McNeil!" Scotty said. "*She's* been waiting for your blood."

"You dumb shit!" Kit shouted. "You don't have any idea what's—"

Wind gusted up from the pit, and Kit stopped as if he had bitten his tongue. Courtney screamed while Scotty laughed like a lunatic. The Children of Uyaga turned to face the pit with eager anticipation.

A bony, taloned hand rose and grasped the rocky edge.

The ground vibrated with a second tremor. Small stones clattered and fell.

"*She's* here! She's here!" Scotty screamed in exultation.

Kit found his voice. "We've got to *go!*" he whispered to Courtney. He knew he wasn't going far, not without a crutch or cane, but that didn't matter. Getting her out was the only thing that did.

"I-I don't understand," Courtney whimpered. "I thought Uyaga needed your blood in order to . . . to—"

Kit nodded his head. "*She* does, but she must have enough blood now to get out of the pit. I think mine might be what she needs in order to leave the cave."

"Th-then what do we do?"

"We're getting the hell out of here," he lied. Only one of them was going to make it.

Edgar Dunley had imprisoned himself in the outer cave as a kind of barrier or threshold—something Uyaga couldn't get past. Edgar was the lock. Kit realized that now. But how had he done it? Kit figured that simply blowing up the cave entrance and dying of thirst inside wasn't sufficient. There had to be something else, something he was missing. He racked his brain trying to remember what he'd read in the journal.

Another tremor crossed the cave, stronger than the previous ones. A second hand clawed at the air before latching on to the rim of the pit.

Kit grabbed Courtney by the shoulders, turned her away from the pit, and forced her to look at him. "You have to run! Back up the tunnel. Get out!"

"But . . . but what about y—"

"No! Don't worry about me! I've been shot. I'll only slow you down."

"I can't leave you!" she screamed, the grim inevitability settling on her.

He stared at her hard, as if he could overpower her will by the sheer intensity of his gaze alone. "You *have* to. For Jillian and Whitney."

Courtney started to weep. Her hair was streaked with dirt, and dried blood freckled her face. Tears cut paths through the dust on her cheeks.

"Hen'yehmoak taan! Uyaga! Uyaga!" Scotty shrieked as he fell to his knees. Saliva bubbled on his lips.

Jimmy Earl began to scream.

Courtney grabbed Kit, burying her face in his chest. "No! No! No!"

With his arms around her, Kit had no way to cover his eyes. He gaped as terror flayed his mind like a cat-o'-nine-tails. Uyaga climbed from the pit and stood, looking down at them with vacant black sockets.

Not even the visions had prepared Kit for the abomination that towered at least fifteen feet above him. The head was malformed and lumpy as if it had been pulled and twisted like warm taffy. Gaping pits just below the eyes were the only indication of a nose. Far beneath them was a wide mouth lined with needlelike teeth. Strands of pure white hair floated in the wind.

The body was emaciated, the pelvic bone prominent through the cottage cheese skin. Taloned hands dangled at the end of arms that were simian-like in their length. There was no indication of sex despite the journal's reference to *her* as female.

Kit trembled as he held Courtney. He was transfixed, not by the shape or smell of the hideous blasphemy, but by the *mouths*. All over Uyaga's body, blackened mouths appeared and disappeared. They formed out of her flesh. Cracked and peeling lips, broken teeth, and rancid gums moaned and blubbered, producing no recognizable words. After a moment, each mouth disappeared, only to reappear somewhere else. The air was thick with a cacophonous, unintelligible keening.

"Oh . . . my . . . God," Kit managed to say.

The cave rumbled again, and dust drifted from the darkness. Jimmy Earl hobbled around the perimeter of the cave. He no longer screamed but made senseless noises as he felt his way along the wall, one arm angled across his eyes.

Uyaga stared at Kit with eyeless sockets. "God? *God?*" Her voice was part loathing, part arrogance. It sounded like a hammer against bone. "Oh no, not the Great Spirit nor the godling of Nazareth nor any of the other false gods created by your kind. I have been around much, much longer. Across this insignificant terrestrial ball from time immemorial, I have been. I always will be."

"Wh-wh-what are you?" Kit stammered.

"Hen'yehmoak taan! Uyaga! Uyaga! Hen'yehmoak taan! Uyaga! Uyaga!" Still kneeling, Scotty paid obeisance to her.

Jimmy Earl fled, blubbering, up the tunnel.

"What *am* I, little worm? I am more than you can imagine. I am from everlasting to everlasting. In China, I am Jiutian Xuannü. In ancient Egypt, I was Min, Celestial goddess of fertility. In the Nordic countries, I am Svart jordsmor. The Greeks worshiped me as Demeter. In Africa, I am Asase Ya. The Canaanites and the Phoenicians named me Ashtoreth. To the Celts, I was Nantosuelta. The natives of this land feared me as *Nitib-pingwi Manitou*, the Black Earth Spirit. The Cherokee hid their faces when they dared to whisper my name."

"Hen'yehmoak taan! Uyaga! Uyaga!" Scotty shrieked.

Uyaga continued, "Cultures have honored me. People have given offerings in exchange for my blessing. Kings have proclaimed my power. Priests and shamans have bowed before me. Your species has invoked me for their bodies and crops, seeking fertility and rich harvests. They have danced before my glory and composed songs to my thousand names.

"But I am *more*, so much more! I am the Mother of a Thousand Wombs and the Twilight of Leng'tuan. Those who are barren call me Comamatos. In languages long dead, I was spoken of as Bastershurn-Kal. I am the Black Goa—"

"No, you're not!" Kit shocked himself with the outburst. Where had *that* come from?

Uyaga hissed. "What did you say, little worm?" She stepped forward, fingers twitching like spider legs.

Scotty turned his head and stared at Kit with furious contempt.

"I *know* you," Kit continued. Maybe if he could keep this thing focused on him, Courtney might be able to make a run for it. "You sent me visions, remember? And I've read Edgar's journal. You're not immortal. You're not a god. You're just an evil, twisted monstrosity that the Cherokee stuck down in that damn hole!"

Uyaga roared. She lashed out with one hand, her nails digging furrows in the rock just above Kit's and Courtney's heads. They ducked and covered themselves to block the falling debris.

"To me, my children!" Uyaga bellowed.

As the rocks and dust settled, Daniel, Lena, and Lydia walked toward Uyaga. They gathered around her legs and hugged them. Slowly, all three were reabsorbed into Uyaga's pallid flesh with a sound like phlegm being raked from the back of the throat.

"Now I am complete. And as for you, little worm, have you not enjoyed the gift I bestowed upon you? Has it not been glorious being part of my great work?"

"*Gift?* Fuck you! You ruined my life and killed people! All for your own twisted delight!"

Uyaga grinned, displaying far too many ice pick teeth. "Of course. Is that not my purpose, little worm—to ruin that which is good, to sow misery, and to feast on suffering?"

Scotty stood. There was nothing but madness in his eyes.

Courtney hadn't moved. She cowered against the wall.

Kit's mind raced, trying to grasp why *Nitib-pingwi Manitou* had done all these things and still furiously seeking what he'd missed in Edgar's journal. If Edgar was the lock, was there a key? And if so, what was it?

"Shall I kill her for you, Mother? I can wound her if you prefer. That way you can keep her on you forever." Scotty had the Taurus trained on Courtney.

The thought came so hard and fast that Kit almost flinched at its vividness.

"No," Uyaga declared. "I will consume this one." She started toward Courtney.

Kit pushed himself away from the wall. He *had* to get out of here! He staggered and limped as quickly as he could around the pit. The pain sent sparks across his vision. He gritted his teeth and tried to block it out.

*The tunnel! I've got to get to the tunnel! Got to get—*

Uyaga stopped, seeming amused by Kit's juddering and handicapped flight. Scotty fired. Kit heard the rock behind him crack under the bullet's impact. He forced himself to go faster. The sparks in his vision became miniature explosions.

Scotty fired again and missed, cackling as if he were playing a carnival game.

• • •

Uyaga's leechlike tongue flicked from her mouth as she sneered at Courtney. "You are forsaken. He does what all little worms do when they cannot comprehend who and what I am. He flees. He is a coward. I have known this since I touched him those many years ago. It is who he is and who he shall always be. Come now and be joined with me."

Scotty twittered.

*Nitib-pingwi Manitou*'s bony hands reached out. Courtney shrank back against the wall and screamed. She screamed at the unknown fate of her daughters and at the impossible horror in front of her. She screamed at what was about to happen. And she screamed in hopeless agony as Kit disappeared up the tunnel.

# 26

## THE FINISHING TOUCH

*Wednesday, June 15, 2011*

**K**it stumbled through the tunnel. He saw no sign of Jimmy Earl, and more than once collided with stalagmites and rocks. He was not sure if the aurora of light ahead of him was the first cave or his pain-shocked vision.

*Hold on! Hold on! Just a little bit longer. Please, please, please, let me do this right!*

Kit almost fell going up the slope. His footsteps sounded puny and distant in his ears. He reached the first cave. Ahead of him lay the climb to the exit, and a part of him wanted to just keep going like Jimmy Earl had. He could still hear the storm outside, the thunder growling around the sides of the mountain like an angry bear.

He had remembered something from the journal: *a key for the lock.*

*So there is a key of some sort.*

To his left, the dead watched him approach with unseeing eyes. Kit limped between stones and corpses. He saw where he had landed earlier on the torso of Tyson Collinsworth. It was nothing but a rotting morass of maggots and pulpy tissue. Kit couldn't help looking at the remains of Melody Sellers. How would things be different if he and Troy had told someone what they had seen that summer day?

The bones of Edgar, Daniel, Lena, and Lydia—along with at least one other who would probably never be identified—lay half-buried in the dirt

234 · J. TODD KINGREA

and rock. Kit grabbed a nearby lantern and set it among the bones. Their pep-
pery-gray coloration turned garishly white in the fluorescence.

He could not kneel, so he slid down a boulder to the dirt. He scattered
the bones about like a child knocking down a sandcastle. The journal said
that Edgar had written it down somewhere else. It wasn't in the journal, but
where—

Kit knew where it was. He had seen it here earlier, except he had thought
it was just an oddly discolored scrap of clothing. But it wasn't! Scratching
frantically through the desiccated bones and bits of nineteenth-century clothing, his fingers closed around the brittle piece of paper he had mistaken for
cloth.

Trembling from relief and blood loss, Kit unfolded the paper as carefully
as he could. It was the same size as the journal pages, no doubt ripped from
it. Bits of the edges flaked off.

*No, no, please don't fall apart!*

To his great relief, the interior of the paper was in halfway-decent shape.
Only the margins were crumbling. He read the words Edgar had scrawled
across it.

Now if he could only hang on long enough to get back to the pit.

• • •

Courtney cowered as Uyaga bent down over her and sniffed. A grin of
malicious pleasure split Uyaga's face. "Yes, *yes*," Uyaga hissed. "I can smell
your suffering." The myriad orifices across her body licked their ruined teeth,
and their impossible ululations invaded Courtney's ears. Courtney hugged
her knees to her chest and sobbed into her arms. All she could think of was
Jillian and Whitney.

And Kit, who had abandoned her.

Uyaga's gaunt fingers began to close around Courtney.

Courtney found a reservoir of strength and tried to resist, but her kicking and flailing made no difference. Picking up a stone, Courtney bashed it
against the hand that held her. Uyaga's flesh absorbed the blow as if it were a
sponge.

Scotty watched with manic glee. Uyaga lifted Courtney off the ground.

Courtney couldn't move. Uyaga's hand was wrapped around her body, pinning her arms tight. Uyaga held Courtney, kicking and screaming, over her head like a barbell. The sound of bones snapping filled the cave as Uyaga's head tilted back and distended. The empty eye sockets flattened and began to recede up her forehead to her scalp. At the same time, her mouth enlarged, becoming a cavernous circle that occupied nearly all of her head.

Courtney screamed as she stared down Uyaga's gullet. Saliva glistened on spiny teeth, and Uyaga's tongue wiggled like a plump maggot. The stench pouring from Uyaga's throat smelled like dirt, putrefaction, and sour milk. Courtney would have gagged or even vomited if she wasn't busy shrieking.

Uyaga positioned Courtney upside down with her head and shoulders hanging above the yawning mouth that appeared as big as a garage door. She lowered Courtney toward it.

• • •

Kit stumbled into Uyaga's cave, carrying a femur he'd grabbed to use as a weapon. He saw the monster pick Courtney up off the ground and saw Scotty enthralled by the grisly spectacle. Kit approached Scotty from behind. He was terrified that Scotty would turn around, especially since Kit was moving with all the stealth and grace of a three-legged colt on marbles. Kit edged closer. Scotty didn't move, completely focused on watching Uyaga feast.

Kit swung the femur as hard as he could. He didn't know if the loud crack came from Scotty's head or the bone as it splintered to pieces. Kit hoped it was the first.

Scotty pitched forward with a moan. As soon as he was down, Kit searched him. He found the Taurus, and using a boulder to help him stand, he aimed at Uyaga. He fired three shots in rapid succession. The gun kicked hard in his sweaty hands, and the explosions stung his ears. For several seconds he couldn't hear the chittering, slavering, wailing mouths across Uyaga's body. The recoil, combined with his bad leg, caused Kit to stagger back against the rock wall.

The rounds penetrated Uyaga's flesh—one in the side, one in the hip, and one in the shoulder. A pus-like, opaline fluid spurted from each, but Uyaga didn't react in pain. Instead, her head swiveled, and that gaping mouth turned toward him.

Kit aimed and pulled the trigger, but the clip was empty.

Uyaga pitched Courtney aside. She hit the cave wall but was still moving. *Thank God!*

"You cannot kill me," Uyaga snarled as she lumbered toward Kit. "Those pitiful things cannot stop me. I am invincible!"

Kit ducked behind a boulder as Uyaga closed the distance, but his leg slowed him down. Her hand swept out, grabbed him, and flung him against the wall. The impact made his head swim, and his vision threatened to go black. Kit collapsed near Courtney. He reached into his pocket and pulled out the paper as he held his head with the other hand.

*Hold on . . . for Courtney! Hold on!* he ordered himself.

Courtney crawled over to him.

Uyaga was coming toward them from the other side of the cave. Her face was little more than a drooling mouth of seemingly endless teeth.

"R-read . . . read it," Kit said through his pain. "Out loud." He stuck the paper into Courtney's hand.

"What? Why?"

"Just . . . do it. Only way. Then . . . give it back to me."

Uyaga towered over them. "This game is over. You cannot escape, and you cannot kill me."

Courtney unfolded the paper and began to read Edgar's writing aloud. Kit knew the words would probably make no sense to her. Most were just guttural gibberish.

"What is that?" Uyaga demanded when she saw the flimsy paper in Courtney's hand. As Courtney did her best to pronounce the words, Uyaga trembled and bellowed. Kit did not know if Uyaga's reaction was from pain or outrage but he was glad of the effect the words seemed to have.

The creature swatted Courtney with the back of her hand. Courtney rolled across the ground, blood flying from her nose and mouth.

The incessant wind from the pit carried the paper along the rocks. Uyaga attempted to grab it but missed. The paper danced on the currents toward Kit.

He snatched it before it could disappear over the edge or be carried up to the ceiling. He forced himself to stand. Grayness hovered at the edges of his vision, and he had no feeling in his leg anymore. The pain had become a muted ache.

*This is it.*

He read the words aloud with authority, nearly spitting them into Uyaga's contorted face, and steeled himself for what he had to do. His final act in this life. A gift for Courtney.

*Nitib-pingwi Manitou* roared and turned her pestilential maw toward him.

Kit heard thunder again, much louder this time. It seemed to go on for too long, but he kept reading Edgar's key. A part of him wondered how the storm had gotten inside. The more he read, the more Uyaga shrieked. She began to convulse.

Did he hear voices amid the thunder?

Uyaga twisted and writhed as if she were being struck from behind by something hard and heavy.

Kit took his eyes off the paper for a moment, just long enough to look at the creature and glance across the pit. His vision must have been playing tricks on him. He couldn't believe what he saw.

Standing in front of the tunnel was TBI Agent Mack and two Black Rock deputies. They fired at Uyaga, pausing only to reload. Agent Mack stayed at the tunnel mouth while the deputies fanned out around the perimeter. Bullets gouged into Uyaga's flesh, spraying creamy fluid into the air.

What he'd been hearing was not thunder at all. Kit grinned although it made his face hurt. He kept reading.

• • •

Kit noticed movement out of the corner of his eye. One of the deputies coming to help him. *Thank God!*

He looked up as Scotty Dunley swung at his head. Unable to react quick enough, Kit felt something cold and hard smash into his skull. His vision went black as he fell backward.

"You ain't takin' this from me!" Scotty screamed. "Uyaga is mine! She gives me power!" Scotty swung again.

Kit barely managed to protect his head. The butt of the gun hit his forearm and glanced off.

"You son of a bitch! I'll kill you! *I'll kill you!*" Scotty yelled. Saliva flew from his mouth.

Kit blinked but his vision remained blurry. Blood trickled down the side of his face, and his head felt like putty.

"Scotty Dunley!" a voice yelled, echoing through the cave. "Freeze! This is the police. Drop the gun!"

Uyaga teetered on the rim of the pit, struggling against unseen forces that tried to pull her back. She screamed and flailed her arms, the mouths across her body shrilling in what might have been fury or fear.

Kit's vision cleared in time to see Uyaga tumble backward into the pit.

Scotty kicked Kit in the ribs. Kit was so numb he hardly felt it, but he did hear something crack. As he looked at Scotty, a burning sensation erupted in his gut. It surged through his heart, then his brain.

A clarity like he'd never known before broke over him—a sudden epiphany that transformed everything.

Kit saw an opportunity.

It wasn't true that a dying person sees his whole life flash before him. At least it didn't work that way for Kit. For him it was the opposite. Realizing the possibility before him, Kit saw his life—the good and the bad—as part of a whole. Instead of a collection of individual mistakes and bad decisions, they were the things that gave him reason to fight, reason to be better today than he had been yesterday. If he were dead, there would be no chance to change. If he were dead, he couldn't appreciate music and laughter and friendship.

He smiled, at peace with this new understanding.

Then in the fog of his mind and the blurriness of his vision, Kit saw his mother. She smiled, and he watched her mouth move as she spoke to him.

In that moment, Kit made one of those critical decisions that alter the trajectory of destiny. He chose to live. With a newfound surge of adrenaline, Kit grit his teeth and managed to stand up. He screamed in defiance as he flung himself into Scotty.

They went down, but just as before, Scotty was back on his feet first. Kit lay on his back while Scotty straddled him and grabbed his shirt. Scotty lifted Kit's torso off the ground. His seething face was inches from Kit's.

"*Dunley!* Last warning! Stop and put your hands in the air!" one of the deputies yelled.

Uyaga's screams still rose from the pit. Her hand thrust up, raking the edge and seeking purchase.

Scotty held Kit and punched him in the face. Kit's head lolled back and forth as if his neck were broken. Blood spattered against the rocks. Scotty punched him again.

It was thundering once more. The gunshots echoed off the walls.

Scotty let go of Kit and arched his back. He grunted in pain as the bullets found their mark.

Kit spit blood and rolled over. He forced himself to his knees, then his feet.

Uyaga's other hand grabbed the edge of the pit, and her head began to rise into view once more.

Kit's whole body quivered. He locked eyes with Scotty. Kit reached out and slammed his hands into Scotty's chest.

Scotty laughed through the blood bubbling from his mouth. "Is that . . . all you got, McNeil?" Scotty's eyes were feral and gleamed with madness.

Kit smirked. "No, asshole. *That* is." His gaze drifted to Scotty's chest.

Scotty looked down. Sticky, coagulating blood covered his shirt. And there was something else. Stuck to the blood was a piece of paper covered with bloody fingerprints and dirt. Its brittle edges fluttered in the wind.

Scotty asked, "What the—"

Kit swung his fist.

Scotty's nose broke, and he staggered back under the impact of the punch. Kit stepped closer and punched Scotty again, knocking his head back. The third punch caught Scotty in the jaw, spinning him around and over the side of the pit.

Scotty screamed as he fell into Uyaga's champing maw. Her teeth shredded him like a thousand ice picks.

Uyaga screamed as the key and the lock entered her. She let go of the rim and plummeted into the darkness.

"Fuck . . . you . . . all the way to hell," Kit spat. The last thing he saw was Agent Mack and the deputies running toward him. Then oblivion beckoned, and he welcomed its embrace.

# 27
## A NEW BEGINNING

*Friday, June 17, 2011*

For a long time, Kit only remembered floating, like the scene in *The Empire Strikes Back* where Luke Skywalker was in the bacta tank after nearly dying on the ice planet Hoth. Except Kit was horizontal, not vertical. It was warm and dark. He didn't know where he was, and he didn't care. On occasion, Kit heard distant, muffled voices but paid them no mind. He wondered how long he had been floating like this.

But he began to realize when it was coming to an end.

At first the sensation was just a tremor, a quick muscle spasm. Then it grew to a faint ache. It troubled him that these things were disturbing his time in the bacta tank. Kit tried to move but was not sure his limbs were working.

After a while Kit relaxed and continued to drift through the soupy blackness, content and at peace. Once more, it did not last. Something tingled, itched, and began to burn like napalm. He wanted it to go away. It subsided for a while, which led him to believe it was all in his mind. He just wouldn't think about it anymore.

The next time it struck it felt like being hammered with a white-hot baseball bat. Kit thought he might have moaned. He heard something that sounded like one anyway. The sensation lessened but not enough to let him drift any longer.

This time he knew that he was moaning. He heard more voices, closer this time.

*Where . . . am I?*

His mind made no sense to him. Flashes of memory and bits of experience tumbled around like socks in a dryer. He attempted to catch one or two, but they always seemed to flip out of his reach at the last moment.

The darkness faded and became charcoal gray. Was it dusk? Early morning? The burning sensation continued. Kit tried to move, to get away, but it followed him. He groaned. Moving his body made it worse.

*What's going on?*

"He's coming out of it," a voice said somewhere in the charcoal.

Kit realized he was lying down and with that awareness came another wave of pain. It felt like waves of fire were washing up and down his body. Charcoal gave way to ash, and that in turn became a diluted white as he lifted his eyelids.

"Mr. McNeil, can you hear me? How do you feel?"

Kit didn't recognize the voice or the face that came with it. He squinted, blinked.

"I'm Dr. Khamavant."

More blurry faces looked down at Kit. He raised one hand to rub his eyes and felt something attached to his finger and arm.

"Just take it easy," Dr. Khamavant said.

The doctor pulled one lid open and waved a bright light in Kit's eye. Kit flinched.

"Yes, I know it's uncomfortable, but you're recovering nicely."

Kit's vision finally cleared, and he saw Dr. Khamavant. She was from India or Pakistan, a Hindu most likely given the red bindi on her forehead. Her jet-black hair was pulled back in a ponytail, and her dark chocolate eyes were framed by long lashes. She smiled in a way that made Kit feel safe as her fingers checked the injuries on his head.

"Hey, buddy!" Troy said.

Kit smiled or thought he did. Troy smiled in return, so he must have succeeded. There was relief on his friend's face.

"Hey there," Courtney said.

"Wh-where—"

Courtney took his left hand. "You're in the hospital."

"H-how'd I . . . get here?" The socks kept spinning just out of his reach.

"It's a long story," Courtney said. "Just take it easy right now." Her concern was like a fuzzy blanket.

Dr. Khamavant touched his leg. Pain flared and Kit grimaced.

"Sorry," the doctor said. "I need to see how this is healing."

Kit watched her undo the bandage that covered his thigh. The flesh around the stitches was red.

*A wound? Stitches?*

"It's looking good, Mr. McNeil," the doctor said. "How's your pain?"

"P-pretty bad." His mouth felt like it was filled with that pink insulation people put in their attics.

"Okay, I'll get you something for it." She left the room only to be replaced by a nurse with an IV bag.

"Besides the pain, how do you feel?" Troy asked.

"Like . . . like I've been run over. By a train. Twice." Kit looked at Courtney. "What happened to me?"

She raised her eyebrows. "You don't remember?"

Kit started to shake his head, but the movement made him nauseous. "No."

"You . . . you were in an accident," she said. "The doctor said that with a concussion as severe as yours, your short-term memory would be affected. But it's not permanent. It'll come back soon."

"I was . . . in an accident? Where? When?"

The nurse adjusted the drip, checked Kit's arm, and instructed him to relax and rest.

"Don't worry. We'll talk later," Courtney said with a smile.

Kit started to respond but felt woozy. The socks spun and the bacta tank enticed him back.

• • •

*Sunday, June 19, 2011*

Kit awoke, ate his lunch—his first solid food in several days—and drifted off to sleep again. He was flipping through television channels when someone knocked, and the door opened. Troy and Courtney were all smiles when they entered.

"Hey," Kit said.

"Hey, yourself," Troy replied.

They pulled chairs beside the bed. "How're you feeling?" Courtney asked.

"Better. I think. Leg still hurts like crazy. Itches too."

"That's good. Means it's healing," Troy said.

Kit grinned. It felt good. In fact, since the fog of the pain medication had lessened, everything felt good. Not physically, of course, but internally. He felt as if he had gone through some kind of rebirth. Even the light streaming in his window seemed brighter. Diaphanous. "And when did you get your medical degree, Dr. Wallace?" Kit teased. They exchanged pleasantries and caught Kit up on the news for a while.

"I can't believe I've been here since Friday," Kit said.

"Thursday, actually," Courtney corrected. "Thursday evening."

Kit was silent a moment. His face grew pensive, his gaze distant as he stared out the window. "I remember it now. All of it."

Courtney took Kit's hand. "I told Troy everything."

"Yeah," Troy replied. "Damn. Who would've ever thought, right? All the crazy stuff about this town all came from—" He didn't need to finish the thought. "Is it . . . is it *dead*?"

Kit shrugged. "I hope to God it is."

"Well, I've heard that the patches of blight are shrinking. Some folks even say it's vanishing altogether," Courtney said.

Suddenly, Kit turned to Courtney, his face pale with fear. "Jillian and Whitney! Are they—"

"They're fine. They're okay," she reassured him. "Well, aside from seeing things that'll traumatize them for the rest of their lives."

"But they screamed," Kit said. "We heard them screaming—"

Courtney nodded. "They ran into the police on the mountain. Agent Mack said you telephoned him just before you left the old school. That was a smart idea. You made it seem like you were on your own but had backup on the way."

"I'm just glad they took me seriously."

"They scared the girls half to death, but one of the officers escorted them off the mountain. They also gave the officers some directions that helped them find the cave quicker," Courtney said.

"I owe them my life then," Kit said. "If Mack and the deputies hadn't arrived when they did—"

"*We* owe *you* our lives," Troy said.

"Agent Mack and Sheriff Owens have been by to check on you a couple of times," Courtney said. She made a pained face. "They've, uh, got some questions."

Kit grinned. "Yeah, I'll bet they do."

"Oh, you know what else?" Troy said. "Your dad has been by too. Twice."

Kit raised his eyebrows. "No shit?"

Troy nodded. "He's been really worried about you."

Kit chewed on this for a moment but was interrupted when Troy spoke again.

"Do you think your . . . curse-thing is gone? You know, about you touching people?"

Kit shrugged. "I hope so. Maybe having the lock and key go straight down *her* throat got rid of it. I guess we'll just have to wait and see if I have any more blackouts." He looked at Courtney. "I need to tell you something—both of you. I'd . . . made up my mind that I wasn't coming back. It was supposed to be *me* in that pit."

Courtney couldn't hide her surprise, and Troy stared at him.

"I figured if Edgar had been able to restrain Uyaga somewhat by just dying in the cave with that paper, then I might be able to do even more . . . by going into the pit."

Tears formed in Courtney's eyes. "Kit, *why?*"

"Come on, you both know why. My life has been one big mess for as long as I can remember. I just . . . I didn't see any other way. If I wasn't around, the curse couldn't affect anyone else. And if there was a chance I could keep that *thing* from doing any of *her* shit again, I thought I had to try. You both know I'd been thinking about . . . killing myself. When I realized what Edgar had done, well . . . "

Silence descended, broken only by the rhythmic beeping of the IV unit. The muted television showed a dog food commercial. A bird flew past the window.

Courtney squeezed Kit's hand. "What changed your mind?"

Kit looked out at the clouds and the brighter-than-before sunshine, then turned back to her. "Just before I was about to go through with it, Scotty started beating the hell out of me. I thought I was about to die." He gave a humorless snort. "I mean, I *was* dying, and . . . and then I saw my mom . . . She was smiling at me." Tears rimmed his eyes. "And for some reason, I don't know why, I suddenly just—"

Courtney kept squeezing his hand. "It's okay, it's okay."

The tears slipped down his cheeks. He used the heel of his hand to wipe them away. "She . . . she . . . spoke to me."

"What'd she say?" Troy asked, his voice just above a whisper.

Despite the tears that kept flowing, Kit smiled. "She . . . she said—" He stared into Courtney's eyes. "She said, 'Change the ending.' And that she loved me."

Courtney put her free hand over her mouth. Tears crept down her cheeks.

Kit wiped his face again and sighed. "That's when I just . . . I got so pissed off at Scotty for beating on me and causing all this. I just . . . didn't want to die anymore. He had so much blood on him. It just came to me to give that son of a bitch the paper."

"Good for you, man," Troy said. "Good for you!"

Courtney pulled a tissue from the box on the bedside tray table and dabbed her eyes. "I am *so* proud of you."

Someone knocked on the door.

"Yeah," Kit said, "come in."

Agent Mack and Sheriff Owens entered.

"Glad to see you're awake," Sheriff Owens said, taking off his hat and offering a smile.

Agent Mack asked how he was doing. Kit told him that he'd suffered a major concussion, two broken ribs, numerous cuts and bruises, and had required surgery on his thigh. The bullet had passed through the tissue, but all the extra exertion he'd put it through had worsened the wound. He had another few days in the hospital before a week in rehab. After that, he'd be able to rehab at home.

"So you're going back to Nashville?" Sheriff Owens asked.

"Yeah. Well, actually, I don't know. I haven't decided," Kit answered.

"Agent Mack and I need you to go over some stuff about what happened up there," Owens continued. "Both of our reports are going to require some"—he worked his mouth from side to side— "*creative embellishment*, but we can do that tomorrow."

"We wanted you to know," Agent Mack said in his deep, rolling voice, "that the cave will be sealed off completely. I've made some calls. We plan to blow up the caves and keep that *horror* buried forever. We'll release a statement to the press that part of the mountain had to be sealed off due to the discovery of cinnabar."

Kit squinted. "What's that?"

Agent Mack crossed his arms. "It's an extremely toxic mineral. It used to be mined primarily for mercury, and it's deadly in large quantities. Even small amounts of exposure can cause significant health issues. The US Geological Survey will—ahem—*confirm* the findings and release their own statement about the actions on Blackpoint."

"A cover-up?" Troy asked, astounded. "You gotta be kidding me."

Kit sighed. "It's either that or the story of an evil Indian monster that lives in a pit and kills people and cursed the town."

"Toxic minerals it is then," Troy agreed with a lopsided smile.

Kit looked at Agent Mack and Sheriff Owens. "Did you catch Jimmy Earl?"

"We did," Sheriff Owens said. "Found him wandering on the mountain. We arrested him, but I don't think he's going to be much help."

"Why's that?" asked Kit.

"He's scheduled for a psych eval, and to be honest, I don't think he even knows what planet he's on anymore. He's completely lost it," said Sheriff Owens.

"Maybe that's for the best," Kit said. "What about your deputies? I mean, what they saw up there—"

Sheriff Owens nodded. "They're on paid leave so they can process and deal with . . . what they saw. They'll get counseling for PTSD. Both of them are strong. They'll be back eventually."

Kit smiled. "That's great. What about the bodies in the cave?"

"They're all at the morgue. Thanks to you, we can close the cases on Melody Sellers, Tyson Collinsworth, and Meredith Walston," the sheriff said.

Agent Mack glanced out the window, then back at Kit. "A forensics team from Nashville is working on the identity of the Hispanic victim, and they're reconstructing all the skeletons. They've got three children so far and figure to have at least that many adults."

Kit nodded. "What about the journal? Did you find it?"

"Yep. It's in evidence lockup now. Why? You want to see it?" Sheriff Owens said with a good-natured smile.

Kit raised his hands to ward off the sheriff. "Hell no!"

Agent Mack and Sheriff Owens laughed. "Listen, we'll come back tomorrow if that's okay," Sheriff Owens said.

"Sure," Kit replied.

"That way we can put this madness behind us once and for all," Owens said. He put his hat back on and paused before going out the door. "You did good, Kit. I can't imagine what you went through up there, but we appreciate it. Thanks."

A warmth spread through Kit's chest. He'd really done something good. Something *right*. He could almost feel his luck changing, and he'd never felt such clarity and wonder about the world around him. Everything he saw now revealed something he'd never noticed before. It felt *good* to be alive.

Kit looked at Courtney. "There's something I'd like to ask you."

She smiled and waited.

"When I get out of here . . . how about you let me take you out to dinner?" The words flowed effortlessly. Kit felt so satisfied that even if she said no, he'd be fine. Rejection didn't bother him now. But he hoped she'd say yes.

A quick glance showed Troy, goggle-eyed and mouth open in a flabbergasted grin. He gave Kit a thumbs-up.

Courtney smiled. Her face reminded him of golden sun dancing on the surface of a lake, pure and precise, blinding in its glorious intensity.

"I'd love that," she said.

• • •

*Wednesday, June 29, 2011*

Kit occupied the passenger seat of Troy's Ford as Troy drove west on County Road 501. They planned to hit Highway 127 and connect with I-40 toward Nashville. Wispy clouds brushed across the sky, and the morning sun forced its heat inside the cab of Troy's truck.

The blight really was disappearing. Kit saw almost none when they drove through town. He hoped it meant Uyaga was well and truly gone.

He'd been discharged last Tuesday. Albert had invited him home with a sincerity Kit hadn't known the man possessed. It seemed his father had changed. Albert had even prepared the living room so Kit wouldn't have to climb up and down the stairs on his bad leg.

Kit still couldn't drive, which was why Troy had taken the day off to shuttle him to his apartment. Kit had decided to stay in Black Rock a little longer. He knew he had to go back to Nashville at some point but was in no hurry. This trip was just so he could put a few affairs in order that had lapsed in his absence.

He'd been using his convalescence to re-evaluate his life and his choices. Once he could stand without the aid of crutches, Kit was going to find another band in need of a guitarist. And this time, he'd be reliable. If he was going to make a career from music, it was well past time to get serious.

Things were going well with Courtney. They'd had their date a week ago and scheduled another for next week. Not only had their shared experience drawn them together but they'd also found a connection with one another that filled their emptiness. Courtney had convinced herself she'd never feel whole and loved again, and Kit had convinced himself that he wasn't worth loving. She was changing that. It made him smile to think about how lucky he was.

*Me, lucky? How about that.*

As they listened to the radio, Troy asked, "Do you know what today is?"

"Wednesday."

"It's June 29." When Kit still looked perplexed, Troy added, "It was thirty years ago *today* that we saw Melody Sellers in the woods with Greg and Jeff Dunley."

Kit thought for a moment. "Wow, yeah, you're right."

That was all either needed to say.

• • •

*Friday, July 1, 2011*

South of Melvine, east of Upper East Valley Road, and just inside the southern border of Scarburn County, the hamlet of Crocketville prepared for its annual Fourth of July celebration. Twelve-year-old Madelyn Greenwood sat outside the community center while her parents worked inside on the decorations. Cell to her ear, she talked to her best friend, Hannah, about her crush, Cameron Dalton. Madelyn walked around the concrete building and through the gravel parking lot, lost in conversation.

Trees bordered one side of the property, and she ambled along them, swatting the low-hanging leaves. Something squelched under her shoe.

"Oh, *gross*!" Madelyn said.

"What?" Hannah asked in her ear.

Madelyn wiped her shoe on the grass. "Ugh, I just stepped in something!" Behind her, a pale, spongy growth about the size of a CD bore her footprint.

"Maddy? Hey! You still there? What's going on?"

The brown-haired preteen lifted the phone. "Yeah, I'm here."

"What was it? Dog shit?"

"No, it's white. Looks like somebody spilled ranch dressing. *Ugh!* And God, does it stink!"

## ACKNOWLEDGMENTS

My grateful thanks and appreciation go out to Vern and Joni Firestone, publishers extraordinaire, and to my editor, Stephanie Bennett, at BHC Press. It's an honor and privilege to be part of such a fantastic company.

To my wife, Felicia, for her help, support, encouragement, and love.

And to you, the reader: thank you for your time! There are so many books out there and I'm grateful that you've given this one your attention.

Please feel free to contact me at jtoddkingrea@yahoo.com, on Facebook, Twitter, or Instagram, and share your experience with it.

# ABOUT THE AUTHOR

J. Todd Kingrea is the author of the Deiparian Saga trilogy: *The Witchfinder* (nominated for a 2021 Pushcart Prize), *The Crimson Fathers*, and *Bane of the Witch* (slated for a 2024 release). He's also written two nonfiction books and writes movie reviews for *Screem* magazine.

When not writing he enjoys collecting and watching movies, reading, lurking in dusty old bookstores, and wishing for some distant relative that he doesn't know to bequeath him a decrepit trunk full of Eldritch Tomes and a beach house. Until such a time, he and his wife live outside Chattanooga, Tennessee with their two dogs.